THE
CAVERN
UNDER THE
LAKE

A.D. DOWNTON

ISBN: 978-1-0686616-0-0

DEDICATION

To my family and friends...

It is finished.

Ruins

Northward
Forest

The Four
Sisters

The Bridge over
the Everflow

Lake
Tväre

Everflow
Wood

Northern Valley Railway

Forest

Levi Larson

CONTENTS

Part One

The Blizzard

A gentle breeze brushed over the surface of the frozen Lake, whipping up the powdery snow that had settled upon it overnight. In the depths of the carved arctic valley, the wind was calm and casual... but up in the great heights of the surrounding ice-capped mountains, the wind was dangerous and unpredictable. Piercingly cold gusts roared over the ridged backbone of the Thorhorn, the largest of the valley's guardian mountains, blasting the snowdrifts from the peak and over onto the nearby slopes. A lone moose lifted its head curiously, watching as a new bank of snow began to build in front of him, another reminder of the harshness that was winter.

A deep grunt of a fellow moose came from further down the snowbank, a signal to retreat as the heavy winds grew in power. The moose acknowledged the call and began to withdraw from the height of the mountain. As he began the treacherous journey down, he saw a faint glow deep within the valley. Down by the Lake, if you could still call the frozen mass of snow-covered ice a Lake, was a gathering of a thousand tiny lights. The settlement of those two-legged hardy creatures that use the skin of other animals to keep warm, and cut down trees to use as shelter... The moose didn't understand, then again, he didn't really care. As long as he could graze, he was happy.

*

1

Lake Tväre, to put it very simply, was a solid mass of ice and dirt. In the summertime, the Lake was a beautiful and twinkling surface, with little waves gently flowing towards the west. Though it had to get very warm for it to appear like that... and here in Tväre, very warm was not warm at all. The cold was normal, the freezing was a typical winter, and the darkest night could sometimes bring a cold unlike any other in the world. It was only in the very deepest of winter the weather became so bad that even the locals stayed inside.

Levi had found this out the hard way. He was a traveller from the south... a long way south as it happens, and he'd been in Tväre for about two weeks now, having arrived via the newly installed Northern Valley Railway system direct from Stockholm. Hailing from England, the wondrous centre of the British Empire, Levi had experienced a very different childhood than most. His father was English, and his mother was Danish, thus Levi had spent many of his early years constantly journeying between the two cities of London and Copenhagen, though it was the Danish capital that secretly had his heart, not that he dared tell his father...

Despite being only twenty-five years in age, Levi was already quite the extensive traveller for his time, having explored much of Europe in the early 1880s and even partaken in a trip to northern Africa a few years later, following in the adventurous footsteps of his father. His bright blue eyes had seen many an impressive sight, from the infamous circular structures of stone in his home country, to the heavenly landscapes of Switzerland. He simply loved exploration, taking any chance he could to add to his collection of hand-drawn maps. It was his dream to one day showcase a huge book of his travels to the world... and the unique findings that came with them. Therefore, the opportunity to venture into the far north to the quaint town of Tväre wasn't one to be ignored. It was isolated and distinctive, a humble town that was only just learning of the world's great industrial revolution. Later this evening, however, Levi was going to learn an important lesson about the harshness of the little wintery town.

Levi sat within the confines of a small tavern, the wooden support beams hovering above his dark head of hair. He was wrapped within a thick jacket and long trousers, both lined with an additional layer of wool for extra warmth. The long room glowed in the light of the many torches that were balanced on the walls, and little displays of mugs and paintings were mounted all around him. The place was unlike any other in this town, as if someone had flipped an ancient Viking longship over and then filled it with tables, chairs and barrels... many, many barrels. Levi stared at them all, lined up against the back of the room. It seems this town has quite a severe drinking problem if they needed all that... Levi hummed, returning his gaze to a little sketch of his latest map in front of him. Using a pencil, which he'd sharpened with a small knife, he carefully added some extra detail to the sketch, outlining where the tavern lay on a small map of the town.

A looming shadow fell over him, the light of the torches suddenly vanishing. Levi glanced up to see a rather sizable woman, complete with an equally large apron, standing in front of him. Her name was Hervor, and she was the heavyset owner of said tavern, having been the one to have served him and the other locals for the first half of the evening. She was a gentle giant at heart, but currently her intimidating stance was matched with a stubborn nature.

> Hervor: Here.

She dumped a small mug on his table. Levi stared at the wooden cup, slowly playing with the stylus in his hand.

> Levi: What is this?

Hervor replied with her trademark sarcasm.

> Hervor: It's called a drink. It's the main reason why people hide in places such as this.

Levi smirked to himself.

> Levi: Thanks for the education. But I didn't ask for this...

Hervor huffed a reply.

> Hervor: Oh I'm fully aware. But you've come in here for the last couple of nights and the most exciting thing you've ordered was water taken from the

3

height of the Thorhorn. I thought I'd bring you something a bit more exciting...

Levi suddenly understood.

Levi: You mean something a bit more expensive.

Hervor: You catch on quick.

The young cartographer nodded to himself before attempting to make his case.

Levi: I appreciate the effort, but I don't drink whilst I'm working. It'll go right through me, and then I risk making a mistake that I can't correct.

Hervor glanced down at the detailed map, intrigued by the strange symbolic set of work. Cartography wasn't the type of occupation often seen in such a small town, so it was surprising to see someone take such care over it... but that didn't matter to her as much as money did.

Hervor: It is fascinating work, I'll admit... But if that's the case, I'm going to have to ask you to complete it elsewhere.

Levi almost smiled in disbelief.

Levi: You're going to kick me out for not being drunk enough?

Hervor: Not at all. I'm kicking you out because you're not providing fair business. You see those men over there?

She pointed towards the other end of the room, where a group of four great burly men sat around one of the tables, drinking themselves into oblivion. Their eyes were rolling back into their heads as they drank and choked, beer and mead flooding into their curly, matted beards.

Hervor: Those four loggers came into town a few days ago. Like you, they're here for work. But unlike you, most of their daily wage ends up in my pocket instead of their own. I may have to pick them up out of a pool of vomit and drool at the end of the night, but right now, they're my best customers.

4

Levi turned his eyes away for a moment, allowing the barwoman to continue.

Hervor: I'm not asking for you to match them, not that you would be able to come close...

She glanced up and down at Levi's skinny frame.

Hervor: But you have to give me a reason to let you and your odd little maps stay put.

Levi balanced his mapping stylus upon his finger, pausing before he replied.

Levi: I guess that's fair. Alright then, allow me a bit more time to finish my work and I promise I'll order something that is both exciting and expensive before I go.

Hervor smiled.

Hervor: I'll come back in a short while then.

Levi: Keep a sharp eye though; it looks like one of your 'best customers' might need some help getting up off the floor.

Levi indicated towards one of the four men as his sweating head smacked against the wall. His eyes remained wide open, as if he were having some sort of out of body experience. Hervor shrugged it off.

Hervor: Nothing I haven't handled before.

Right on cue, the drunken man stood to his feet, balanced himself for a second and then collapsed, much to the amusement of his friends. Hervor stared as a rather sizable mug of drink spilled right across her clean floorboards. Levi flashed her a guilty smile as she exhaled in frustration, grabbing a mop from the corner to deal with the new chore now on her list. One of the other loggers dozily lifted his head as she approached, reaching out for her arm.

Logger: Hey big lady. You on offer too?

Hervor quickly flicked the handle of the mop, catching the logger in the face and sending him sprawling. Several other locals in the tavern scowled, shaking their heads at the stupidity of these outsiders. It was common knowledge that

5

Hervor could stand her ground without any help. You did not want to end up on the wrong side of her. After a short while, and a filled mug of cloudberry mead later, Levi got to his feet and paid for his drinks, bidding Hervor good night.

Hervor: Take care on your way back; the wind sounds like it's picking up a bit.

Levi: I'm only around the corner, I'll be alright. Thanks again.

He now strolled through the dimly lit streets, making use of the evening to discover more about the town and the rugged people that lived there. A few flakes of snow were falling, covering the gravelly paths with a wispy layer of white powder. But the random gusts of wind were beginning to grow in strength. A heavy thump came from above, and Levi glanced up to see a large white bird watching him from one of the rooftops. It followed him with large yellow eyes before taking flight and disappearing into the darkness.

A sharp chill in the wind caused Levi to flinch. He'd been staring at the peak of the Thorhorn mountain in the moonlight, which lay to the south of the town, but now the sky was thick with dark clouds. A heavy mist seemed to be descending upon Tväre, obscuring more and more of the night-time view. Even the furthermost houses of Tväre seemed to have vanished, and the town had fallen deathly quiet…

Suddenly, the wind began to transform, turning from a brief gust to a colossal roar. Within seconds, Levi was caught in a blizzard, the roughest of the season. The white storm had seemingly come from nowhere, blasting across the roads and forcing the few drunks that were on the streets back inside their houses. The young explorer threw his hands up to his face, protecting his bare skin from the sharp knives of the snowflakes, the tiny blades of ice slicing across his cheeks. He tried to take another step, but even his own leather boots seemed to have vanished from view, becoming buried under a layer of new snow.

Levi glanced around, his eyes wide and wild, looking for any kind of landmark or building that might help him identify where he was. His sense of direction was normally so precise, so perfect that he could navigate his way blindfolded. But this was unlike anything else; it was a complete whiteout, and now he was beginning to panic. He whirled around anxiously, knowing that he needed to find some form of shelter urgently. He'd heard of blizzards like this before. Some of them could last for minutes whereas others lasted for days, and he did not want to be in one of those stories as a traveller that froze to death. He crashed his hands against walls that seemed to appear and then vanish just as quickly. He couldn't see a thing. It was as if the buildings of the town centre had completely disappeared, leaving him alone in the vast icy wilderness.

A sudden moment of silence fell over him. The roar of the wind stopped, and the whip of the snowstorm went quiet. Levi glanced around in a state of complete confusion; the blizzard continued, as harsh as ever before, but it was as if all the sounds of the world had been stripped away. The snow still battered Levi's eyes and face, and the wind still cut itself across his skin. There was just no sound travelling with them. Then, in the far distance where the frozen Lake lay still, came a bright blue glow. Levi stopped, staring at the strange apparition of light that appeared before him, the rays breaking through the ice of the distant Lake and soaring up into the sky, like the light from an erupting volcano. Then it was gone. And the sounds of the wind and snow returned, worse than ever before, stripping him of his vision and his senses...

A hand reached out, grasping Levi by the shoulder and pulling him in a new direction. The piercing cold and blasts of wind instantly vanished, exchanged for the calming warmth of a humble fireplace. The door to the house slammed shut, and Levi brushed the snow from his face, opening his eyes to see a pretty, young woman standing before him, a look of disbelief on her face.

> Elvera: What the hell are you doing out there!?

Levi attempted to gather himself, the shock of the blizzard rendering him silent.

> Elvera: Not even a scarf to cover your face! What were you thinking!? Are you drunk!?

Levi: No, no... I'm not drunk.

Elvera helped him remove his coat, gently taking his shoulder bag and placing it on the floor.

> Elvera: Just disorderly then. If you hadn't crashed against my door, I wouldn't have known to look outside. Another few minutes and you'd have lost some fingers for sure, if not more...

She lifted his snow-covered coat and placed it on a wooden rack by the fireplace. Despite the raging wind buffeting down the chimney every so often, the fire remained warm and powerful, and Levi's coat quickly began to steam. Levi stood unmoving, still in shock from the impact of the sudden whiteout. He stared at his rescuer, trying to get back to reality. Her brunette hair glowed with the light of the fire, and her brown eyes were fierce and bright.

> Elvera: You alright?

> Levi: Yeah... I'm just...

> Elvera: In shock?

She finished the sentence for him. Levi sighed and nodded, rubbing warmth into his hands and fingers.

> Levi: I'm not used to feeling so lost...

Elvera hummed, a small smile appearing on her lips.

> Elvera: How long have you been here?

> Levi: Just over a week, more or less. I arrived from Stockholm about eight days ago.

Elvera scoffed.

> Elvera: It's a different world up here, so few people seem to realise that. No wonder you're nearly frozen!

Levi rubbed his cheeks, soothing the windburn. Elvera seemed to soften, realising that his fault was due to ignorance rather than idiocy.

> Elvera: Well. at least you're safe. Come. You might as well sit by the fire and try to warm up. You won't be able to go anywhere for a while.

8

Levi stared after the young woman as she disappeared. He glanced around at the modest living room, the beautifully carved table in the middle clearly the defining factor. Laying upon it were several pieces of paper that appeared to be a child's drawings, each of them held down with little wooden figures. Levi carefully sifted through the drawings as he sat down, his curious nature tempting him in.

The top page depicted two great Viking longships sailing down a vast fjord, one coloured black, the other left in white. The pages beneath varied between pencilled forests and slanted style houses, each of them depicting a single, lone figure. They were all inaccurately drawn and coloured in with the whimsical imagination of a child. He glanced up quickly as Elvera eventually returned, holding a steaming wooden mug filled to the brim with warmed wine.

> Elvera: Oh, don't mind those; my son has a bit of a wild imagination. Here.

She handed him the mug, and Levi wrapped his hands around it, feeling the frost of the outdoors finally leaving his fingers. Despite her rather direct impression, Levi realised Elvera was actually a very caring person, especially if she was willing to let a complete stranger into her home in the middle of a storm.

> Levi: Thanks.

He sipped the wine gratefully, the very sweet yet very strong taste storming across his tongue. Unless he was mistaken, there was a hint of raisin to it too. As he drank, he could feel the warmth flow down his throat and through his body, expelling every essence of cold that remained.

> Levi: This is good... Your own recipe?

Elvera nodded as Levi correctly identified the famed Nordic winter drink, sitting herself down opposite.

> Elvera: My family's. Although it's practically the same as everyone else's.

> Levi: Well, this is one of the best I've had so far.

He took another sip, only now realising that he hadn't yet done the courteous and most important thing.

9

Levi: Thank you by the way. For saving me out there.

Elvera: No need. Any reasonable person would have done the same. It would have been shameful to have just left you out there to join the snowdrifts.

Levi chuckled.

Levi: Shameful or not, if you hadn't, I think my adventures would have come to a very swift end. So, I mean it... Thanks.

Elvera: You're very welcome.

She smiled and got to her feet, wandering over to the small stairway near to the wall. She called up the stairs to someone that Levi could not see.

Elvera: Sigmund! Come down now please.

Levi heard the soft voice of a young boy as he muttered a retort.

Sigmund: Why?

Stubbornness ran in the family it seemed. Elvera spoke again. Her voice was raised but not punishing.

Elvera: Now Sigmund. You have to clear up your things if you want to use them again. That's our deal!

Elvera disappeared into the kitchen as the heavy clumps of a reluctant child stomped down the stairs, the excessive noise almost acting as a form of protest. Levi watched as the boy came into view, pitch black hair falling across a grouchy expression. Sigmund stopped suddenly when he got to the bottom, his eyes landing on Levi for the first time, who raised a friendly hand in greeting.

Levi: Hello.

Sigmund didn't move. He could only have been eleven or twelve years in age and he hadn't quite grasped polite greetings.

Sigmund: I don't know you...

Levi: No, you don't. My name's Levi.

Sigmund eyed him cautiously continuing his no-nonsense interrogation.

Sigmund: Why are you here?

Levi: Your mum saved me from the storm outside.

Sigmund lifted his head, listening to the blizzard rage outside their house. In the silence between the questions, its raging power was much more prominent.

Sigmund: Why weren't you back at your own house?

Levi leant back in his chair.

Levi: Because I'm the adventurous kind… and I got lost.

He chortled to himself, changing the subject.

Levi: Are these yours?

He pointed at the drawings upon the scratched firwood table, to which Sigmund slowly nodded.

Levi: They're very good. I draw myself.

Sigmund: You do?

Levi smiled.

Levi: Come. Take a look.

The cartographer reached down for his own shoulder bag, quickly withdrawing a padded folder which stored a few carefully folded pages. Elvera returned to the warmth of the room, setting a small plate of what looked like a bread bun sliced in half on the table and watched as Levi spread out several of his own drawings, all of them sketched with an incredible preciseness. Some of them were simple, just a small map outlining where the town of Tväre was located within the local valley. Whereas others were amazingly accurate, with every path and river noted down to a precise mark.

Levi: These are what I draw. Not as imaginative as yours but I'm sure you know what they are?

He gently posed the question as Sigmund slowly wandered over to the table.

Sigmund: They're maps.

Levi: That's right. From all over the world. Everywhere I've ever visited. Good, aren't they?

The young boy scanned the various charts that Levi was so excited about, his expression unmoving.

Sigmund: They're different to the ones in the library...

Levi raised his eyebrows hopefully.

Levi: Really? Are they any better?

Sigmund frowned and looked Levi straight in the eye.

Sigmund: No... Those ones aren't boring.

Elvera: Sigmund!

Elvera immediately chastised her son, but Levi just laughed.

Levi: Why are mine so boring?

Sigmund: There's no pictures. The ones in the library have ships and monsters on them. Yours don't have anything.

Levi stiffened slightly, dropping to a somewhat firmer tone.

Levi: I'm afraid maps have evolved a fair bit since the old days. It's all about navigation and information now. No room for legends or monsters anymore...

They fell into a short silence, the wind, once again, howling at the door as if shouting to be let inside. Sigmund muttered a response, fiddling with the corner of Levi's map.

Sigmund: What about ghosts?

It was Levi's turn to shrug.

Levi: Not a problem for me. I don't believe in them.

Sigmund: You should. There's one that comes out from the Everflow every night and walks across the lake.

Levi paused.

Levi: The Everflow?

He glanced uncertainly towards Elvera, who spoke up to help him out.

Elvera: It's a part of the lake that never freezes, even in the middle of winter. It's nothing but a small stream in reality, but it's quite special to us and the town.

Sigmund: It stays in the same place every year. Right there...

The young boy now leaned across the table, pinpointing a spot upon one of Levi's maps with his finger, right towards the edge of Lake Tväre.

Sigmund: No-one believes me, but I know it's because of the ghost. Whenever it's dark and the clouds are heavy, I look out my window and he's there staring at me...

Elvera shifted uncomfortably in the corner, but Levi decided to play along, albeit slightly sarcastically.

Levi: Hmm... Well, it sounds like I need to go and visit that part of the lake again. See if this ghost will make an appearance for me or not.

Sigmund perked up.

Sigmund: I could show you where it is?

Levi: Maybe you could. But shouldn't you check if an adventure like that is okay with your mum first?

Sigmund's gaze fell instantly.

Sigmund: She never lets me go...

Elvera quickly waded in, trying to save some face in front of Levi.

Elvera: That's not true and you know it. I just never let you go by yourself.

Sigmund kept his head low.

Elvera: Anyway, it's time to head up for bed. We're not missing another weekend's lesson again. Torsten expects you to be there.

The addition of this terrible news made the young boy even more moody.

Sigmund: But there's a blizzard outside!

Elvera: Which might clear up by tomorrow. Bedtime, now. No excuses.

Sigmund's face turned dark.

Sigmund: Fine.

He plodded back towards the stairs.

Elvera: And I see you haven't cleaned your things up, like I asked.

Her tone was playful but also firm. Sigmund sulkily cleaned up the drawings and carved figures, storing them in neat little piles beneath the table. Without even a wave goodnight, he disappeared up the stairs.

Elvera: That's for you by the way.

She pointed towards the sliced bread bun that remained on the table. Levi looked at her in surprise; her generosity towards a random stranger unlike anything he'd experienced before. Elvera followed her son up the stairs. Now alone, Levi stared at the red-hot embers in the fireplace, the roar of the blizzard outside occasionally buffeting down the chimney.

*

Elvera: I'm sorry about Sigmund. He's not normally so impolite.

Levi shook his head.

Levi: It's nothing at all. I was the same when I was his age.

He and Elvera sat downstairs, watching as the fire desperately fought to stay alive as the wind channelled down the stack of the chimney. Elvera had refilled Levi's mug with warmed wine, as well as filling one of her own.

The wind continued to howl outside, the hurricane of snowflakes whipping against Elvera's modest, little house.

Levi: Is it just you and him?

Elvera nodded curtly.

Elvera: His father had an accident whilst out working by the lake. Sigmund was only three at the time.

Levi: That must have been difficult...

Elvera sighed, her eyes dropping to the floor.

Elvera: It still is. The house feels... empty at times. Sometimes it's alright, other times, Sigmund can take it quite hard. He struggles to get to sleep most nights as it is, even without a storm to keep him awake. But we're lucky, our town looks out for us. Whatever we need...

Levi lowered his gaze and sipped his wine. The wooden mug had no handles, which was a bit of a new experience for Levi, whose own upbringing was very different to Elvera's style of living. Then again, he was a long way from home...

Levi: I don't have to stay tonight—

Elvera: Don't be stupid. You think you can go back outside in that!?

Elvera's stubborn tone returned as she cut across, the wind continuing to smash against it like an intruder trying to gain entry.

Elvera: The last thing I want is pity. As I've already said, I'd have let you freeze to death if I wasn't happy with you being here.

Levi held his hands up, Elvera's honesty making him smile.

Levi: Alright, my apologies. But I'll be damned if I don't repay you for at least saving my life. Not to mention all the additional services you've provided.

He waved towards the empty plate on the table. Elvera thought for a moment, staring at the fire as one of the logs collapsed into the flaming ashes.

Elvera: Were you being sincere when you offered Sigmund the chance to accompany you to the Everflow?

Levi nodded several times.

Levi: Of course. It'd be no inconvenience.

Elvera: He might not appreciate your craft, but he loves the outdoors. He doesn't have many friends; there are so few children here. Maybe when the weather lets up, we can come along with you for a time...

Levi: For sure, I'd welcome the company. Besides, nothing better than local knowledge.

Elvera raised her eyebrows.

Elvera: Even if it's about ghosts wandering across a frozen lake?

Her comment made Levi chuckle.

Levi: Even that.

Elvera sipped her wine, before hesitantly asking a question of Levi.

Elvera: So you don't believe in anything mystical then? Not even ghosts?

Levi: Not especially. I've got quite the cynical mind, which helps in this respect.

He patted the maps that remained atop Elvera's table.

Levi: If I'm to be a famous explorer, I have to play by the rules. No drawing office is going to publish a map showing things that aren't real... Mystical maps don't sell.

He sighed reflectively.

Levi: What about yourself?

Elvera pursed her lips for a moment before answering.

Elvera: I like to think that certain things could be real. Stories of the great Northern wolves that roam and protect old villages, or ghosts walking on the lake. But it's the idea of them that really matters, isn't it? Our way of staying connected to the stories of our ancestors...

She sounded tired, and confirmed this a moment later by getting to her feet.

> Elvera: I'm going to head upstairs. I'm right in guessing that this is your first real blizzard?

> Levi: I've survived a storm or two in my time. But no, nothing like this.

> Elvera: Okay, then let me reassure you. If the wind and snow sounds like it's going to tear the house apart, it's not and we're fine.

She paused.

> Elvera: But if it does begin to fall apart, I'll run down and help you try and survive.

Levi laughed.

> Levi: I'll make sure I'm ready.

> Elvera: Enjoy your stay.

Elvera smiled and disappeared up the stairs. Levi glanced back at the fire one last time, soaking up as much warmth as he could before he settled himself more comfortably in the soft leather chair. He buried himself underneath the fur that had once belonged to a local reindeer, feeling cosy at last. The wind bellowed and whistled around him, all the more prominent now there was silence. And with that, Levi fell asleep to the maelstrom of wind and snow.

**

The surface of the Lake echoed and growled with the sound of moving ice. The heaving mass formed one minor part in a huge river system, gradually flowing from the mountains and valleys of the east all the way through towards the Atlantic Ocean in the west. It wasn't unusual for the ice to gently shift and groan every now and again... but this was an unusual time.

*

Levi stared out across the expanse of the shining Lake; a blanket of gleaming snow having been laid across the surface during the night. As the clouds flew across the sky, they took turns covering the rays of light that emerged from the moving sun. The result was a glittering scene of white and blue, as if someone had thrown millions of diamonds into the depths of the valley.

The raging nature of the blizzard had calmed during the night. Levi couldn't remember a point when the wind wasn't howling outside but when he awoke, the silence had been very welcome. Elvera had been up for a half hour already, choosing to let Levi sleep whilst she prepared breakfast of loaf buns spread with a fine yellow jam. Levi had taken one bite of the extremely tangy paste and politely asked what it was made of. Elvera had informed him of the cloudberry, a common fruit picked, mixed with a little sugar and stored during the summer months. To her, it was no big deal but to Levi, the taste was unlike anything he'd had before. It was nothing like the sharpness of the mead he'd had at the tavern the night before; this time the taste was smooth and sweet.

Levi pressed his boot curiously into the fresh bank of snow, listening to the strange groan as he compacted it down with his foot.

Elvera: Are you all set?

Elvera poked her head out the strong wooden door, breaking Levi's concentration. He turned and nodded politely, watching as she and Sigmund pulled on their boots and headed out the door.

Earlier that morning, Elvera had quietly asked whether Levi wished to join her and Sigmund for their weekly trip to the local church. The day was Sunday, and the clocktower in the village rang out across the new layers of snow as the bell tolled nine, the sound echoing throughout the frozen valley. Levi said he'd be delighted to join, wanting to learn as much about the town of Tväre as possible, which was much easier when you knew someone. He had occasionally visited his local church, when residing in either England or Copenhagen, before taking up his travels and wanted to see how the hardy northerners practiced Christianity here. He

18

had never really called himself a Christian, but he occasionally weighed deep philosophical questions in his mind, often wondering if there was more to life beyond the simple sights of his eyes.

In a quaint street, not far from the town's newest addition of the railway station, was Elvera's house. It was smaller than most; filling only a small section of the entire complex that led down the incline of the road. It was by no means poor, which Levi had seen far worse of back in Britain, just smaller than the rest of the unique shelters scattered within and around Tväre. The status was hardly reflected in her attitude however, for Elvera now hummed cheerfully while she walked. Flecks of snow were still falling, and Levi could feel them landing upon his face.

Elvera: I'm almost afraid to ask...

Elvera began to speak, conversing with Levi whilst they slowly ambled through the snowy streets, their boots crunching on the frosty layer of ice below.

Elvera: But where is it you said you were from?

Levi sighed, a small smile appearing on his face.

Levi: I'm guessing there's a wrong answer to this?

Elvera shrugged her shoulders.

Elvera: Not wrong. Just one that you might want to keep quiet if it turns out to be true...

Levi: Ah, I see.

Elvera quickly tried to recover some ground.

Elvera: It's not any problem with me by the way. I'm just thinking about the rest of the town. You've already seen how much they *love* outsiders, but if word got out that I gave shelter to a *Dane*...

She said the word almost as if it were a curse.

Elvera: Well, I'd never hear the end of it.

Levi: Even this far north, you Swedes still don't like us huh?

Elvera glanced over, worried she might have caused offence by pointing out Levi's Danish nationality. Levi didn't reciprocate the look, choosing instead to stare at the peak of the Thorhorn mountain close by.

Elvera: Come on, not all neighbours are meant to get along. Besides, it's not without cause; we've had our share of wars, and raids. And you've stolen lots of things from us over the years...

Levi: And you stole Norway from us. I think that makes it even.

They both stared hard at each other, before breaking out into smiles. Elvera paused, bending down to quickly readjust the scarf around Sigmund's neck as Levi continued the conversation.

Levi: What if I was only half a Dane? Would that help alleviate my local status in any way?

Elvera: Depends on what your other half is...

Levi: How about English?

Elvera raised her eyebrows and Levi's faced dropped slightly.

Levi: Why? Don't tell me that Englishmen are also disliked around here...

Elvera rolled her eyes.

Elvera: Every stranger is disliked in this town. That's just a barrier you have to live with until we get to know you... But no, the English half of you is fine.

She picked herself up, Sigmund instantly tugging at the tightened scarf around his neck as his mother pulled away. Levi tucked his hands into the pockets of his coat as the cold air began to get through the skin.

Elvera: So, half English, half Danish... Where did you grow up?

Levi: I flitted between the two really. I lived in Copenhagen the longest, but never long enough to settle properly...

Elvera nodded, humming in agreement.

Elvera: Very different to somewhere like here then. Where you're born, grow up and die in the exact same place.

That made Levi laugh. They continued walking in a comfortable silence after that. Levi glanced around, taking in the true remoteness of the town now that the fog and mist had lifted. The Thorhorn mountain soared up to the sky in the near distance, overlooking the town and the Lake like a natural guardian. Every house had a slanted roof, built to survive the heavy onslaught of snow that came every few days. Windowsills glittered with icicles, some hanging over a metre in length, owed to the thawing and refreezing of meltwater in the gentle sunlight of each day. Over towards the north, the valley was filled with frosty trees, their green leaves and branches now the colour of sparkling white.

Elvera: Watch the road please, Sigmund.

The firm command cut across Levi as Sigmund meandered his way towards the cobblestone street. He kicked the newly formed banks of snow without much enthusiasm, responding moodily to his mother.

Sigmund: I'm fine!

Elvera exhaled heavily through her nose, making her frustration clear. Horses and wagons frequently made their way along these streets and every local had to constantly be on their guard, or risk learning the hard way...

The little wintery town suddenly began to feel a lot busier. As the trio ambled into the central square of Tväre, Levi found himself spotting more and more people, all of them dressed in thick coats and gloves as they shovelled and conversed, clearing the sidewalks with huge shovels and dumping the excess snow in massive piles around the roads. One such townsman shouted out as he worked, clearing the snow from his doorway.

Townsman: Bit of ice-fishing later today Edvin?

A large, hefty man grunted a reply as he passed on through the square.

Edvin: A bit? I'm planning on spending the rest of the day down there. Didn't catch a thing yesterday.

Townsman: Nothing at all!?

Edvin: Nope. Not a bite. The lake better not have run itself dry; I need something to eat for supper.

Edvin continued on his way, greeting Elvera politely as she and Sigmund passed him by. Levi didn't get much more than a curious sideways glance... but that was normal to him now.

Up ahead, the door to a quaint shop opened and then closed, ringing a little bell. Another woman, clearly quite a few years older than Elvera, stepped out into the street and greeted them.

Freja: Good morning Elvera!

Elvera: Good morning Freja. Everything okay after last night? It's the first blizzard to hit your new roof, isn't it?

She indicated towards the building with the shop, glancing towards the slanted roof.

Freja: Oh, no problems whatsoever, it's been perfect. We could barely even hear the wind during the night, it's like the entire house is brand new.

Elvera: Ah, that's good to hear.

Freja didn't stop there. She was clearly an excitable woman, emphasising her words with hand gestures and exaggerations. Levi didn't know what to make of her.

Freja: Honestly, I was anxious about the amount beforehand; it was a much larger payment than we'd ever thought we'd agree to, but getting that loan was the best decision we ever made. I mean, I know we've always been a bit wary of southerners in the past, but this one is definitely one of the good ones. And...

She glanced over her shoulder guiltily, lowering her voice.

Freja: He's absolutely gorgeous. Makes me wish I wasn't married.

22

Elvera: Freja!

There was a cheeky smile on the face of the older woman.

Freja: Just for a day... or an evening...

Elvera shook her head in mock disbelief, her friend's attitude almost comical. Freja turned her attention towards Levi, who'd been politely standing nearby.

Freja: Who's this young man? I don't recognise him.

Elvera: Another outsider as it happens.

Levi gave a small wave.

Levi: Pleased to meet you.

Freja raised her eyebrows.

Freja: Oh, an accent too! Where are you from?

Elvera: English! He's English...

Elvera jumped in with an incredibly quick answer.

Elvera: He's just here for a short stay while he completes some work.

Levi frowned slightly as Freja seemed to examine his physique with her bright, wide eyes.

Freja: You don't look much like a logger... Are you one of Avarson's?

Levi: I'm doing some work for him, but I don't work for him. Just making that clear.

Freja: Ah, I see. Nice catch.

She winked at Elvera.

Elvera: Come off it. Go back to your deeply fulfilling husband and get yourself to church.

Freja: Oh, I will. A woman has to fulfill her needs somehow.

She grinned once again, and then made her way off down the street. Elvera glanced at Levi; this time it was her turn to be slightly embarrassed. The braying of a horse was heard in the distance, along with the growing claps of

23

hooves upon cobblestones, but neither sound caught anyone's attention.

Elvera: Sorry about her.

Levi: No problem. She seemed simply delightful.

Elvera made to continue but was immediately cut short by her son's antics.

The young boy had clearly gotten bored during the rather adult conversation and had returned to playing with the newly formed roadside snowdrifts... but danger was rapidly headed towards him. Levi lunged forward, dragging Sigmund away by the shoulder just in time. Two great horses came barrelling down the road, leading a large carriage that clattered along the cobblestones, sending snow in all directions. It was beautifully carved, with lots of clever spirals and decorations engraved into the wooden structure, and the wheels were lined with a sparkling silver shine. The carriage continued rattling down the road, causing many of the wandering locals to quickly jump out of the way.

Levi: Damn. Someone's in a hurry.

Elvera huffed as the carriage trundled away, holding onto Sigmund protectively with a gloved hand.

Elvera: That 'someone' is your employer.

Levi fell quiet and stared after the carriage as it turned at the edge of the town square, heading off down into the valley. The tracks left in the newly accumulated snow were the only scarred reminders of its presence. Elvera began to march forward, muttering to herself more than anyone else.

Elvera: Come on, we're going to be late...

*

THE STATE OF AFFAIRS

In the very centre of the town stood a majestic building, the largest by far within the remote arctic valley. Built over a thousand years ago as an ancient Viking shelter, the substantial structure had been repaired and strengthened by every generation that had followed. With great wooden doors, and an extreme slanted roof, the building was known as Tväre's Hall of Memory. A tie to the ancestral roots of the wilderness. In the square outside, standing guard on either side of the central pathway, were two statues, each of them depicting a Viking warrior. One was a male, with a stoic shield and a beard to match; the other a female, with long braided hair falling around a gigantic sword. The plaques beneath each statue described the two warrior Vikings that had ruled the frozen lands many centuries ago, battling hard to keep the town protected from neighbouring barbarian clans before being lost on one of their great explorations.

Sigmund leant against one of these two great statues, hiding in the darkness of its shadow as the sun rose into the sky. The stone figures seemed to loom over him, their angry faces roaring curses and insults, as if he were currently under their judgement. Elvera and Levi stood nearby, shivering in the breeze as they watched the rest of the town head east to church.

> Levi: Who is it we're waiting for?

> Elvera: A man named Torsten. Our unofficial leader and the closest thing we have to a politician.

Levi glanced over towards the Hall of Memory, the unique architecture and design catching his eye.

> Levi: Is that why we're here? Politics?

Elvera chuckled.

> Elvera: Technically, yes. Every Sunday, the leader of the town mentors the children of Tväre in the ways of the council. Making decisions, learning to negotiate, preparing for the future...

She lowered her head, her voice dropping.

> Elvera: We had a few tough years a while back... Not many children were born. Sigmund's the only one old enough to learn, but it means he's on his own.

The single mother stared towards her despondent son as he leaned against the frozen stone of the Viking statue, his head low.

> Elvera: It's been a bit of a struggle convincing him to do it.

Levi nodded, beginning to understand the plights that both Elvera and Sigmund were facing. He looked out across the sparkling brilliance that was the Tväre landscape. He loved the folk's connection to their ancient culture, and it pleased him that so much of their history had been preserved. A lot of his travels had shown him a harsher approach to history, with people raiding, burning and selling off a lot of their own ancestry for the sake of guns or money. This new approach to life was refreshing, but clearly it came with its own set of troubles.

> Levi: It's human nature to want to be with others. Even with the beauty and wonder of this land around you every day, it's hard to stay cheerful when you feel alone...

Elvera stared at Levi for a moment, almost in awe.

> Levi: What?

> Elvera: It's just strange to hear an outside perspective for once. It's not something we get a lot of here, especially when most folk would have sooner let you freeze your Danish nose off than risk talking to you.

She gave a small laugh, though there wasn't much humour behind it. She joined Levi in staring across the snowy rooftops of her little mountainside town.

> Elvera: Most of us live out our entire lives here, never venturing further than the hills we see. We wake up and our eyes gloss over the lake and the trees every day, year after year...

She sighed again.

Elvera: But build something out of bricks and stone on the far shores, and suddenly it's the talk of the town.

She stared into the far distance, and Levi's eyes turned to see a horrible blight on the landscape, one which he'd seen many times already but often avoided staring at. Formed from a mess of orange bricks and black stones was an unsightly factory, exhibiting two ugly chimneys that speared their way into the blue sky. It wasn't colossal by any means, not compared to huge factories of Victorian London, but large enough that it still blighted the beauty of the valley. The snow around it was dirty and brown, as if its very presence stained the land it lay upon. Huge silver pipes lead away across the landscape, disappearing down into the ground. The factory was a relatively new addition to the town, having been completed only a few months ago, one of several that had been set up throughout the north to serve the newly upcoming logging industry that was now dominating the country.

Elvera began to enlighten Levi on the town's apparent gossip, a hint of sarcasm evident in her voice.

Elvera: The owner of that great masterpiece, your employer, is taking guardianship of the forests around Tväre in a few days time. More and more of his workers arrive every day. It's getting a lot more crowded than we're used to...

Levi pondered that thought.

Levi: Educate me. What is guardianship?

Elvera: You've never heard that term before?

Levi shook his head and Elvera happily filled him in.

Elvera: Every town in the Northern Valleys has a version. It's sort of like an agreement of trust. Someone manages or takes care of the land on your behalf and takes a small portion for their trouble. If someone like a farmer, or a herder, gets injured or sick, then it's a good agreement to have. But, in this case, it's not a farm... more the entire forest.

Levi gave the factory one more glance.

Levi: You sound like you don't approve of the plans...

The young woman shrugged and plunged her hands deep within her coat.

Elvera: I don't know what I think really. I was skeptical initially, but so was everyone. Then the railway opened and...

She stopped herself, closing her eyes fretfully.

Elvera: It's just a lot of changes... Too much at once for a small northern town like ours. But that's the way it is. It's what our Municipal Council voted for, so I can't argue.

Levi: I know that frustration. I've found there's no such thing as an honest councillor.

He laughed but he was on his own this time. Elvera muttered a curt reply.

Elvera: I'm on the council.

Levi bit his lip... and tried to hide his embarrassment.

A hefty thump from behind suddenly drew their attention towards the Hall of Memory. From the double set of great wooden doors came a large, powerfully built man, covered in pelts of thick brown fur for warmth. His eyes were grey and stern, and he grunted with every alternate step, as if the movement caused him pain. This must be the man Elvera had spoken of: Torsten. The unofficial leader of Tväre's Municipal Council. Though he didn't look like any politician Levi had ever seen; he actually appeared to know what he was supposed to be doing.

Sigmund stood upright as Torsten approached and passed him by, receiving only the briefest glance of recognition from the muscular man in return.

Torsten: I'm sorry to keep you waiting in the freezing cold Elvera. We've been dealing with the aftermath of the storm all night. Only just sorted out today's equipment...

His voice was tired and gravelly, a notable feature that frequently resulted in a lot of mocking from his fellow townsfolk. It sounded oddly like the man had filled his throat with pebbles and stones and then attempted to talk through them. He didn't smile nor did he seem upset, he was just plain grouchy.

> Elvera: I see. Are you still taking Sigmund with you this morning?

She sounded almost hopeful, but her face fell as Torsten responded.

> Torsten: Can't today, I'm afraid. Far too much to do. We've got to check and repair all the lake markers first and foremost. That's going to take all morning already.

> Elvera: Can't you bring him with you on that? Surely, he can be of some help. It'd be good for him…

Torsten lowered his voice.

> Torsten: I can't, Elvera. It's not that I don't want to, and I don't wish offence on you or your family by saying this, but Sigmund's a liability. He never shows any initiative, nor any willingness to help provide for the town. He's simply not a leader, and it would be a poor use of time to continue preparing him as one…

As he spoke, Elvera's breath became somewhat short.

> Elvera: What of the carnival…?

> Torsten: The honour of the Firelog is meant for those who stand by its values. At this point, we're going to have to choose another… someone more willing.

He withdrew from her, lowering his gaze.

> Torsten: I'm sorry.

And with that, he left, moving on to the next chore that was required of him but not before he spared a suspicious glance towards Levi. Elvera turned her face away from them both, staring down into the snow... After taking a long, deep breath, she spoke towards her son.

> Elvera: Sigmund?

The young boy glanced over.

Elvera: Come on.

Sigmund sullenly rejoined Levi and his mother. Without another word, they began the short walk through the snow to church...

*

A heavy carriage lumbered along the road of the town, passing more and more of the local townsfolk as they gathered together, ambling their way to the Sunday service. The great carved beast came to an eventual stop in a small yard, leaving deep marks in the snowy plain around it. From the beautifully fashioned door stepped a pair of pristine leather boots, the owner pausing as the soles descended into the snow below.

*

Levi: I'm guessing it's that church-looking building there?

Levi pointed towards a small courtyard that housed a lovely stone church, the steeple shooting up into the sky like a pointed needle. The walls were painted a pale white, with no signs of fading or peeling anywhere, complimented by the darkly coloured windows and doorframe. The paths had been salted and the heavy snow of the previous night shovelled neatly aside, allowing nearly the entirety of the local townsfolk to gather before the entrance, conversing with one another before the service began.

Levi: It's very well kept... How long has it been here?

Elvera: A few hundred years, at least. Probably even more... It's the only building that's technically owned by the people.

Levi furrowed his brow.

Levi: How did that happen?

Elvera: It belonged to the family that built it. But the last of them died without anyone to take the inheritance. So, she left it to the trust of the town. It belongs to everyone, and everyone takes care of it.

As Levi passed through the throng of thick coats, he noticed the people seemed to be crowded around a tall, proud man, dressed in fine clothes and a perfect ushanka styled hat, the kind that wrapped around the top of his head like a blanket, making him appear taller than he actually was. Several locks of perfect blonde hair snuck out from beneath the brown fur, a bright yellow stain on his forehead. Upon his hands were a pair of unmarked leather gloves, and Levi could see the glint of a gold watchchain poking out of the waistcoat that hid under his fur coverings.

The man's name was Avarson, and he was a wealthy industrialist set on transforming the humble little town into an economic paradise of the far north. He had first arrived well over a year ago, having presented himself as the owner and self-representative of the new Northern Valley Railway. Tväre had been one of the many towns he chose to add to his new network, linking the north to the south by a coal-powered railway for the first time in their histories. The trains weren't the only commodity that Avarson had dipped his wealthy hands in though.

Across the frozen surface of the Lake, on the far side of the valley, the great, ugly factory stared back. The huge and horrible blight was Avarson's crowning jewel within the Northern Valleys, though there was nothing sparkling about it. The railway came first, but it was merely a support network for transporting and delivering the produce of the great factory, which was specifically designed for one purpose: tree logging. It was Avarson's plan to become the key trader in logging exportation for the entirety of the Northern Valleys, and he had spent a great deal of money, time and energy into linking it all together... and in gaining the trust of each and every town to let him manage their forests on their behalf. The towns would get enough logs and subsidies to survive any winter that could ever hit them, and if Avarson earned a little profit on the side, no one really minded.

It was because of all this that Avarson's presence had gradually become a regularity in Tväre, though why he'd stayed so long in the quaint little town, no-one could quite figure out. Maybe it was to keep an eye on his projects personally, who knew for sure except for him? But despite his outward appearance of wealth and perfection, and the subtly arrogant way about him, the townsfolk believed he had their own interests at heart and was simply trying his best to just fit in with them and their unique culture. He spoke to many of them now, a cheerful smile adorning his face.

Avarson: Believe me, it never gets tiring. Wherever my work takes me, the message of the Bible comes with it. Like a heavy blizzard, once you're caught in it, you can't avoid it!

The townsfolk laughed along with him.

Avarson: I am very impressed though. I've been here throughout all four of the seasons now, and your amazing town is still capable of surprising me. Even after the nightmare that was last night, here you all are the next day, not even a minute late!

An elderly man named Almarr spoke up. He was a spirit of great energy, beloved by all in the town.

Almarr: Ah, a little storm doesn't stop us that easy!

Avarson: I don't doubt it. It'll take a lot more than nature to put you down old man!

Again, everyone laughed as Avarson threw his hands up in defense.

Avarson: I'm joking, I'm joking. I honestly just appreciate you all for letting me get so involved here. Trust is a hard thing to dig up nowadays, so it is really pleasing to find so much of it here.

Everyone nodded. Several women in the crowd, including Freja, vocalised their support.

Freja: You're welcome anytime!

Annali: Hear hear! You're a part of this town now.

Beyond the inner ring of the small crowd stood Levi, Elvera and Sigmund, who had shifted closer to overhear Avarson's kindly words. Levi gently pointed him out to Elvera, keeping his voice low.

Levi: That's the man who's hired me... Avarson.

Elvera nodded.

Elvera: I thought as much.

Levi: He lives here!?

Levi quietly exclaimed, but Elvera quickly frowned.

Elvera: Oh, not at all. He only appeared on our doorstep a year or so ago. The factory and the railway quickly followed. Now it's like he's our own personal saviour.

The nearby townsfolk chuckled again as Avarson made yet another joke.

Levi: Clearly there's a lot of love for him.

Elvera narrowed her eyes.

Elvera: They love his words.

Sigmund pulled on Elvera's sleeve, and she bent down to listen to him. He seemed slightly distressed by something, but Levi could not hear anything over the mutterings of the crowd. At that moment, the bells of the church rang out again and the Minister appeared at the entrance, ready to welcome everyone who hadn't already entered.

As they approached the church together, Elvera briefly spoke with another woman, Annali, who introduced herself to Levi as Elvera's rather excitable younger sister. They exchanged quick promises of a dinner together later that day and began to pass beneath the humble entrance of the church, the small building emanating a feeling of hope and warmth as more and more of the town gathered inside. Levi turned and laid his eyes on the dark skin tone of an aged African man, who smiled and greeted every single person that passed him by.

His full name was Benjamin Aigetoro, but he had shortened it himself to ease the pronunciation for the locals. And since that moment, the nickname 'Minister Toro' had stuck. After giving Elvera a quick hug and leaning down to jokingly shake Sigmund's hand like an adult, he grasped Levi's hand warmly, welcoming him to the church. His voice had the faint element of a thick accent, grown from a country much further south than here.

> Minister Toro: Hello. Welcome. I think I recognise you from around town, but I don't believe we've met...

> Levi: No sir, we haven't. Call me Levi.

The old Minister smiled, pleased at the chance to introduce himself to someone new.

> Minister Toro: Benjamin Toro. Forgive me if I'm wrong, but you are a visitor to the far north, yes? I haven't been ignoring you for twenty years, have I?

He nervously chuckled as Elvera quickly chimed in.

> Elvera: He's with me.

> Levi: I travelled up here a week ago. Drawn by promise of work from Avarson.

Levi nodded back towards the small crowd outside, where Avarson continued to entertain.

> Levi: I got lost during the blizzard last night and Elvera took me in. She then invited me to come along this morning and... here I am.

> Minister Toro: Ah well, it's always good to see new faces, even if some of the other folk remain wary of them. Where have you travelled from, may I ask?

Levi gave Elvera a quick, hinting look before answering.

> Levi: England.

Minister Toro raised his eyebrows.

> Minister Toro: Quite the journey then! I'm a traveller myself of sorts... obviously.

He indicated towards his exposed skin and chuckled. Being the only person of colour to live in the town of Tväre, it was obvious that Minister Toro stood out among his brethren. With his short and grey curly hair, there had been the odd stare when he had first appeared many years ago, travelling

34

up through the country for work and exploration with several others. The folk of such a remote culture had been somewhat cautious, but the town had welcomed him in once they felt his kindness and friendship, enough so that he'd stayed ever since, settling into the church as their Minister.

> Minister Toro: I used to think the nights of the desert were cold, but I've learnt that the word has its own meaning up here.

Minister Toro held up his hand, proudly displaying an old scar that ran across his palm and onto his fingers. It was clearly a sign of early onset frostbite, an injury that he had since healed from, though the scar still remained as a painful reminder. Levi winced at the sight.

> Levi: Oof... I was lucky not to come away with worse than wind burn. If not for Elvera, there'd be a funeral today instead of a service.

He laughed nervously at the thought.

> Minister Toro: Lucky, maybe. Or it was God looking out for you.

> Levi: Maybe...

They both smiled as the Minister turned his attention to the next awaiting visitor in line. Levi and Elvera moved into the interior of the church, finding a wooden pew that still had room upon it and began conversing with the others of the town they hadn't yet spoken to.

Avarson was the last to enter, his leather boots clumping on the floor. He looked around the interior of the church and smiled, taking a long and deep breath.

> Avarson: I do love that old church smell.

The kindly Minister interrupted his embrace.

> Minister Toro: Good to have you back Avarson.

> Avarson: Good to be back.

> Minister Toro: Your trip south worked out well, I trust?

Avarson stared at the congregation as he spoke, as if watching over them.

Avarson: It did. It did indeed.

They both smiled, though each smile was very different to the other. Avarson moved on ahead, after getting in a final word.

Avarson: I look forward to hearing you speak, Father.

He strode to the front of the church, taking one of the prime seats in the front row. He shifted a pillow nearby underneath him for comfort, the other occupiers gently moving up the pew to allow him to sit down. He threw his huge fur coat forward out of the way of himself, getting comfortable as Minister Toro approached the ancient carved pulpit at the front.

Minister Toro: Welcome, all. Let us begin, as we should, in prayer.

Everyone, except Avarson, bowed their heads...

**

The ice in the Lake ran deep, creaking and groaning as it tried to settle. At its lowest temperatures, Lake Tväre would completely freeze. Thousands of tonnes of water would suddenly become trapped in the valley, fed even more each day by the near-freezing river. The pressure from the weight of the ice would build, and eventually snap, the resulting effect creating shuddering cracks in the ice that ran deep into the earth. No-one knew what was down there, no-one dared to find out. The unknown depths were not worth the risk, and hundreds of stories from the ancestral past repeatedly warned the town that it was better to keep your distance... and respect the will of the Lake.

These stories, however, had no effect upon the two men that were now trudging through the snowdrifts that bordered the desolate surface of the Lake. The wind, although calm, still had the occasional chilling gust to it, and the men shielded their faces while they walked. One carried a heavy shovel and the other a stack of long wooden rods. They came across a similarly large thin rod, this one

36

protruding out from within the snowy ground. The rod had snapped at some point in the night, leaving the other half buried somewhere unknown.

A strong, wolf-like dog, with fur of grey, brown and black, sniffed the broken tip of the pole, and then lay down in the snow for a rest. The cold didn't bother the cheerful animal, who sat there smiling and panting as the two men stopped by the broken marker themselves. Without any prompting, they readied the shovel and began to dig out the rest of the broken marker from the confines of the ground. The larger of the two grunted out a question.

> Torsten: How many left?

His younger brother, Vargard, shifted the stack of markers he'd been carrying over his shoulder. All of them had a red band tied around the top of them for identification.

> Vargard: I think there's ten markers to go on this trail…

Torsten gritted his teeth.

> Torsten: And how many do we have left!?

The youngest brother looked through the stack again.

> Vargard: Uh… Eight.

> Torsten: Right. Not all of them will be broken, so we should have enough for the ones that are left.

Vargard nodded. They were both getting tired from their work on the Lake, but it was essential that they complete it. The markers were there as indicators, separating the edge of the land from the ice. Whilst many of the town often walked upon the Lake in winter, either for ice-fishing, training their dogs, or just a morning walk, there was always the risk of collapse, especially when the spring thaw began. The snow of the land and the ice of the Lake appeared identical, and it was almost impossible to distinguish the two masses apart… unless the markers were there.

Vargard examined the broken pole closely, shocked by the damage.

Vargard: The wind's properly snapped this one in half...

Torsten: I'm not surprised... It was like a war out here last night. Worst one this year so far, that's for sure.

Vargard managed to pull the broken marker from the snowy ground. He breathed heavily, his scarf flapping gently in the wind. His dozing dog lifted its head curiously, thinking he might be offering something.

Vargard: What do you want? You want this?

Vargard held up the broken pole, the ears of his faithful dog springing to attention at the sight of the new toy.

Vargard: Go on then.

He launched the remains of the pole over the dog's head, sending him flying into the snow-covered grasslands, where the dog immediately began rolling and wriggling on the ground.

Vargard: Daft dog...

Vargard muttered to himself before turning back to the job at hand.

Vargard: Was any of the main town damaged this morning?

Torsten paused to think, reading the next marker for burial.

Torsten: Uh... Not that I could see. Only small parts, like these annoying things. Though I did see the railway clearing the tracks earlier this morning.

Vargard looked up curiously.

Vargard: Oh yeah? It's about time those workers did something useful.

Torsten: Oh no, they weren't doing anything. I meant the railway itself. Someone had attached this huge metal 'cage' to the front of the metal beast.

He held out his free hand, demonstrating the motion.

Torsten: As it went past, it just threw all the snow out the way as if it wasn't there. Just incredible...

Torsten placed the marker alongside the old marker's empty hole, gently hammering it down into the ground using a small hammer that he'd withdrawn from his bag.

Vargard: I'd never have thought we'd get anything like that here. Think how easy it'll be to get to the next town over once it's open to us. We'll be able to get to Järven in less than an hour...

Torsten lowered the hammer.

Torsten: Is this about that girl again? Tanya! That was it! The one who visited halfway through autumn from Järven!? It is, isn't it!?

Vargard blushed; he'd been caught.

Vargard: Fine, yeah maybe...

Torsten, like the typical older brother, capitalised on his brother's emotions.

Torsten: You realise she's probably already married right? Unless she's younger than you said she was?

Vargard: No, she said she wasn't.

The older brother rolled his eyes.

Torsten: Women will say anything, especially ones from Järven. Were you selling any of your firelogs at the time? She might have just been trying to get a better deal out of you.

Vargard: Alright, can you leave it alone now!?

Torsten returned to the task at hand, the marker descending into the deep snow with every blow of his hammer.

Torsten: I'm just looking out for you brother.

Vargard: No, you're not. You're just jealous...

With that slightest provocation, the two brothers descended into an argument, their voices becoming sharp and fast.

Torsten: Oh, come off it. Why would I be jealous of you?

Vargard: Because I might actually get to choose who I spend my life with.

Torsten lowered his voice. Not in a gentle way, but one that was much calmer, and much more dangerous.

Torsten: Careful what you say next Vargard...

Vargard: Oh, what are you gonna do? Stop me from going to Järven like you did the last time!?

Torsten: I wasn't trying—

A deafening, echoing crack reverberated from under their feet. The worrying kind of sound, like the ones heard under sleeping mountains before they wake up with fiery fountains of fire and ash... The two brothers, immediately on alert, looked across the Lake's surface. A deep fissure had opened up within the ice, leading off into the distance where Avarson's ugly factory lay on the shoreline. The tiny ravine was by no means large, for it was only noticeable when one stood directly above it, but the sound it had made wasn't one to be taken lightly... Vargard's faithful dog raised its head in the distance, sensing something unusual.

Vargard: Was that us...?

Torsten didn't reply. He instead lowered the hammer and moved onto the surface of the Lake itself, kicking the thin layer of snow and peering down at the newly formed crack in the ice. For the briefest of moments, there was a shining blue aura glowing within the depths, but then it went black.

Vargard: Torsten...What is it?

Torsten took a deep, controlling breath.

Torsten: It's just a crack.

Vargard: Are you sure? It sounded a lot worse than that...

Torsten replied to his fearful brother. He tried to sound confident, but uncertainty ran through his voice.

Torsten: Yeah, I'm sure. Come on, let's finish marking out the shoreline.

They hesitantly returned to their task at hand, neither of them raising so much as another word.

**

Minister Toro: I'd like to start with a story I was told when I grew up.

The old Minister's deep and powerful voice echoed around the small church. Everyone sat in their respective seat, transfixed by the words of the African preacher. He was so different to them: his name, his mannerisms, his origins... but they respected him more than any other in their town. Minister Toro had brought hope and meaning to the church when he had first arrived, especially since the town had lacked such spiritual guidance due to their previously ancient pastor finally returning to the ground. Minister Toro had first arrived with two other missionaries, all of whom were making their way through the Northern Valleys to talk with the local churches and share the gospel to the towns and villages that had no such links. But upon seeing the companionship and friendliness of the town of Tväre, and the vacant spot in their ministry, he had decided to stay long past the few months put aside for his travels. Nearly two decades later, he was still preaching in that little church, promoting care and love, and challenging the people to do better for one another.

Minister Toro: A Shoebill, which is a rather ugly bird found in my homeland, was tending to its young chicks. As they grew, the chicks would cry out for water, and the Shoebill would deliver some. As they grew more, the chicks would cry out for food, and again the Shoebill would provide. Then one day, the Shoebill was late to return... and in panic, the chicks fled the nest...

He rested to take a breath. The congregation didn't move, all of them caught in the eloquence of his delivery. There was no struggle in understanding him, nor any hint of hesitation or a stutter.

41

Minister Toro: It is the hardest of trials, to keep your faith strong when times get hard... To be patient and wait, instead of fleeing the nest and taking it all on ourselves. We think we are good enough to solve problems without God, OR we might think that he's abandoned us...

He paused, the townsfolk hanging onto his every word.

Minister Toro: It's easier to just dismiss the idea of a God, especially when there's so much else happening in this world. Why do evil things happen? Why do our businesses and livelihoods struggle...?

The congregation nodded in agreement as Minister Toro reeled off his selection of difficult questions. Avarson, however, smiled smugly to himself.

Minister Toro: We can quickly forget the blessings we've been given because we take them for granted. Sometimes, we need not look further than our own front pew.

The folk chuckled as Avarson raised his head and looked around with a big grin on his face, clearly relishing in the love of the people.

Minister Toro: And sometimes, the blessings are hidden... behind the darkness that lives in our society...

**

The congregation filed out of the church in unison, chatting about the morning's message and their individual plans for the remainder of the day, mostly involving either preparing food or clearing their paths and lands from the buildup of snow. The sun now poked through the clouds and the rays were reflecting across the frosted surface of Lake Tväre, bouncing off the sparkling layer of ice and back into the sky.

A heavy whistle shot through the air, the kind that pierces through the ears, turning the heads of many of the local townsfolk towards its source. A jet of black smoke began to surge upwards in the distance, billowing near the western reaches of the Lake. As the people turned and watched, the powerful shadow of a coal-powered train charged across the land, followed by carriage after carriage. The great machine dominated the landscape; all eyes watching its screeching movements.

Avarson: Revolutionary, isn't it.

Avarson's smooth voice sounded out from behind the small crowd, once again gathering their attention. He emphasised every sentence he spoke, almost commanding over the town as their leader and guide.

Avarson: My hope is to have the Northern Valley Railway coming in two or three times a day once the factory is in full operation. Imagine that. Being able to travel all the way to the heights of Stockholm in just a single day and night at any time of the year you wish. You're finally connected to the rest of the world.

One curious townsperson spoke up.

Townsman: The factory's been smoking away for months now. Isn't it up and running already?

Avarson: Oh, my good man, hardly. What you're seeing is just a third of what it can do! A few select trees from Järven's valleys, along with several from the west river, are all that's being processed right now. But when it reaches max capacity, the railway will join its pace, and we'll all be benefiting from the fruits of the forests!

The townsfolk muttered in appreciation. The very idea of travelling across the country so easily was merely a playful dream to such a remote town. Yet, as they looked out across the landscape, that dream was flying past them, the shriek of its whistle announcing its presence to all around. One of the young women from earlier, Elvera's sister, probed Avarson further.

Annali: When do you think we'll be able to board it ourselves then?

Avarson: You seem eager. Are you trying to get away from everyone here?

Limited laughter met his little joke before he continued.

Avarson: Just as long as the signing of Guardianship goes ahead next week, I can't see why it won't be any more than a few weeks. So, enjoy the view! It's a sign of good times.

The people hummed intriguingly. But from the front of the admiring group came a small and unappreciative mutter.

Sigmund: It looks ugly...

Avarson shot his head round, his bright blue eyes searching like a spotlight for the mumbling voice that had interrupted his perfect moment.

Avarson: Who said that!?

Elvera quickly reached down and took Sigmund's hand, gently pulling him away. Avarson immediately spotted them, charging towards their direction as he hunted Sigmund down. Levi stood and watched nearby, somewhat concerned by the sudden change in Avarson's expression.

The industrialist quickly reached the mother and son pair, his persuasive and articulate tone now replaced by one that was a bit more reactive.

Avarson: Wait! Was that you son?

Elvera stood her ground.

Elvera: He didn't mean any insult. He was just saying what he thinks—

Avarson held up his hand, instantly silencing her.

Avarson: It's okay... I'm sure he can answer for himself.

He turned back to Sigmund, crouching down to join him on his level.

Avarson: I'm just curious why you would say such a thing my boy. This railway is the new pride of your town. It's bringing you into the new world. This is your future!

Sigmund looked up at him, with all the wonderful defiance of a young boy who didn't care for his words.

Sigmund: It looks ugly.

Avarson blinked in shock.

> Avarson: Son. That is what success looks like. Hmm? It's not ugly. It's good. And you should be grateful; you're getting it all given to you... Don't you see that!?

Sigmund looked away uncaringly. Avarson's cheeks began to grow slightly red, his patience being driven hard by Sigmund's attitude. Elvera now took control, leading Sigmund away.

> Elvera: We should go... Sigmund, come on.

Avarson let them go without another complaint. He stayed crouched for a moment; his gloved hands gripped into fists. He rose up and faced the crowd, now realising they had remained to watch the incident unfold for themselves. Avarson immediately put on a fake smile.

> Avarson: Children eh?

He forced a weak laugh and then waved his hands, silently ordering the crowd to move apart to let him through. His locks of perfect blonde hair shone in the sun as he disappeared and then the rest of the congregation finally dispersed.

***

The Inevitable

The view was pristine. Thousands of trees populated the valley around Lake Tväre, all of them twinkling in the sunlight, the light reflected by each individual crystal of snow that had made their homes on the branches of every fir tree. Occasionally, the layers of snow would fall away in a great cloud of white, either disturbed by gravity or by the movement of a clumsy animal.

Levi sat upon his own private balcony, staring out across the wonderous expanse before him from the comfort of his room. The hostel he was staying in was only a small place, fit only for a couple dozen people at best. Whilst, yes, the people of Tväre were somewhat judgemental of outsiders, they did – albeit rarely - entertain visitors from neighbouring northern towns, either for trade, family visits or emergencies. And this hostel was where they often stayed. The generous spirit of Avarson had provided the hostel with a bit of financial support, as he had with several other trades and businesses within Tväre. In return, the industrialist was offered a room to stay in whenever he wanted, despite being perfectly able to stay in his own empty house or sleep in the depths of his factory across the shores. He'd, therefore, given Levi the freedom of the complimentary room while his work was in progress, and that came with the beautiful balcony and accompanying view that Levi now stared at lovingly.

The young cartographer now pulled out a strange wooden contraption, one that unlocked and unfolded to form a sort of portable desk, complete with little holes for inkwells and little pins for securing notes and papers. Levi placed one such manuscript on it now, a beautifully drawn map of Tväre that omitted the accuracy and detail of the land and buildings in exchange for drawings of mountains and animals with stark similarities to the famous maps of old explorers. Withdrawing one of his many styluses, Levi sat himself down and began to add to his map, using the view before him for inspiration. He sat there for well beyond an hour, his drawings precise and accurate, matching the mystery of the land he sat within.

After several minutes of watching the clouds move across the tops of the snowy hills, Levi flicked his eyes to his wristwatch. It was an old style of clock, the face covered by a metal guard to protect it from the elements that Levi often encountered, but the numbers could still be seen through the gaps. The next stage of Avarson's work was due. It was time to return to the task at hand.

*

It was often feared that at the darkest point in winter, an icy figure would be seen skulking across the shifting expanse of the Lake, eyes shining whiter than the sun at midday. Believed to emerge only once a year, the wraith first appeared to protect its unbordered territory from those who dared pose a threat. And if you happened to look out your window, towards the white hills of the Four Sisters in the distance, at the darkest point in the night, you might just spot an emaciated form, shifting its way through the mist…

The legend of the Ice-man was so deeply written into Tväre's community, that the evening of the winter solstice now hosted a small 'Carnival of the Fires' as it was known. A festival of warmth set up to fight against the devastating cold that the frost brought each year. What once began as an offering to the old Norse gods and the ice-wraith for protection had now become an evening of social fun and cheer, mixed with the rather dangerous tradition of placing lit candles in windows. Specially crafted firelogs were carved and hollowed by hand, lit and then placed all around the town, burning and glowing for hours without any assistance. It was truly not to be missed.

As Levi ambled through the little town, the preparations began to make themselves apparent. The square had been cleared of the heavy snow drifts caused by the blizzard and was now thriving with activity. Levi was one of the many townsfolk now walking along one of the central pathways, every direction bringing a new sight. Stalls seemed to spring up like flowers in the spring thaw, the grunts of shovelling and lifting echoed in the valley. All around him, the wooden skeleton of a massive hand-crafted sculpture took on its immense form. It was a colossal tower, as tall

47

as the tallest building in Tväre, rising up like a huge unlit torch. It was only half complete at this moment in time, but Levi was still astounded by the progress. Members of the town hammered in nails and supports, their friendly greetings matched by the occasional argument.

Townsman: A steg to the left... Marc!

An older man shouted up to the younger man above, who was busy helping to assemble the sculpture from above.

Marc: What!?

Townsman: A steg to the left! It's too far over!

Marc quickly lost his patience.

Marc: What the hell is a 'steg'!?

Townsman: It's just under a metre.

Marc: Then just say that then! I'm not a thousand years old!

The old townsman rolled his eyes as his son corrected the work. He then turned and grumpily picked up one of the large wooden beams, leading it away to another part of the town square.

Townsman: Watch it Outsider!

Levi ducked out of the way of the moving beam, narrowly avoiding his head being knocked from his shoulders. He muttered a short apology and continued on his way, the old townsman staring after him in distaste. The folk of Tväre could be awfully blunt, but that was their way; they meant no harm. It was just very different to the overly polite Britishness that Levi had grown up with.

He continued on his way, passing the double statues of the twin Viking heroes. Levi glanced up at them, their stony eyes staring back at him... watching every step that he took as he neared the town's Hall of Memory. The great wooden doors heaved open as he pulled on the heavy handle, ready to delve inside the impressive building.

*

The dimly lit room was full of dusty books, from neatly arranged ledges to random, unbalanced piles in the corners. The shelves within this rather sizable library seemed to show a general progression of age, with the newer shelves and books near the entrance, and the oldest, dustier shelves hidden away towards the back. Levi's footsteps echoed as he left the stairs of the entrance for the cobblestone floor. The torches were lit around the room already, so there was no need for any candles, and Levi could see all the way to the back of every shelving corridor.

He had visited the library that lay below the town several times already, having found the ancient maps of the town, and the terrain of the lands surrounding it, on his first visit. He'd been amazed at how far back the records went, with some drawings and notes written alongside unmistakable Viking runes, detailing the construction of certain buildings or the beginnings of great voyages during the springtime melt. Though he had to take care when handling such documents, for some of them were incredibly old and fragile.

Levi began where he had previously left off, searching the library for any information on land registry that he could find. He'd completed his research into the borders of the forests and was now entering the next stage of his work, which involved the documentation of each patch of land that belonged to each individual currently living in Tväre, from local buildings to the farmlands around the Lake.

Levi was searching through the drawers, when suddenly, he stopped. He could sense something... Something watching him...

He jolted back! A huge shadow flew by his head, nearly colliding with him. Levi glanced around, panicking as adrenalin soared through his veins. What was it that had nearly hit him!? And at such a speed!?

A dark shape caught his attention. In the corner of the room, landing upon the top of an old bookshelf, was a huge grey pigeon-looking thing. The beady-eyed bird steadied itself, turning its head back to stare at Levi. A singular yellow eye bore into him from above, watching his every move. Levi had no idea what to do, or what to think. A pigeon? And in here of all places? It was very strange...

> Levi: Hello Mister Pigeon.

Levi slowly approached the great grey bird. It didn't seem intent on hurting him, and Levi deduced that it was more curious than annoyed by his presence. His feathers weren't puffing out in anger, and he pecked and cleaned his claws in the way relaxed animals do. Levi had always liked animals, always choosing to approach and seeing if he could pet them, before inevitably scaring them off. This explained the occasional scars on his hand, which were owed to the random and slightly aggressive stray dog.

> The Librarian: He doesn't like new people.

Levi whirled around. He was already on such high alert, and this calm new voice had made him jump. The thick, grey eyebrows of an elderly woman shot up, amused by his reaction. Her long grey hair was smooth and straight, tied into a small bun behind her head with a feather poking through it. Additionally, she wore a thick woollen gown that had been hemmed and refitted to be tighter to the skin, secured around her waist by a thin, black sash. The style was very out of place for a town like Tväre, but Levi struggled to place where an outfit such as hers would ever look normal in the world.

The old woman continued, her voice quiet but ever so slightly judgemental.

> The Librarian: Then again, most around here don't like new people...

Levi managed a reply.

> Levi: Are you including yourself in that?

> The Librarian: Yes.

Her own reply was instant. Levi watched tentatively as the strange woman began to slowly walk around him.

> The Librarian: New people mean new troubles. They're unpredictable and often difficult to compromise with.

Levi was a bit taken aback; was this woman insulting him?

> Levi: Well, maybe it's because you don't start by introducing yourself to them first?

The Librarian hummed thoughtfully and moved towards the nearest bookshelf, her long, white hair shining as it moved within the firelight. She reached one wrinkled hand up towards the top shelf, depositing a few little crumbs of biscuit up there. Almost immediately, the large, grey pigeon came waddling over, quickly persuaded by the delivery of food.

> The Librarian: I'm assuming you're looking for a book?

> Levi: That's why I'm in a library.

The sarcastic response wasn't his best choice. The Librarian stared at him for a moment before reaching up to stroke the pigeon, its pluming feathers soft to the touch.

> The Librarian: You see Peckingham, I told you he'd be rude.

The pigeon didn't seem to listen. He was quite happy with his crumbs, pecking at them with incredible greed. Levi took a short breath, composing himself.

> Levi: I didn't mean it like that...

The Librarian continued speaking to Peckingham, almost as if Levi wasn't there.

> The Librarian: Look at him fluster. He's trying to apologise now.

> Levi: Yes, I am! I overreacted. I'm sorry...

The Librarian stared at him again with her unwavering gaze of grey. It was almost haunting. But then, she seemed to forgive him.

> The Librarian: What assistance can I offer?

> Levi: I'm looking for Tväre's land registry, or anything similar. A document or a map that shows the boundaries of land for each building and farm.

The Libarian narrowed her eyes in thought. She finished stroking Peckingham's beautiful feathers, leaving him to enjoy whatever crumbs were left. Turning gracefully, she made her way down one of the corridors, gently commanding Levi to join her.

The Librarian: Follow me then.

Levi tentatively followed, shifting his way past Peckingham's distracted form on the shelf above. The pigeon lifted its head, its yellow eyes staring at Levi as he joined the Librarian at a set of strange desks, each of which held its own built-in drawer. The Librarian pulled on one, opening it to reveal several huge and ancient maps, some showing the buildings of Tväre, some showing the surrounding farmlands, and others showing the routes to the nearest neighbouring towns. Beside these maps lay several leatherbound books, which the old woman gently began to retrieve, speaking slowly as she worked.

> The Librarian: You might be fishing in an empty lake if you're looking for something detailed like a land registry. Family names. That's all there is here. People don't usually concern themselves with exact borders this far north.

She continued rifling through the assortment of documents, her eyes flicking from one book to the next.

> The Librarian: I know, also, that many of the townsfolk have recently taken out loans against their homes from that overbearing southern man... This wouldn't happen to be a link to that, would it?

She gave Levi a perceptive look.

Levi: Not to my knowledge.

The Librarian laughed once.

> The Librarian: Ah! Here we are.

She swiftly withdrew a faded brown book and accompanying map, handing them over to Levi.

> The Librarian: Outlines of the farms and fields around Tväre. I have to inform you that they are a

couple of decades old... Such is the way of a small town.

Levi: No no, that's plenty good enough. Better than I expected.

The Librarian hummed as Levi took the map and laid it out across the nearest desk, scanning its huge size for any potential use it could have in his work. After watching him for several moments, she turned and withdrew a dishevelled looking book from high upon the opposite shelf.

The Librarian: This may also be of some help...

Levi glanced over.

Levi: What is it?

He reached out curiously, carefully taking the book from her wrinkled hand.

The Librarian: A book detailing stories and legends of Tväre. It's not as exciting as a land registry but I have no doubt it might be of some use in your cartographical endeavours.

Levi skimmed through the book, frowning as he came across drawings and sketches of Viking longships and sea dragons, all matched with heavy sections of old Norse text.

Levi: I appreciate the thought, but I'm not a child who hides themselves behind fantasies and stories. There's a reason why modern maps left them behind.

The corner of the Librarian's mouth curled as she curtly replied.

The Librarian: Because you know exactly what kind of maps the world needs...

Levi stared at her for a second. He then closed the book dismissively and went to hand it back, but the Librarian refused.

The Librarian: Give it a read anyway. Who knows, you might soon find yourself questioning that very belief.

With current business concluded, the Librarian turned and began to walk away.

The Librarian: I wish you well in your work, young master Levi.

And before Levi could respond, the old woman disappeared up the entrance steps of the library. Peckingham's little claws scratched on the bookshelf above Levi as he took off, vanishing into the rafters somewhere else. Levi was left alone, somewhat baffled by the curious exchange.

**

Deep within the warm recesses of the Bergskydd Tavern, which remained partially buried under the snowdrifts, there gathered many of the townsfolk. Hervor's tavern was one of the most, if not the most, popular in the town, and once or twice every week, the place was completely rammed with locals. Every seat and table was occupied, and every person had some form of alcohol in front of them, served in beautifully carved wooden mugs of various sizes. One man sat himself at the bar, proudly placing a huge frothing mug down in front of himself, only for the man next to him to be served one that was double the size. Barrels were disappearing from the back wall rapidly, and poor Hervor was being rushed off her feet, desperately trying to quell the impossible thirst of the town.

Up until recently, nights such as these had only come around once every few weeks, with the townsfolk often spreading their evenings of drinking and mischief throughout other days. But with increasing numbers of workers and loggers, all under the employ of Avarson, turning up every day, the local bars and taverns had become full of strangers and unsociable labourers. In a bid to keep the Bergskydd Tavern as a local favourite, and after several predictable and rather hate-fuelled complaints from certain members of the townsfolk, Hervor had agreed to the idea of reserving a couple of nights a week purely for local enjoyment only. Thus outsiders, such as Levi or the loggers, were unwelcome. This was not intended to be in a rude or segregational type of way, it was more like the only solution that the town could think of on such short notice. In any city or large town, such an approach would have been unheard of, but Tväre was unlike any other place in this world. Locals were local and outsiders were kept outside.

Several members of the Municipal Council of Tväre were present, including Torsten, his father Almarr and additionally Elvera, who were all enjoying a drink with their friends. Sigmund was staying the evening with his aunt Annali, who lived just a street away, allowing Elvera an evening of her own every now and again. The folk gossiped and chattered about many different things, the main point of conversation being the upcoming Carnival of the Fires and the preparation that was yet to be completed. But there was also another pressing matter, which Torsten quickly summarised.

> Torsten: So, despite the blizzard, which caused only a small setback, it looks like we're gearing up to have a good carnival this year. A busier one than we were expecting maybe, but we've never had a problem before...

> Jurgen: It's only busier because we've been flooded with those damn loggers.

A grumpy, middle-aged man, known to the community as Jurgen, spoke up. As was the way in most of his conversations, his first sentence was a complaint, as was his second.

> Jurgen: More and more get off that damn rail train each morning, all looking for somewhere to stay. I go for a walk in the square now and I see more people from the south than I do from my own town!

> Torsten: It's not for much longer. Most of them are just contractors. Once the Guardianship papers are signed, they'll do the rest of the work in our forests and then they'll move on.

Jurgen took a sip of his drink.

> Jurgen: The ones who work in the factory will still be here though...

> Torsten: That place looks after itself. It's not exactly close to us, is it.

Jurgen scoffed, his complaints now gathering the attention of others talking around them.

Jurgen: Close enough that it's the first thing I see every morning! Even when the mist is down, those chimneys somehow poke through the clouds. They follow me around, I swear.

Torsten rolled his eyes, giving up the argument.

Torsten: Whatever. You see it as a problem, I see it as a new opportunity for Tväre. We would never have even gotten the railway link had we not agreed to the factory in the first place.

The table fell into silence. Elvera took the opportunity to finally add her thoughts.

Elvera: Have we signed the document ourselves? The Guardianship one?

She glanced around the table, avoiding eye contact with Torsten.

Torsten: Uh, no. Not yet... But as long as it's done before the evening of the carnival, we'll be alright. Otherwise, we might have to deal with those outsiders staying around for a little bit longer...

Torsten aimed the last part as a joke towards Jurgen, who snorted in response. His face remained grouchy, and his forehead was wrinkled with the scars of a life spent frowning. Torsten poked him in the arm.

Torsten: Come on, Jurgen. It'll be fine. Besides, not every outsider is a bad egg. The Minister's been here for so long, he's one of us now, and Avarson's never put a foot wrong since we've known him.

Jurgen grunted uncaringly.

Torsten: Elvera even rescued one of his newly hired hands from the blizzard the other night and, apparently, he was very gracious.

Elvera shot a small frown Torsten's way.

Elvera: How do you know about that?

Torsten: Hervor told me earlier today.

Jurgen: Well, you should have left him outside! He then might have learnt some consequences.

Elvera nearly scoffed at Jurgen's complete disregard for human life.

Elvera: Jurgen...

Jurgen: I'm serious. If they can't handle our way of life, they shouldn't even be here!

His voice began to rise, a change that Elvera matched.

Elvera: Our way of life is not letting a man freeze just because he stumbles. Outsider or not, I couldn't do that to him. Besides, there was barely anything to him anyway, he would have frozen instantly!

Hervor appeared behind everyone, holding two great wooden jugs in either hand, each of them filled to the brim with alcohol.

Hervor: Is that the skinny looking one who makes all those drawings?

Elvera: They're maps, I think. But yeah, that's the one. The only outsider without a beard.

They laughed, all remembering the notable Levi. Hervor began to refill their mugs, raising another question to Elvera.

Hervor: Did you say you took him inside from the blizzard?

Elvera: Yep. He banged on my door by accident. He was completely lost.

Jurgen: Clearly his maps weren't good enough.

Jurgen muttered a retort, getting only a reduced smirk from Torsten. Hervor continued on, ignoring him like most people did.

Hervor: He was in here earlier that same evening. I told him to take care of himself right before he left as the wind was picking up... Looks like he didn't listen.

Torsten: Don't take it personally Hervor. None of us really listen to you either.

Hervor rolled her eyes as everyone laughed again.

Hervor: Well, if you did, you'd find life would become a hell of a lot simpler. I've always said this town was better off without all these supposed blessings. It was hard enough before all the railway men started coming in here to forget their day. Now I'm run off my feet every evening trying to serve them all...

Elvera chimed in, raising a notable perspective.

Elvera: But surely, you're making a lot more money from them all, no? I mean, you're one of the few who hasn't needed some sort of financial help from Avarson, so clearly you're doing well.

Everyone around the table nodded thoughtfully, as Hervor quickly wiped up a spill on the table.

Hervor: Oh, the money is certainly welcome, don't get me wrong. I was just happy with how things were before that ugly factory went up. I hate to say it... but I have to agree with Jurgen.

Everyone at the table chuckled, except for Jurgen of course. Their conversations continued as Hervor returned to her natural position behind the bar. Just as everyone began to forget about the annoyances of their lives outside the tavern, they were all interrupted by the creak of the heavy wooden door, which had been heaved open by a tall, dark figure.

Jurgen: Speak of the devil...

Jurgen muttered once again as Avarson stepped in from the midst of the outside world, garbed in the cleanest, most expensive clothing and furs. He removed his ushanka fur hat, blonde hair falling across his face, and entered the last private domain of the Tväre townsfolk. He glanced around the torchlit room with a smirk, almost happy to see all eyes had turned towards him. He removed a random coat from the entrance hanger, placing it on top of another to make room for his own, and stepped down into the tavern.

58

Avarson: Evening Hervor!

He proclaimed the statement like a bard announcing the arrival of a great lord and made his way through the tables of people, docking himself at the bar. He was taller than most, having to duck slightly to avoid the wooden beams that supported the slanted ceiling above.

Avarson: Busy tonight, isn't it?

He snickered; the only sound heard in the tavern at that moment. Everyone had fallen silent and was glancing awkwardly towards the bar, for reasons clearly unknown to Avarson.

Hervor: It's Tuesday evening Avarson...

Avarson: And that means what? Happy hour, I hope.

He broke out into laughter again, choosing to play ignorant. Hervor couldn't figure out if it was an act or just pure incompetence.

Hervor: Tuesday nights are for locals only. I'm afraid you, Avarson, do not fall into that category.

Avarson put on a false smile, though it was obvious he was a bit surprised to be treated any less than he was expecting.

Avarson: What are you talking about? I've been a part of this town for over a year!

Hervor: Do you live here?

Hervor began interrogating him in her simple but infamous style.

Avarson: I have a house here.

Hervor: And do you live in it?

Avarson: Yes.

Hervor narrowed her eyes.

Hervor: For longer than two weeks at a time?

Avarson rolled his eyes rather dramatically. Several quiet discussions had resumed but most in the tavern waited to see what the end result would be. Avarson began to bargain, a smile of disbelief on his face.

Avarson: Surely you won't kick me out over a technicality? Come on...

He glanced around at the many faces that stared back at him, opting for a different approach instead.

Avarson: What if I were to buy a couple of barrels for everyone to share? Would I have earned my stay then?

There was a brief pause as the nearby folk considered the offer. One of the more drunken townsfolk muttered a response.

Townsman: I quite like the idea...

Avarson: There we have it then!

Hervor paused as Avarson signalled for her to move, hesitation filling her voice.

Hervor: Really? Two barrels?

Avarson nodded.

Hervor: And you're happy paying for those...?

Avarson: That I am. Like I said, it's not a problem for me.

Avarson pulled out a wallet from within his waistcoat, handing over a rather large amount of paper money as if meant nothing to him. Hervor hesitantly took it, before leaving to retrieve two barrels from the cellar below. Avarson waited for her to return, watching as she struggled to lift the first of the heavy kegs to a central table in the long, communal room. He smiled smugly as Hervor released the first barrel, stepping forward to break it open.

Avarson: Lovely. Look at that.

He opened the tap that was linked to the barrel and poured himself a small amount of mead. He turned and addressed the entirety of the Tavern.

Avarson: Keep a hold of your mugs everyone. Refills are free for all tonight!

He tapped the top of the barrel as several people smiled and politely cheered in thanks, though it wasn't quite the standing ovation Avarson was hoping for. The one townsman who was much more drunk than the others, cheered louder than the rest and surged forward to abuse the free barrel, nearly barreling Avarson out the way, causing the industrialist to briefly grimace.

Back at Elvera's table, the occupants rolled their eyes at one another, amused by Avarson's antics. Jurgen was the first to voice his opinion.

Jurgen: Well. That's one way to get everyone to like you.

Elvera: It's a bit much though, isn't it?

Elvera responded as Torsten spoke up, defending Avarson's rather forward antics.

Torsten: He's trying at least. I'd rather that instead of him staying distant.

Jurgen: True...

They glanced back at Avarson, who was enjoying the sight of different townsfolk taking advantage of his alcoholic gift. As each member approached, he leaned in for a quick and rather pointless conversation, similar to when a politician tries to win an easy vote.

Torsten: He is a bit blunt, but he's harmless really.

And so, the evening continued. The townsfolk enjoyed their free mead and eventually, as the night wore into the earliest hours of the morning, they all began the long stumble home. For many, home was only a street or two away, but they all kept an eye on each other, lest someone end up unconscious and upside down within a snowdrift.

As Avarson left the torchlight of the tavern behind him, he approached his pristine, wooden chariot, which had been parked, rather impetuously, in the middle of the street. Another man, this one short with a sneering expression, stood outside the carriage, smoking the rolled paper of a cigarette. He glanced up as Avarson approached, throwing the remainder of cigarette into the snow. His voice was snide and calculating, quite the opposite to Avarson's great prideful bellows.

Regan: Ready to go, Sir?

Avarson: That I am. Make it as quick as possible, I'm freezing!

Regen: Will try my best.

Regan stepped forward and opened the door to the carriage, allowing Avarson to climb inside, before he moved towards the horses at the front. With a quick whip, he stirred them into action, pulling the carriage along the snow-trodden roads and away into the darkness.

***

The streets were cold and quiet. Wind whistled through the rafters of the nearby houses, cutting through the shards of ice that the residents hadn't quite knocked down from their houses. In the uppermost street of Tväre lay the town's only school, catering to the few children that lived within the humble town. It was a bit of a walk up the snowy paths, but the townsfolk didn't mind, and it meant that the parents could join together and socialise on their walks twice a day. Though currently, there were few who did... The school itself was capable of caring for up to twenty children at any one time, but at the moment, there were only three. None of whom were the same age.

In the depths of the empty school yard, Sigmund sat alone. He tucked into a sandwich that Elvera had lovingly prepared for him, today's special consisting of small slices of venison, along with some fresh berries to follow. The two other children were much too young for Sigmund, choosing to remain inside and play their imaginary games away from the bite of the cold. It was the blessing and the curse of living in such a small town. Few children meant peace and quiet for those that wanted it, but it also meant few friends for those that craved them.

Sigmund remained by himself, as he did each and every day, holding one of his wooden, whittled horses in his gloved hands. He didn't feel like imagining today...

*

Sigmund shoved his hands deep into his coat pockets as he walked down the hill from the school. Elvera glanced at him, hoping that he'd at least reply with a smile, but his face was empty and glum as always. They slowed their walk as the path became slightly steeper. The way was always icy during these months of the year, and you always had to have your wits about you. The Municipal Council did their best to organise the spreading of salt across the most popular pathways every evening, but sometimes those who fulfilled the duty missed a spot, and it was usually the evening drunks that paid the price. The primary responsibility of the town's salting lay in the hands of Edvin, who greeted the mother and son as they passed by. He was dressed in a thick overcoat and pulled a heavy cart full of salt crystals.

Edvin: Afternoon, Elvera.

Elvera: Afternoon, Edvin.

The large man pointed to the steps further down the hill, a huge cloud of water vapour billowing from his mouth as he struggled to breathe and talk at the same time.

Edvin: It might be better if you cross the road. The steps on this side haven't been salted yet.

Elvera: Okay. Thanks for letting us know.

The pair crossed the road and continued down the hill, taking careful, calculated steps. Neither of them said a word to each other. Not out of rudeness or anger, there was just nothing to be said. Sigmund didn't seem to care. He gazed emptily ahead as they walked, but Elvera watched her son almost mournfully, wondering if anything was wrong, and if there was, how she could help...

Elvera knew of Sigmund's difficulties the way only a mother can tell. He exhibited a strange mixture of independence and loneliness, as if he craved companionship but he couldn't take the first step towards finding it. Elvera wished she could help him, but she felt helpless in this. Something was missing, but she didn't know what. All she could do was provide the food and friendship that she could and pray that things will work themselves out. Maybe Levi's offer of adventure might distract him... At least, until the dreariness of winter wore away.

She looked down into the valley ahead of them, her eyes naturally drifting towards the strange, grey roof of the newly built railway station. Maybe Sigmund's life and future lay outside of Tväre... Maybe this new railway was the way to get the connections that Sigmund desperately missed. Torsten had made it clear that his future in the town wasn't in leadership or service, but if the town leader wouldn't take him on, who else would? She sighed to herself, annoyed at her own self-accusing uselessness. They continued on home, the sun already beginning to lower itself over the snow of the distant mountains.

***

Levi breathed deeply, his warm breath dispersing in the cold air. His eyes were shut, as if he were meditating. And then he opened them, taking in the beauty of the landscape before him.

He pressed his eye against a moderately sized telescope, docked on a simple wooden tripod, and stared out towards the distant hill that lay upon the opposite side of Lake Tväre. By adjusting the little metal dials on the incredibly nifty piece of equipment, Levi was able to focus the magnification, and see the trees at the top of the hill as if he were standing right next to them. Even the snowflakes upon the branches could be examined with amazing clarity. The tripod was not Levi's own design, though he had made his own amendments to the hinges and legs to fit his own comfort. He'd, in fact, bought the tripod from a small shop in the dirty streets of London, having argued down the massively over inflated price for the item. The telescope, however, he'd received directly from his father for his eighteenth birthday.

Sigmund: Can I have a look?

Sigmund peered up at Levi from below the clever array of instruments.

Levi: Of course you can.

Levi carefully lowered the tripod to Sigmund's level and turned the telescope, adjusting the dials to focus the image in front of him. Sigmund pressed his eye against the telescope.

Levi: Careful you don't knock it... It's incredibly sensitive.

Sigmund squinted, struggling to work the strange device.

Levi: Can you see anything?

Sigmund: I think... maybe the trees... There's green but it's blurry.

Levi quickly adjusted one of the dials on the side.

Levi: Let me play with the settings a bit. What about now?

Sigmund frowned, twisting his head to try and get a better view.

Sigmund: I don't see anything...

The boy pulled aside to compare the telescope's view to normality, blinking in confusion as his sight readjusted. Levi chuckled at the boy's reaction.

Levi: Don't worry, you'll get it eventually. Even I struggle sometimes.

Sigmund gave a resigned smile and turned to Elvera, who stood watching nearby.

Sigmund: Can I go and look at the lake?

Elvera: Do you remember your promise?

Sigmund lowered his head, muttering the memorised set of words.

Sigmund: Keep close and stay away from the red markers...

Elvera nodded, granting her son permission.

Elvera: Okay then.

Sigmund's eyes lit up and he quickly turned and strode towards the edge of the Lake, which was a short walk away from the forest clearing. There were subtle markings in the snow that indicated the presence of a path, but Sigmund casually sauntered around them, his boots randomly sinking into pockets of much deeper snow.

Levi returned the tripod to its original level, resetting the dials and balance of his equipment, returning the telescope to its original stance. His portable desk, ready with a pre-drawn map and a stylus, stood in the snow nearby, waiting for him to return to work. Levi held his breath, checked the telescope again and then carefully added to the detailed map of the Lake and the surrounding forest. Every little detail was there, from the stone ruins at the top of the Northward Forest to the disfigurements in the snow where a small avalanche had occurred. Even the modest little bridge, way over to his right-hand side, was drawn and labelled. In the corner, was a neat and simple compass drawing, pointing the way to the north. Levi had noted where the north star was on his very first night in the town, despite having access to his own compass, and hadn't forgotten his natural sense of direction since... Except for that one night with the blizzard.

His rescuer, Elvera, stood by him now, observing his unique work. The drawings intrigued her greatly, for she had never seen her homeland drawn in this unique way before. Whilst it lacked the wonder and magic of strange sketches and pictures that accompanied ancient maps, it made up for it with impressive detail and pencilled perfection. It was unlike any other map she'd seen before. Her attention, however, was quickly diverted by the antics of her son.

Elvera: Sigmund! Come away from the edge!

She yelled out across the snowy landscape towards Sigmund, who was wandering out of the shelter of the trees and off onto the ice of the Lake. Levi looked up to see Sigmund backing away from the subtle dip in the snow that hinted where the land met the ice, the red markers of the shore blaring nearby.

Levi: Is it dangerous?

Elvera glanced at him.

Elvera: On the lake? Not especially. It depends upon the season. The lake is completely frozen at this time of year and our horses and gatherers make crossings almost every day. I just don't want him to get used to the idea that it's always safe.

Levi nodded agreeably.

> Levi: Do you know how thick it goes? I'd believe you if you told me the ice went all the way down…

> Elvera: And some in this town will say exactly that, but I wouldn't trust them. Besides, the Everflow and the ice-fishing holes already prove them wrong. That's what the blue markers are. Those ones way out there.

She pointed out across the surface of the Lake. Beyond the little red poles that mapped out the Lake's shoreline were several little blue ones, spread out across the shallower areas of ice just beyond the shores.

> Elvera: I guess it's the idea of such deep ice that fascinates everyone. It makes it seem cold… mysterious…

> Levi: And beautiful.

Levi finished the sentence for her, staring out across the shining expanse. He had never seen anything like this before in his life. Despite his young age, he had travelled more than many older than him, seeing sights that would appear as fantasy to those who had never dared to venture further than their town pub. A frozen Lake so stable that horses could walk upon it? That was a new experience for him, and Elvera could tell.

> Elvera: Do your lakes not freeze in winter then?

> Levi: Oh they do, but never to this extent. In my patch of the world, people try and walk across the ones that do, but they usually end up swimming… and then drowning.

Elvera laughed softly at Levi's playful response.

> Elvera: We've had a few of those happen too, usually in the springtime thaw. And that's the point of the red markers.

The young woman once again pointed towards the Lake's edge, where Levi could see two or three wooden poles speared into the ground, each with a red tape-like band strapped to the top.

Elvera: Even in the coldest point of winter, we still have to be careful of what's underfoot. It's essential they're in the right place, sort of like the lines on your maps I guess...

Levi hummed and rubbed his chin. He returned his gaze to his work, completing a quick calculation in a little notebook. Elvera watched him, her interest piqued by the strange ritual.

Elvera: Explain it to me.

Her request caused Levi to pause.

Elvera: I mean, obviously I know it's a telescope, with some other bits attached, but what are you using it for?

Levi raised his eyebrows, shrewdly.

Levi: In simple terms?

Elvera: Preferably.

Levi smiled, quite happy to explain the process.

Levi: It's all just simple mathematics really. The maps are my own designs, a combination of those in the town's library and my own explorations. But they lack elevation. I use the telescope to pinpoint a position. The theodolite tells me the angle of elevation, and without even having to climb the mountain, I can figure out the height by calculation.

He showed off his notes, which were a selection of trigonometric calculations alongside sketches of the surrounding hillsides.

Levi: And then I simply put them on the map. It's almost effortless once you know what you're doing. But the people who don't, pay a lot for the people that do.

Elvera: Like Avarson?

Levi nodded knowingly.

Levi: Exactly. And if he's too busy, or too lazy, to complete all the other bits that go along with it, then it's a larger paycheck for me.

Elvera stared out across the shining landscape, the sun's weak winter rays twinkling off the snowflakes. She squinted, trying to connect Levi's black and white map to the real world around her.

Elvera: So... That's the hill there?

Elvera pointed gently at Levi's sketch.

Levi: Correct.

Elvera: And we're stood here?

Levi: Just... here.

Levi gently moved her gloved finger across the map, not too firm. Elvera smiled ever so slightly at the brief contact. She leant over, reading Levi's notes and calculations, without really understanding them.

Elvera: So, how do you know you're drawing it correctly?

Levi shrugged.

Levi: The same way I know when I've drawn it incorrectly.

Elvera bit her lip.

Elvera: I don't follow...

Levi: Ah, it's difficult to explain... My brain works in a particularly abnormal way. It makes sense to me, but not to anyone else.

It was a weak excuse, and Elvera didn't accept it.

Elvera: Everyone's brain is like that in some quantity. Try me. I might understand.

Levi stared down at his work, following the detailed markings of the forests and the nearby hills with his eyes. When he finally spoke, his voice was quiet and much more reflective, having lost that touch of mischief that was often present in his tone.

Levi: I see things differently than the way everyone else does... When I sit somewhere and breathe it in, I feel like I can see it all. The obvious, the secretive, the hidden... It's like everything is drawn already in my mind. And I just have to copy it down.

Levi pointed to his current work, picking out the features for Elvera's benefit.

Levi: Look here. There are clearings between the trees, but there's even more. The snowdrifts follow the ridges and breaks in the land, showing me the crevices where the meltwater flows down and into the Lake. And below them, markings in the dirt. A sign that the snow might give way and fall...

He spoke so passionately; it was clear to Elvera that he loved his work.

Elvera: I thought you said you didn't sketch stories and legends? That mystical maps weren't worth the time?

She leaned forward and lifted a small pad of sketches that were attached to Levi's mapping desk. Cartoonish drawings of the Lake, the Thorhorn and Avarson's factory lay hidden beneath one another, revealing themselves as Elvera looked through them. Levi narrowed his eyes, matching Elvera's playful tone.

Levi: I said mystical maps don't sell. That doesn't mean I don't like drawing the stories.

He smiled and returned to his drawing.

Elvera: So this is what you do. Even when you're not after a paycheck. You try and make the perfect map?

Levi gave a short laugh and quickly corrected her.

Levi: There's no such thing as a perfect map. I only want mine to be the best people see. I want people to know that mine are honest to the world they represent. Stories or not... My contribution to the cartographical world.

He droned off, the conversation nearing unknown territory. It was rare that Levi spoke of his thoughts and aspirations, and it was rarer for him to share them with someone he did not know well. He cleared his throat, quickly returning his focus to the work at hand. His reply was very well thought out, and Elvera nodded in silent awe. She turned and looked out across the Lake again... but something was missing this time...

She gasped.

Elvera: Where's Sigmund!?

Levi glanced up, immediately on his guard.

Levi: I don't know, wasn't he just there!?

Levi stared across the landscape. The edge of the Lake was now completely empty, as if the young boy had never been there in the first place.

Elvera: Sigmund!?

Elvera marched towards the spot where Sigmund was last seen, staring in every direction for any slight movement that might give her son away. There were footprints in the snow, but nothing that showed any clear direction.

Elvera: SIGMUND!

She called again, this time with a lot more fear and worry in her voice, but no reply came. Elvera made a snap decision and began to charge into the depths of the snowy forest. Levi rushed to join her, before pausing and turning back to his mapping desk, where his bag and equipment lay completely unguarded.

Levi: Ah...

Levi was loathe to leave all his things behind, but this was an emergency.

Levi: Oh... It'll be fine...

He rushed through the snow in an attempt to catch up to Elvera's striding figure, which was already growing smaller within the forest. Her shouts for her son rang out across the valley, echoing and rebounding off the white, shining hills.

*

Little plumes of snow danced across the surface of the icy Lake, spiralling and swirling in the breeze. Sigmund leaned against a set of polished wooden beams, staring down at the trickling water below. The beams belonged to a neat little bridge, which led across the bottleneck point in the valley where the Lake became a river. Beneath the bridge lay the Everflow: a forever moving stream of water that, for reasons unknown to the townsfolk, seemed unable to freeze. Sigmund now watched it intently, the neighbouring layers of ice being continually washed clean by the flowing waters, revealing the variety of blue shades within them. Tiny pebbles bounced and rolled as the water flowed over the shallow riverbed, taking yet another step on their endless journey through the world.

Sigmund gently pushed one of his little horse models along the supporting beam of the bridge, the tiny hooves of the proud stallion eroding the snow below it. There was no real enjoyment in its movement; it was mostly a mixture of feeling glum and boredom. He suddenly looked up, hearing a voice in the air. It sounded like his mother shouting his name, but Sigmund didn't move a muscle. He sighed to himself, unsure why he was feeling so glum. He didn't understand and he didn't try to. Only the quiet, picturesque view of the forest and the hills made him feel any sort of cheer. But as he looked up now, all he could see wafting on the breeze was a grim, expanding cloud of smoke and steam…

Avarson's great factory, built on the opposite end of the narrow Lake, chucked out a heavy black cloud from one of its two chimneys. After a month or so at work, the smokey plume of the factory was now a common daily sight, though it quickly dissipated as it rose further into the sky. But as the trees from nearby valleys piled in, the small plume was quickly becoming accompanied by the unmistakable screech of the railway. Sigmund looked to the left, over to where dirty tracks dug into the land, as another blast of the whistle pierced the air. The train was on its way, taking the excess logs from the factory down to the country's southern regions, ready to be sold to whoever had ordered them. The young boy stared as another hundred or so trees left their home of a thousand years… never to return.

He sighed deeply at the thought, though he did not know why. His mother, and the entire town for that matter, had used the local trees for fire fuel their whole lives... but never on this scale. Maybe that was the difference. The town of Tväre had once relied heavily on the proud treegatherers: a group of the strong and abled whose job was to go out and find the best trees to meet their needs. They were regimented in their ways, cutting only a few down from each area and never touching the largest ones. As he had learned in school, their ancestors believed the tallest trees to be like Eden's Tree of Life; to look at in awe, but never touch, as were the oldest on the Earth. Though now, since the opening of the new factory and the new methods of forest management, the treegatherers had very little work available to them. Avarson had proudly stated that the factory could cut and strip a tree and have the whole town basking in the warmth of a fire within a single morning... but this felt different.

Sigmund took a deep breath, mournfully gazing into the murky haze ahead of him. A slow grumble began to grow from the Lake below, causing Sigmund to glance down towards the trickling waters of the Everflow. It was like the creak and groan of a gently shifting glacier; nothing was moving, yet the sound was definitely there. Forgetting his little model for the sake of curiosity, Sigmund slowly left the bridge and crept down the snowy hill, leaving a tiny set of footprints in the white powder behind him. The groans of the ground seemed to get louder as Sigmund approached, and for a moment, the young boy thought he saw the concoction of snow and ice shift slightly.

Lake Tväre had awoken.

*

Elvera: SIGMUND!

The young mother's voice was becoming hoarse. She had been screaming the name for what seemed like hours, though it could easily have only been a few minutes. She became more and more desperate in her calls, searching behind every tree, in every ditch and even venturing onto Lake Tväre itself. She now charged towards the Bridge over the Everflow... Sigmund's favourite spot.

In the near distance came Levi, who struggled to keep up with Elvera's panicked state. The incredible depth of the snow was not helping, and Levi could feel it going into his boots as each foot sank and rose from the ground.

Levi: Elvera...! Elvera!

Elvera: What!?

Levi caught up with her.

Levi: Might it be easier if I returned to the town and got help? The police or something?

Elvera replied, her breath short.

Elvera: That'll take hours! It'll do no good anyway; we only have one policewoman... We need to find him now!

Levi: One policewoman!?

Levi repeated the disbelieving statement back to himself as Elvera muttered to herself desperately.

Elvera: I bet he's just on the bridge... He must be. Where else would he go?

She charged towards the quaint wooden structure.

Elvera: Sigmund, where are you? Why would you do this? We talked about this...

Levi slowed down, trying to catch his breath. He wasn't exactly the lazy type, but Elvera had the superhuman energy of a distressed parent, and Levi could barely keep pace with that. He considered himself relatively fit, but clearly, he had overestimated his abilities in the cold of the winter. As he recovered his breath, he happened to glance towards the ground, noticing something.

Levi: Elvera...

Elvera marched on towards the bridge, her ears deaf to any cries, loud or quiet. Levi looked down at the footprints in the snow. They were small and belonged to a child, leading down the hill, away from the bridge and towards the edge of Lake Tväre.

Heavy footsteps thundered upon the old wooden planks as Elvera landed on the bridge, the wood below her feet thudding and groaning. She looked around frantically for any sign of her son, but there was no-one here. Then something small, something that shouldn't be there, caught her eye...

Levi followed the small footprints down the hill, visualising Sigmund's short journey down as he moved. He could see the slip in the snow, the handprint where he'd steadied himself and the gentle approach towards a strange depression in the snow.

Elvera slowly walked towards the wooden support beam of the bridge, her face wracked with desperation and worry. She reached out and picked up the little model horse that remained balanced on the bridge's support beams, running her hand down the smooth, carved mane. The last sign of Sigmund's presence. Elvera held it close to her chest and then slumped against the side of the bridge, her panic and anxiety now overtaking her will to continue. She didn't say a word, nor make a tearful sound. She just sat there silently, the light in her eyes becoming faint...

Levi stared at the unbroken snow in the ground. It didn't make sense. The footprints led perfectly up to this point, and then suddenly, there was nothing...

Sigmund had vanished...

***

Part Two

The Lost Viking

His eyes flashed open, but all Sigmund could see was darkness. He shifted his head. Cold bedrock brushed against his face. He recoiled; the floor freezing cold to the touch. Now suddenly alert, Sigmund reached out and ran his hand over the cold, wet stone, which was coated in a strange mixture of water and ice. He sat himself up, his eyes adjusting to a weird blueish light that emanated from the ceiling high above. The weird new world slowly began to reveal itself as the darkness cleared from around him.

Sigmund sat within a huge cavern, filled with soaring spires of rock and ice that seemed to grow down from the ceiling and up from the bedrock floor. The roof was made from thick, dirty ice with a large central pinnacle that acted as the apparent source of the pulsing blue light. The rest of the cavern was made of an unusually dark type of rock, and when Sigmund peered closer, he saw tiny crystals had formed within the stone itself, each of them glittering and shining. Icy streams had frozen their way down the walls, appearing like waterfalls that had stopped in time. The air was freezing, and Sigmund could see his dissipating breath every time exhaled... but strangely enough, he didn't even feel cold.

Instead of instantly panicking, as every adult would, the young boy picked himself up and began to explore. Any thought of home was gone for the moment; this was a new horizon and Sigmund wanted to see what secrets it held, even if he couldn't recall how he'd gotten here... His footsteps echoed through the immense chamber, and Sigmund tested the acoustics by throwing little pebbles at the icy sculptures that ran down the walls. The tapping of the rock as it struck the ice echoed around him in response, shuddering against the ceiling of frozen water.

At the far end of the cavern lay a small tunnel, leading deeper into the subsurface world. The blue light faded slightly as Sigmund entered, but he could see a second, fainter version emanating from further within, pulsing and beating as if it were calling out to him. Sigmund followed the passage deeper, the walls decorated in strange brown paintings. Sigmund rubbed his hand against them as he passed by, touching ancient tales of men fighting against wolves and bears, and sitting around a fire in harmony. They were incredible paintings, truly an archaeologist's dream discovery, but Sigmund paid them very little mind. He was being drawn in by something else.

The end of the tunnel appeared, and Sigmund entered a much smaller cavern, lit again by the blue light of the ceiling. Sigmund glanced at some further cave paintings, one depicting a strange warrior garbed in skin of blue, defeating and killing a whole swath of sea monsters, from huge krakens to what looked like whales with sharp teeth. They reminded Sigmund of his drawings back at home. Even the odd way the eyes were drawn seemed to match his own imaginations.

Sigmund turned again, and froze. He stared towards the wall of the little cavern, into the withered face of a frozen corpse...

The eyes of the long dead Ice-Man were closed, and his mouth hung slightly open. He was clearly incredibly old, as the frozen fabric and fur he wore for clothing were exactly like the ones Sigmund had seen in Tväre's Hall of Memory. The frostbitten skin of the dead man was like that of a rotten berry, and every bit of hair, or what once was hair, was now a tiny needle of pure ice, all coming together to form a wraith. The same wraith that Sigmund sometimes heard the elders talk about... But unlike the tales and horror stories that every child of Tväre had ever heard, this wraith didn't scream. Nor did it move, or even blink... It remained frozen into the wall of the cavern, stiff blue arms by its side. It was by all means harmless, but still just as horrifying...

Sigmund slowly backed away, keeping his footsteps low so as not to awaken the frozen man. Tiny rocks shifted and clicked along the floor as the young boy retreated. And then, once he was clear of the smaller cave, he turned and ran, the delayed panic of being lost and alone finally forcing its way into his mind. He sprinted across the floor of the huge, main cavern, the thumps of his feet booming around him. When he reached the other side, he found nothing but rock. No secret tunnel that got him here. No way out. No escape...

A rumble boomed around the cavern. The kind that sounded like the earth itself was cracking open. Sigmund paused... and slowly turned around. The tunnel at the other end of the cavern was pulsing with an even greater aura of deep blue light. Sigmund scrambled to hide in any corner of the cavern he could find. A boulder, a stalagmite, anything. Another rumble crackled its way through the vast space, this one louder, like glass being shattered... or icy restraints breaking. Sigmund hid behind one of the large spires that surged from the bedrock floor, clutching his hands to his chin.

> Sigmund: Please God... Help me...

Sigmund kept his eyes shut tight, muttering and praying the words to himself over and over again.

> Sigmund: It's not real. It's not real...

From the depths of the pulsing blue darkness came a skulking figure. Cold, blistered feet stepped across the bedrock, a thin layer of transparent ice appeared like a protective layer, wrapping around the heel and toes each time they landed on the ground. It sought out Sigmund like a hawk, following a direct path that led right towards his hiding place...

The crackle of the footsteps eventually slowed... and then stopped.

Sigmund opened his eyes slowly. He feared what he would see, but simply had to know what was there. He lifted his blue eyes upwards, and saw a frozen hand outstretched. The eyes of a frostbitten man stared back at him; the crystals of his frozen eyebrows raised in curiosity. His skin was a solid blue and his eyes burned white with a ferocious intensity. His head was completely bald, marked with what looked like old Viking tattoos, and his clothes now hung loose around his limbs. Despite all this, his expression radiated warmth and care, and his burning eyes appeared almost curious.

The Ice-Man: Sssig... Ssssig...

The Ice-Man seemed to struggle with the word. He cleaned his frostbitten lips with his teeth, trying to clear the thin layer of ice that coated them.

The Ice-Man: Ssssig...

Sigmund didn't move. The Ice-Man began to cough and choke, becoming more and more animated as he did so. He turned away and began to smack himself on the back, coughing up a phlegm of ice-crystals and small stones. The Ice-Man cleared his throat, spitting the last flecks from his mouth, and turned back to Sigmund.

The Ice-Man: Ugh. Well... That broke the ice.

His face contorted into a huge, comedic grin, his eyes now twinkling in the strange light that emanated from the roof of the cavern.

The Ice-Man: Hello Sigmund. It's good to finally meet you!

*

The Ice-Man stared down at the cowering boy, as if oblivious to what was causing him such distress. Sigmund pressed himself against the bedrock wall of the cavern and lay perfectly still. He stared up at the frostbitten face, not even risking a single blink. The expression of the icy figure changed from one of confusion to one of sympathy; the torn skin and bone still very capable of displaying emotion.

The Ice-Man held out an emaciated hand, opening the palm for Sigmund to see. Then, like magic stripped from an ancient fantasy story, a tiny tornado of snow and ice emerged and grew within the Ice-man's skinny palm. As Sigmund watched, the little crystal whirlwind took the form of a tiny horse, solidifying into a lump of solid, blue ice. An exact replica of his own wooden toy that he'd left behind on the bridge...

In an offer of friendship, the little horse was held out to Sigmund. The young boy paused at first, but eventually, his intrigue won him over. He warily reached out, taking the carved model of ice by the fingertips, and felt an overwhelming feeling of warmth rush through his body. The cold of the ice seemed to have no effect on his small fingers, and his bodily warmth caused no melting of the horse in return. As Sigmund held the gift, the Ice-Man sat himself down, lowering himself to meet Sigmund's eyeline. He spoke again, this time much more gently.

> The Ice-Man: I have a favourite one too.

Again, he opened up his palm and the mysterious magic took form, this time growing into the shape of a howling arctic wolf.

> The Ice-Man: I almost had the entire collection. The wolf, the fox... the arctic pigeon. Though I never really liked the horse one. I can't stand horses. Can't sit on them either!

He grinned, snorting slightly at his own joke. Despite his frankly horrifying appearance, the Ice-Man's impish voice and playful mannerisms granted him a somewhat mellow and easygoing aura. One that drew Sigmund in instead of pushing him away. The young boy finally gained the courage to reply, his words quick and nervous.

> Sigmund: ...Why?

The Ice-Man smiled.

> The Ice-Man: I was horribly allergic to horses. I'd go within twenty metres of one and that was it, I couldn't even breathe! It brought great shame to my family...

80

The Ice-Man wheezed again, but his face fell a bit. Sigmund stared at the frozen figure, finally taking in his strange appearance. The tattoos on his bald head had faded over time but were still quite distinguished. They were like runes, almost spelling out unknown words across his head. His clothes were ancient, as if the man had stripped them from a museum or the exhibits in Tväre's own Hall of Memory. They consisted of rotten, torn garments of leather and wool, all of which hung from the Ice-Man's skinny frame in an ill-fitting design. If Sigmund focused his eyes, he could see a hint of green and red dye around the hems, the woollen strands now fraying and shedding after a thousand years beneath the ice.

> The Ice-Man: Times have got a bit backward since then... From what I've been able to see anyway. What are you, eleven years old?

Sigmund timidly nodded.

> The Ice-Man: See. I'd killed my third barbarian by the time I was your age. Now you don't even learn the basic life skills. Defensive tactics in a snowstorm, or how to stop getting scurvy for a second time...

He waved his hands emphatically as he droned off. In the moment of silence that followed, Sigmund ventured a question that had been on his mind since he'd first woken up, surrounded by the deep walls of the earth.

> Sigmund: Is this... Is this real? Are you real...?

The frozen corpse somehow managed to frown.

> The Ice-Man: I do hope so...

The Ice-Man patted his skeletal body, his fingers tapping his protruding ribcage.

> The Ice-Man: I certainly feel real... though that isn't enough for some people. But then, what *is* real?

The Ice-Man leaned down into Sigmund's face.

> The Ice-Man: What if I'm the one who's real? And you're the one who's not?

He tapped Sigmund's forehead, cackling at his mischief. It seemed the Ice-Man could keep talking for eternity if he wanted to. And Sigmund may have let him, were it not for him wanting answers of his own.

Sigmund: Then... where am I?

The Ice-Man: My lad, where do you think you are!? Have you not even looked at the ceiling yet?

Sigmund glanced upwards, looking again at the vast layer of ice that encompassed the place of the sky. It almost sat upon the supportive bedrock walls, the same way a lid settles itself upon a cooking pot. As Sigmund's eyes widened, the Ice-Man smiled.

The Ice-Man: My name is Fendal. And this is my home. Under Lake Tväre.

***

The sunlight fell beyond the peaks of the Four Sisters, a group of ice-capped mountains that sat on the horizon of Tväre's neighbouring valley. The conflicting battle between the sunlight and the shade fought its way across each of the four peaks, the growing darkness slowly winning a victory as the sunlight was forced to retreat.

Elvera sat upon the snowy wooden steps that led up to the small bridge, comforted by a middle-aged woman who was wearing a blue uniformed jacket. After finding Sigmund's toy model on the railing, Elvera had fallen into a state of silent shock. Levi had been loath to leave her there, but help was urgently needed. He'd run to the road, hoping to come across anyone who was passing through, either by foot or by horse and carriage. After flagging down a local herder, Levi had shared the news of Sigmund's mysterious disappearance, the man quickly agreeing to spread the word once he reached Tväre. He'd promised to return with the help of the local authorities... which consisted of a single policewoman and her son. Chief Magnhilda was the one who now comforted Elvera, whilst her son, Här, did an examination of Sigmund's footprints and questioned the apprehensive Levi about the course of events that had led up to the boy's disappearance.

82

Whether fortunate or unfortunate, depending on who you were, half the town had seemingly joined them at the scene, drawn by the curiosity of such an odd and tragic occurrence. It was rare that anything significant happened in Tväre, the last notable event being the opening of the new railway station some months earlier. So, when anything out of the ordinary did happen, most of the inquisitive townsfolk were almost always there to see it for themselves. Many of them, however, had also volunteered their services in the hunt for the small boy, very much aware that the first few hours of his disappearance were the most critical time to find him, especially before the cold of the night set in. As the sun gradually fell lower in the sky, the light on the faces of the people dimmed in parallel, their collective expressions appearing like a group of worried ghosts...

Elvera muttered broken answers into Magnhilda's ear, answering each of her calm and composed questions as best she could.

> Elvera: He loves it here... This is where he should be...

> Magnhilda: Okay, okay. We're going to try and find him, okay? We've got lots of people here to help. See?

The grey-haired police chief indicated towards the crowd around her. The nearest ones were able to overhear and nodded in agreement, trying to encourage Elvera through this dark moment.

> Magnhilda: Här!

Magnhilda called out to her son, who sat talking with Levi a little further away. His young face glanced up in response to his mother's call.

> Magnhilda: Can you come and be helpful please!?

Här gestured towards Levi to show that he was trying to work, but a quick glare from his mother summoned him immediately. He folded up his notebook and returned to Magnhilda's side.

> Här: I'm busy taking down answers—

Magnhilda: We'll sort that out later. Can you take care of Elvera while I try and get a fraction of control in this crowd?

Här nodded, crouching down to Elvera's level to offer what comfort he could. Magnhilda shouted towards the people in the snowy clearing.

Magnhilda: Alright...! ALRIGHT!

She bellowed, finally getting their attention. They gathered around closer, eager to begin.

Magnhilda: We need to cover as much ground as we can before night falls! We only have a few hours left, if that! Divide up into groups, I don't care who you're with, and report to me where you're searching!

The townsfolk began to murmur and talk amongst themselves.

Magnhilda: Cover the lake, both the forests, and anywhere else you can! Check ditches, ponds and up trees. If there's any breaks in the ice, river or lake, I need to know about it!

Magnhilda paused, almost reluctant to vocalise her final theory.

Magnhilda: ...And if you see or hear anything suspicious, no matter how small you think it is, report it back as soon as possible.

She clapped her hands together.

Magnhilda: Right, go on then! Grab a torch and get moving!

The townsfolk fell into their many different directions, some crossing the bridge, some scouring the Lake and others heading towards the road. Between themselves, they made sure that not a single square inch of the nearby area would go unsearched. With the search having begun, Magnhilda turned back to Elvera.

Magnhilda: Här can take you home... Elvera?

Elvera glanced up.

Elvera: Hmm...?

Magnhilda: Här can take you home. Or anywhere else you'd feel comfortable. Is that okay?

Elvera shook her head defiantly. She'd spent the last hour of her life coming to terms with what was happening, and her strong will had taken an incredible hit... but it wasn't gone just yet.

Elvera: I'm staying here.

Magnhilda: Elvera...

The police chief didn't get a chance to continue as Elvera surged onward.

Elvera: No! This is where my son disappeared. Even if it gets colder than hell, I'm not leaving here until I've got him back.

Magnhilda sighed, talking carefully.

Magnhilda: The sun is dropping fast Elvera. I can't leave you here in the dark...

Elvera: What if it were your child?

Här gave his mother a quick glance.

Elvera: What would you do then?

Magnhilda paused for a moment, aware that her own child was carefully listening.

Magnhilda: I can't say what I'd do...

Elvera: I know that you wouldn't dare go home. Not until you had him back. And I'm no different. I'm staying here.

Elvera turned her gaze away. A look of concern crossed Magnhilda's face. It had been many years since she'd had to face a task of this magnitude, but she hadn't forgotten how to deal with the victims.

Magnhilda: You're still going through the shock of this Elvera. It's freezing cold and look at you, you're already shivering. I have to care for you as well as trying to find Sigmund.

Elvera: You can care for me here.

Magnhilda sighed; Elvera's stubbornness had won.

Magnhilda: Okay.

She exhaled heavily, before turning back towards the dispersing groups, beginning to coordinate the search. As the parties slowly dissipated across the land, the tired face of the old policewoman turned towards the retreating sunlight, which was now beginning to dip below the hills of the west.

Magnhilda: Här? How many torches do we have?

Här: More than enough for everyone. Oil included.

Magnhilda nodded slowly.

Magnhilda: I'll stay with Elvera. You start distributing the rest of the torches and oil. Give every group enough to last the night.

Här: The entire night!?

Magnhilda's hard stare was enough of an answer, and Här nodded.

Här: ...Yes, Chief.

He went away to hand out the torches to the remaining search parties, Magnhilda turned back to face the sun. She watched it slowly fall away, knowing that if they didn't find Sigmund soon, they probably never would...

*

Wooden stakes, burning with fierce flames, were held aloft by every person. The group of searches had spread out into a long line, marching through the deep snow as fast as their legs would allow. The temperature had dropped rapidly as soon as night began, and the forest had become glazed in a fresh layer of frost. But the townsfolk were not deterred by the darkness, nor by the depths of the snow. They endeavored to search every bit of land that they could, scavenging for any clue that might lead them to Sigmund's whereabouts.

Minister Toro stared out from the entrance of his church, praying silently to the Lord. He looked out into the darkness, watching as the forests around Tväre thrived with the most activity it had ever seen. The lights from the walking flames travelled off in every direction, glowing like fireflies in the forest. Out they spread, across the Lake and beyond the hills. In every neighbouring valley and on the Thorhorn mountain itself. It was truly a tremendous sight.

***

Fendal: Come on then! We can't just sit around all day and night.

The frozen corpse had very quickly gotten bored with just sitting still, and immediately sprung back to his full height, leaving the little ice figure of the wolf on the ground. Before Sigmund could even reply, Fendal had turned heel and begun to stride away.

Fendal: Hurry yourself lad. There is much you need to see!

Sigmund's every instinct shouted at him to remain sat against the wall, clutching the figure of the horse for reassurance. It was the safe place to be... or safest anyway. But Fendal's enthusiastic smile, and the strange warmth that Sigmund felt when the Ice-Man was around him, gradually put his mind at ease. The boy slowly got to his feet, glancing around at the vast, empty cavern, in wonder. Spires towered around him, pointing up towards the glowing aura of the icy ceiling. Frozen footsteps, where Fendal had been walking, were stuck to the ground, like animal tracks preserved in ice. Sigmund tentatively followed the icy figure, who was clearly waiting to show off his subterranean home. The earlier heavy feeling of fear and dread had now gone, and the blue aura that lit the cavern above Sigmund now felt calm and cosy.

Up ahead, Fendal walked along the edge of the cavern wall, seemingly looking for the first stop on his grand tour. As Sigmund finally rejoined him, he began to narrate his way around, whether for Sigmund's benefit or his own... it wasn't clear.

Fendal: It is rented accommodation. Sadly, I don't own this place myself. I was only supposed to be here for a short while, but it ended up being hundreds of years...

He suddenly stopped, a look of annoyance appearing on his frostbitten face. Sigmund joined him in staring up at the nearest wall, which was awash with an amazing variety of cave paintings. Mammoths and wolves chasing thin little men with spears... or were the men chasing the animals? It was hard to tell. Around the drawings were a selection of handprints outlined in a shade of red. Some large, some tiny...

Fendal: The last owner put these in. Some sort of art enthusiast, I think. I've been meaning to redecorate for a while, but I haven't exactly got a steady hand...

Fendal held up his frostbitten limb, which trembled slightly in the air. He quickly moved on, completely ignoring the significance of the historical discovery before him. Sigmund gave it one final look, placing his own small hand in the space over one of the smaller handprints... It fitted perfectly.

They continued on further into the cavern, circling back to where Sigmund had first explored himself, a time that felt like hours ago. Long before the cheerful zombie had awoken from his icy pedestal.

Fendal: Just through here.

He bent his head low, entering the short tunnel and emerging through the small archway that led to his original resting place. It wasn't low enough however, and Fendal smacked his head on the rocky beam above.

Fendal: AGH!

Fendal rubbed his bald head, which was now indented with the rocky shape of the archway above. He focused his mind for a moment, his bright eyes closing, and his skull gradually regrew back into shape, sending a spree of tiny snowflakes that gently fell to the ground. He muttered to himself.

Fendal: Every year... Every bloody year...

88

He noted Sigmund's worried look, and quickly put on a smile.

Fendal: Fear not my lad, there's not much in here anyway.

Fendal chuckled and tapped his rebuilt skull before ducking through the archway. With Sigmund in tow, he continued his narration, all the while rubbing the faded runes on his bruised head.

Fendal: You've already had a glance at the bedrooms I know, but I wrote it as part of the tour, and I can't break from the schedule. I'll get lost otherwise. Here is my room, but you knew that already...

Sigmund followed Fendal's gaze, which settled on a simple frozen podium. He could still see the footprints in the little pond of ice, along with the outline in the rocky background where Fendal's body had been locked away... Yet now the frozen man smiled and skipped along with the life and confidence of a real person. He couldn't be real. And yet here he was!

Fendal: And yours is just over there. Room three!

Sigmund peered into a small gap in the cavern wall, spying a quaint little room. The space mirrored his home back in Tväre perfectly, as if Fendal had taken his room and copied it exactly... except that every bit of furniture was carved from blocks of pure ice. From the bed to even the books on the shelves, everything was frozen solid.

Fendal: I hope it's to your liking. Bedsheets are changed once every five days and there's a little nightlight in the ceiling. The lake above provides some nice ambient sounds too. Helps me get to sleep each year at least.

Sigmund peered upwards, seeing a sort of narrow chimney in the ceiling that led all the way up to the underside of the frozen Lake Tväre. The blue aura fired its way down, shining like a cosy spotlight over the room. Sigmund tested the bed with his finger, shocked to find the block of ice to spring up and down just like a normal mattress.

Fendal: I've added an ice-place for you as well.
Though I will warn you, I haven't got much fuel left...

Sigmund turned from the sight of his underground room to see Fendal standing over what appeared to be a makeshift fireplace, complete with a rocky grate. Except that instead of flames, there was a huge block of ice.

Fendal: And that should be it! Well, for the time being anyway. We don't want to spoil the surprises!

He turned to face Sigmund, who remained quiet and unresponsive.

Fendal: So, do you have any questions?

Sigmund didn't move.

Fendal: Nothing!? I won't be offended if you do. Stupid or not, it's the tour guide code to answer every question that comes their way.

Again; there was no response. A look of concern crossed Fendal's dark blue face as he finally understood the reality of Sigmund's position.

Fendal: What is it my lad? What's on your mind?

The young boy took a deep breath.

Sigmund: I want to go home...

Fendal blinked, the realism of Sigmund's hesitant statement hitting home.

Sigmund: I don't want to be down here. I want to go back home...

Fendal immediately began to soften, the heavy feeling of being lost in a dark and strange location all too familiar himself. Despite the frostbite, the tattoos and the glowing eyes, the frozen man still managed to create the appearance of someone who was caring and compassionate.

Fendal: I wish that you could... Honestly, I do. If I still had the ability, I would have you back by the warmth of your living room fire before the night even fell...

Sigmund: Then why can't you? Why am I even here!?

Emotion flowed through Sigmund's desperate questions. But Fendal could only answer with a sympathetic smile, his blue lips becoming thin.

Fendal: The same reason I am. Because we dared to step upon the ice. We attempted a crossing, and the lake decided not to let us pass... I'm sorry Sigmund.

Sigmund's face fell.

Fendal: But hey, at least we're stuck down here together! And who knows, it's never too late for things to change, and that means all is not lost yet!

He laughed weakly at the darkness, trying to lift Sigmund's mood as best as he could. Then, a great idea crossed his mind.

Fendal: Anyway, the tour is far from finished. This is but the top of the iceberg, just wait until you see the bottom!

Fendal launched to his feet and encouraged Sigmund to follow him.

Fendal: Come. Let me introduce you to the rest of the fallen four!

**

Fendal: BEHOLD! The great Ice-log of Lake Tväre!

Sigmund was the only other soul within the cavern, yet Fendal bellowed the announcement as if he were talking to hundreds of other onlookers. His frosty beard twinkled in the blue light as whilst he stood by one of the far walls, patting the bedrock as if he were feeling around for something... but nothing happened.

Fendal: Damn this thing to Thor and his goats...

Fendal muttered to himself as he examined the wall, eventually finding a great stone lever, previously hidden from view by the rest of the rockface in perfect camouflage. His scarred hand pulled down on it hard.

The cavern began to tremble and shake. Tiny stones and pebbles bounced upon the floor around Sigmund's feet as the young boy looked up, watching as the wall ahead of him sank directly into the ground. Shards of stone and ice flew in all directions as the barrier of bedrock disappeared with a tremendous roar, revealing a wondrous sight. A colossal construction of stone stood within the hidden cave. A great sculpture of ice designed to appear exactly like one of the firelogs that lit the streets around Tväre, only much larger. Atop the stone tower, taking the position of the flames, were huge shards of ice, shooting out in all directions like an almighty crown. From the centre of the Ice-log, a blue aura glowed, powering the light within the rest of the cavern.

But, despite the power living within the great nest of shards, the ice appeared discoloured and dirty. Like unclean glass, the sculpture had the potential to be so much more. Capable of grandeur unlike any other... Yet, instead, the sculpture seemed to be tired and drained, as if the life and power were being slowly lost to the world.

> Fendal: Designed after the original great Firelog of Tväre, as constructed in 956 AD for the Midwinter Festival. It is our symbol of power to our enemies, but of unity to our friends. A memory of the bond made between the lake and the land thousands of years ago...

The blue aura pulsed with Fendal's praise, but Sigmund didn't seem impressed.

> Sigmund: What's wrong with it?

Fendal frowned, the icy flecks in his eyebrows scrunching together.

> Fendal: What do you mean 'what's wrong with it'? It's beautiful!

It was Sigmund's turn to frown.

> Sigmund: Well, firstly, you said it'd be bigger...

> Fendal: Huh... I was always told size didn't matter...

Fendal muttered a reply. Sigmund stared at the sculpture before continuing, the ice almost hypnotising him.

Sigmund: And it doesn't look well. It feels... empty...

He shivered as a wave of cold rippled across his body, glancing up to see that Fendal was actually smiling.

Sigmund: What?

Fendal: You're noticing the right things.

Fendal strode forward and spun around, his vibrant attitude instantly returning.

Fendal: But there is one thing that you haven't noticed. Or, as it happens, two things.

He waved a frozen hand across the air, and the blue aura above hummed and pulsed. From within the shadows, on either side of the Ice-log tower, came forth two statues, made entirely of the purest ice. Each of them screaming their raging battle cries. Sigmund had seen these two statues before, cast in their original stone as they watched over Tväre's central square. They were a core part of the history within the Northern Valleys, having conquered much of it during their explorations, and the arctic townsfolk honoured them as the heroes and ancestors they were.

Fendal: The two most valiant warriors the settlement of Tväre ever produced!

Sigmund watched as Fendal now approached the two statues, a great power emanating from each of his frosty palms. As gentle as a snowflake on the wind, Fendal touched each statue where their hearts would be, the power dancing across his boney fingers, passing from him into them. The icy figures began to vibrate and tremble. And with a great roar, the two statues came to life, charging into battle. Sigmund took a short breath, stepping back as their heavy shouts reverberated around the cavern. But upon seeing their master standing in front of them, the roars of the two statues instantly faded away into an awkward silence. A great smile appeared upon Fendal's face as he embraced the subjects of his subterranean kingdom.

Fendal: Sigmund! I'd like you to meet the famed brother and sister duo, Alaf and Olaf!

He dropped his voice to a whisper, but still loud enough that all could hear.

Fendal: Alaf's the girl, Olaf's the guy. In case you couldn't tell them apart.

Fendal laughed cheekily, wrapping his arms around the two Vikings, much to their annoyance.

Fendal: These two here are your ancestors! Believed to be the most fearsome warriors to ever hail from the Northern Valleys. Capable of fighting ten men at a time, captaining the longships in the Atlas Sea, and defending their homes with honour and loyalty.

Fendal patted each of the statues on the back.

Fendal: Only half of which is true of course. In reality, they marched all the way to the western coastline, readied their longship for sail and then immediately shipwrecked it in a Norwegian Fjord...

Alaf gave Fendal a somewhat spiteful look.

Fendal: Still, better to be remembered as warriors! As long as you've got a good storyteller lined up after you die, it doesn't matter what you did or didn't do in life!

He laughed again, sighing when no-one else joined in with him. He addressed the two statues now, talking to them more gently.

Fendal: And to you two, allow me to introduce our newest recruit. Sigmund, son of Elvera! Other titles pending...

The two Vikings stared wide-eyed at Fendal, and then turned to face Sigmund directly. Alaf pushed Fendal's arm away and made a series of silent gestures, finishing with an accusing point in Sigmund's direction, to which Fendal responded.

Fendal: Yes, him. Trust me, this isn't a mistake.

Alaf rolled her eyes with great exaggeration, making another silent exclamation.

Fendal: I know you don't like it. But it's not in our hands anymore.

Alaf had already separated herself from her master before he could even finish. She walked menacingly towards Sigmund, her expression cold and fierce, and that wasn't just because of the ice. Frosted braids whipped around her shoulders as she bent down to face the young boy, glaring at him through ice-carved eyes. It was incredible how much body language could be read from their faces, especially considering what they were made from. The colour of the ice seemed to split into different shades across their bodies, highlighting their various features, from their eyes right down to their beards.

A few short hairs poked out from Alaf's chin and Sigmund couldn't stop himself looking at them. He held his ground against the Viking warrioress as she silently examined him, fighting back in his own simple way.

Sigmund: You need to shave.

Fendal guffawed once in the background, causing Alaf's expression to harden even further. She snorted once, and then let Sigmund be, turning back towards the Ice-log sculpture. She ignored Fendal as she passed him by and returned to her duty, planting a hand against the sculpture, which glowed slightly more brightly than before. The other statue, Olaf, gave Sigmund a little wave and a resigned smile, before rejoining his sister beside the sculpture. Again, at his touch, the icy shards above grew brighter still. Fendal stared at them for a second, his white eyes twinkling. He then returned to Sigmund's side.

Fendal: I apologise for Alaf. She's always had a shorter fuse than most, so try not to judge her too harshly.

Sigmund: She judges me that way.

Sigmund muttered a retort, to which Fendal nodded.

Fendal: And I'll talk to her about it. But I'll give her some time to cool off first. It may not appear like it, but we're in the midst of a war down here. And Alaf hoped our next recruit would be a fighter. Someone that would help turn the tide instead of surrendering to it.

Fendal shook his head.

Fendal: She doesn't appreciate that the lake has made a different choice.

Sigmund: A war against who...?

Hesitation filled Sigmund's voice as he looked up into the face of his frozen guardian, who spoke softly.

Fendal: It feels like it's against everyone...

***

The corridors within the Hall of Memory felt colder today. The freezing air had managed to penetrate the thick, granite walls, and the flaming torches that lit the corridors and rooms seemed to be devoid of warmth. It made the passageways feel smaller and tighter than normal. Usually, the light of the short winter sun would pour through the windows, but the day was horribly grey. Thick, heavy clouds hung over the town, as if the sky were sharing in the shock of Sigmund's disappearance. Altogether, it made the town feel so much colder, and so much darker.

Chief Magnhilda walked through one of these empty corridors, her breath billowing out in front of her as she sighed. The night had been long and hard, not just for her but for many of the townsfolk who had spent the dark hours searching through snow and ice for any sign of Sigmund's whereabouts. It was Magnhilda, however, who'd had to remain awake the longest, ensuring that she took in every last report from every search group that had ventured out in the wilderness. The resulting work had left her completely exhausted, and the light of the corridor torches highlighted the bags under her eyes. Despite all this, she was determined to keep going. Pulling up her thick fur coat for warmth, Magnhilda pushed through a set of double doors, striding past a display case that held a huge, ancient Viking axe, and entered a large meeting room.

Several pairs of eyes turned to face her, all of them concerned and worried. This was the Municipal Council of Tväre, the group elected by those in the town, who could be bothered, to discuss, debate and vote on the decisions that would affect the majority. These included the controversial installation of Avarson's factory, the subsequent installation of the railway and the team selection for Tväre in the annual Northern Valley Ice Hockey tournament held in the neighbouring town of Järven. The council had been the leading force of the arctic town for hundreds of years, dating back to the later Viking eras... But now its latest discussion was to be a sorrowful one.

Torsten detached his large frame from the group of five, bringing Magnhilda a cup of warmed wine to heat her up.

> Torsten: You look exhausted.

Magnhilda scoffed, replying in kind.

> Magnhilda: Thanks. You look great as well.

> Torsten: Have you slept at all since last night?

She nodded whilst sipping her mug, grateful for the warmth it provided.

> Magnhilda: Här took care of things this morning. I got a few hours down then.

Torsten smiled softly, his short, curly beard shifting.

> Torsten: Good. You know we can help coordinate anything if you need us to.

> Magnhilda: I know, but it's easier when it's just me. If too many people try taking control, we'll be like rabbits running around with no direction. And then we don't stand a chance of finding him.

The oldest man in the room spoke up, interrupting the two of them with his horrible pessimism.

> Almarr: It's been a night and half-day already. We all know there's no chance now.

> Torsten: There's no need for that Father!

Almarr shrugged grimly.

Almarr: Everyone's too afraid to admit it.

The council members fell into silence, all of them confronting the bare truth in Almarr's words. The old man threw a few more logs in the great fireplace, instantly brightening up the room. Torsten sighed heavily and then broke the silence with his deep, gravelly voice.

Torsten: I'll start, shall I? I'm sure you've all heard yesterday's news from one source or another so there's no need to go over it. Magnhilda, can you update us on the search?

Magnhilda nodded, her own voice ragged in comparison. It was impressive how she kept herself dignified despite it all.

Magnhilda: Every patch of land, from the bridge to the town, has been searched through by at least two different groups. Through every snowbank and every hidden stream… We've found no sign of the boy.

Jurgen had made it nearly three sentences through the conversation before making a grumpy comment. That peace ended now.

Jurgen: Seriously? No sign of anything!?

Magnhilda: Not completely… One group found a hidden cache of tools on Leif's farm, most of them stolen from the shared use sheds in the centre of town, so we'll have to deal with that after all this. But no, nothing even remotely indicating the whereabouts of Sigmund…

The council sighed collectively. Saffi now entered the discussion. The middle-aged woman was the one who ran the town school and had shed her share of tears when she'd learned of Sigmund's disappearance. Whilst her voice remained steady, her red eyes gave away the deep anxiety that often plagued her.

Saffi: What of the lake?

Magnhilda: A few groups scanned the lake as well. Two of them made a crossing. There's no reports of broken ice, and no new holes around the bridge or the river.

Torsten: And we've definitely not missed anything?

Magnhilda sighed frustratedly; she'd answered Torsten's question over a hundred times already in the last twenty-four hours. Maybe not quite that many, but it certainly felt like it.

Magnhilda: There's always a chance we have but that chance is very low. The folk have been searching all night and we've triple checked every square metre around the Everflow... We've got nothing...

She leant back in the chair, giving in to the comfort it provided. The council, however, tensed up, the reality of the situation sinking in. Jurgen took it upon himself to fill the silence with even more positivity.

Jurgen: I know no-one wants to consider this... And it's something we won't know unless we ask the right questions...

He spoke carefully, eyeing each member in the room.

Jurgen: But is there a chance that someone has done this on purpose?

Saffi: Who would even consider such a thing!?

Saffi exclaimed, causing Jurgen to give her a hard stare.

Jurgen: Some people would... and do.

The group fell into a spell of shock and low mutterings. Saffi continued to defend humanity, whilst Almarr took the other approach.

Saffi: Not in this town surely!

Almarr: I've heard of people doing worse...

Jurgen held up his hands, silencing them.

Jurgen: I'm not meaning to accuse anyone. I just want to be sure we've explored every option.

Saffi: I'm sorry, Jurgen, but isn't that Hilda's job?

Everyone faced Magnhilda to see her response. The old police chief bit her lip.

Magnhilda: I haven't ruled out the possibility. But there's no evidence to indicate such an act has occurred. If there were any tracks indicating a third party, they were completely destroyed when the townsfolk arrived.

Jurgen: So, there may have been a cause... but your inability to manage the situation may have lost any evidence of it!?

The rest of the council glanced awkwardly at Jurgen as he made his accusation. Magnhilda, however, leant forward, her face darkening.

Magnhilda: Have you ever tried to manage a group of people Jurgen? They're uncontrollable, like standing in front of an avalanche. You didn't cause it. You can't stop it. They go where they want, when they want... But at least they came and offered help. You accuse me of incompetence, but where were you when this tragedy occurred!? Another early night was it!?

Jurgen held his tongue and backed down. There was no getting into a fight with Magnhilda, even if she was on less than three hours sleep. Many of the people in Tväre had learnt that the hard way.

Saffi: No one's blaming you, Hilda.

Magnhilda: Clearly.

She shot Jurgen a snide look. The final member of the council, aside from the absent Elvera, entered the discussion. The tavern-keeper Hervor had been quietly listening in the background, but now she thought it right to enter.

Hervor: Have we considered how this might affect the Carnival?

Jurgen: It's too late to cancel. The stalls are already set up!

Saffi began to get infuriated with Jurgen, snapping at him sharply.

Saffi: It's never too late to cancel. What if we had another blizzard!? We'd have no choice then would we!?

Almarr raised a second, but equally valuable point.

Almarr: And I doubt Avarson would be all too pleased if we delayed the Guardianship signing...

Saffi: He's not the priority here though, is he!? I think we should focus on ourselves for once, instead of what he wants.

The council went quiet. Torsten quickly changed the subject, reverting back to the topic that mattered.

Torsten: What step do you recommend we take next then, Chief?

The light of the fire began to dim as one of Almarr's logs collapsed into the centre, instantly killing off the flames. Shadows of the council members danced on the walls of the meeting room as the glow of the embers took over.

Magnhilda: I can't ask any more of the folk than they've already given. Everyone's exhausted and spent. But without them, it's just me and Här, and there's no way we can keep up the search with just the two of us.

Torsten: Don't worry about the folk. They'll give what they can when they can. Just tell us, what else can we do?

Magnhilda smiled softly.

Magnhilda: There's nothing to suggest Sigmund was taken against his will. But that doesn't mean it didn't happen. If anyone knows anything about where Sigmund might be, then I'll find out what it is.

The council nodded slowly, but Magnhilda wasn't finished.

Magnhilda: In the meantime, we continue on the basis that he is lost, and reduce the search to the wider areas with what volunteers we can. We must find him, with what little time we might have remaining...

101

Saffi: One more thing I must ask Magnhilda...

Magnhilda: Yes?

Saffi paused, worriedly vocalising her most feared thought.

Saffi: How is Elvera?

Silence fell upon them all. As their thoughts drifted to that of the grieving mother, the logs of the fire hissed and spat, struggling to catch alight in the freezing cold of the hall...

**

The soft, white fur of a snout gently brushed the top of a small snowdrift. The large dog took a sniff, testing the snowflakes for anything unusual. But after a few moments he continued on his mission, detecting nothing out of the ordinary. The dog's heightened senses took him along the shoreline of the frozen Lake, all the way back to the Bridge over the Everflow where his loving owner, Vargard, stood nearby.

The discerning northerner stared out across the frozen Lake, trying to think of anything that the search parties may have missed. The young boy had vanished right where he was standing. Where could he have gone from here? His face screwed up and tightened as a cold gust blew across his face, distracting him from thinking clearly. Vargard had been hoping that his faithful dog would find the missing piece, the break in the case, but so far there'd been nothing. His husky had practically gone in circles, constantly crossing the wooden bridge over and over again, never quite settling on any clear direction... And now it was getting too cold for them both.

With a quick whistle from Vargard's mouth, the husky gave up its detective duties and sprinted back to his loyal owner. Vargard rubbed his dog's head affectionately.

Vargard: Couldn't find anything huh?

The husky whined sadly and began to pant.

Vargard: Yeah, I know... I thought we'd find him too.

He looked up, seeing his brother Torsten in the distance on the other side of the bridge. He had a shovel with him and was uncovering every odd bit of snow that he could see, just in case something had been missed. As Vargard watched, his brother stopped moving and threw down the shovel, breathing heavily and angrily.

Vargard: Seems grumpy old Torsten hasn't found anything either...

He rubbed the dog's thick fur, burying his hand in the black and white strands. The wind blew again, whistling as the freezing gusts cut across Vargard's face causing him to wince slightly.

Vargard: Brr. I wish had your fur buddy. You can just keep going and going. It's getting too cold out here for me...

He sighed, his breath billowing out in the cold air.

Vargard: Come on. Let's go retrieve the older brother before he starts attacking other things.

The husky snorted and looked out across the Lake. Vargard followed his gaze, which crossed over the Everflow and landed upon the plumes of the factory in the distance. One of its two chimneys was pumping out a putrid, black smoke, which was now the daily norm for Tväre. Vargard stared at it for a few moments, the smoke gracefully riding the breeze towards his hometown.

***

The tracks reeled and screeched as the train rumbled over metal rails. The snowy bushes and trees passed by incredibly fast, the colours blurring together into one shining mess. In the distance, Lake Tväre glowed with a subtle hint of blue, the shades changing in colour as the shadows of clouds moved in front of the sun.

Levi looked out of the carriage window, the shriek of the whistle echoing across the valley. The view was outstanding, the kind of sight you'd find on a cartoon postcard in a grimy sea resort back in Britain. To anyone who'd never trekked this far north, such a place could easily be dismissed as fictitious, and Levi knew that if he ever wrote in his charts about the unique beauty that was Tväre, there would be many who would accuse him of fabricating such a place. Either way, Levi knew what he was viewing at that moment was very special, despite the sorrowful circumstances.

The train screeched again, changing direction as it curved across the countryside. Avarson's great factory stood ugly and tall in the near distance, the train's destination for this particular journey. Levi's work was finally complete. His maps had been drawn, his notes written in full, and the historical documents from Tväre's Hall of Memory had been summarised and presented neatly in a folder. Now came the time for Levi to submit his work to Avarson, a task that required him to travel all the way to the wealthy man's main office, which was very inconveniently placed across the Lake in the heights of his factory. When Levi had first arrived, he had simply disembarked at Tväre's railway station, met with Avarson there and then proceeded to freely begin his work. But the schedules and needs of a wealthy industrialist change without warning, and Levi had been called to take the short train journey across the valley to hand over everything in person.

The windowpane in Levi's little cabin rattled as the train finally began to grind to a stop. This side of the valley was somewhat darker than Tväre's own hillside, and the train now settled itself in the shade. Levi realised, once he'd stepped down from the great mechanical beast, that it was the factory itself creating this vast shadow, and that the train had come to rest right within the underbelly of the dirty building. A single worker glanced at Levi as he exited the carriage, carrying nothing except his faithful shoulder bag.

Levi: Hello good sir. I have a meeting with Avars—

The worker grunted, instantly cutting Levi off mid-sentence.

Worker: Go that way.

He pointed towards a stairwell, which seemingly led from the small in-built station up into the belly of the factory. Levi muttered a short response.

Levi: Okay... Thanks.

He hastily followed the enclosing stairway of grey stone and ascended up towards the upper floors, passing many different doors that led to many different places. One of them hung slightly open and Levi, being the curious person he was, decided to take a peek in the room within. The door creaked as Levi pushed it open. Hidden inside was row after row of cage-like bunk beds, such as those seen in the barracks of an army. Hundreds of them it seemed, all in a row, each and every one of them identical in appearance.

Skalham: Who the hell are you!?

Levi whirled around, coming face to face with a huge, rather ugly, factory worker. He wore a set of hefty, brown trousers held up by a pair of grimy suspenders, matched with a dirty rag of a shirt that lay underneath... and he wasn't happy.

Skalham: New workers sign in with me! Then you get told where you can go!

Skalham glared down at Levi, but despite the brutal nature of this man, the young cartographer was not intimidated.

Levi: Well, that's two things you've already got wrong. I'm not a new worker, and I only go where I want to go.

Levi tried to resist smirking as the heavyset logger blinked.

Skalham: You already work here?!

Levi: That's right.

Skalham's brow wrinkled with skepticism.

Skalham: You're too scrawny to be a logger...

Levi: Scrawny?!

Levi protested as Skalham continued to examine him, his eyes narrowing as the gears in his brain slowly clicked together.

Skalham: Why are you here?

Levi: To meet Avarson. Not all work is logging and grumbling you know...

Skalham snorted heavily at the arrogant comment. The stench of his vile breath washed over Levi like a wave, causing him to grimace.

Skalham: Fine... But I'm not letting you out my sight.

Levi: I wouldn't dream of it.

And with that, Skalham began to guide Levi through the winding brick-wall corridors, constantly checking over his shoulder that the scrawny cartographer was still behind him. Without another word between them, they finally charged through a set of double doors, entering into a dark, dimly lit office. The walls were strangely angled across the corners, giving Levi the horrible feeling of being surrounded.

The dominating desk that lay in the room's centre mirrored the style, taking the form of a sort-of crescent shape. The fire had been lit earlier in the day but now only a thick group of red embers remained. The room had no windows and the torches mounted on the walls were the only source of any light. They too had fallen into a state of ashy decline, producing a passive red glow that filled the entirety of the room.

Avarson glanced up from his chair behind the desk as the two men entered his domain, his expression lifting upon Levi's arrival.

Avarson: Ah, the Man of Maps! I'm glad you've finally arrived!

He turned his head disapprovingly to face Skalham, as if his presence in the office was unwelcome.

Avarson: What's the problem now Skalham?

The logger slowly pointed towards Levi.

Skalham: This little man wanted to see you...

Avarson: And now he's here. So...?

Avarson rather condescendingly pointed out the door that stood behind Skalham, clearly inviting him to leave. The logger sighed again, leaving the two men to their work.

Avarson: There we go.

Avarson watched him go before facing Levi.

Avarson: I'm guessing you got a bit lost?

Levi: Only slightly. I was just being curious.

Avarson gave a short, harsh laugh.

Avarson: Curiosity is a useful but dangerous trait to have. People prefer to keep their privacy private, myself included. The explorers that break that rule are often the ones that go missing...

Levi paused, unsure if and how he could respond to Avarson's wordplay. It almost sounded like a threat. The industrialist smirked as he returned to his beautiful chair, breathing out in relaxation as he sat himself down, leaving Levi to remain standing.

Avarson: I trust you enjoyed the convenience of the railway? I've found it to be much more comfortable than traversing through the wilderness in just a pair of dirty boots, especially without even the protection of a scarf...

Levi smiled, a brief memory of Elvera saying the same thing popping into his mind.

Levi: I would hardly call it a wilderness. I always think to myself that if there's a road and a settlement nearby, you're often quite safe. Much less likely to go missing.

Avarson: And yet people still do...

As Avarson lay back in his fur-covered, sequined throne, Levi almost felt like he was in trouble. He'd always hated bureaucracy; the idea of spending the majority of one's life hidden behind a desk always made him shudder. Yet here he stood, buried within another creepy and uncomfortable office, as if it were an inevitable aspect of life. Avarson shrugged, breaking his hard stare.

Avarson: Wilderness or not, it's freezing cold and a hell of a long way to walk. You've got to be a rather brash individual to find enjoyment in such things. Choosing to trade in comfort and security for a distant and lonely way of life... I'll never understand it.

Levi hummed, considering an alternative point.

Levi: I think a person can be brash but also be intelligent.

Avarson: That is true... But such a person is a rare commodity. In fact, it is one of the reasons why I chose to hire your services when we first met back in Stockholm. Services, which I'm hoping, are now finished?

Levi: That they are.

Levi pulled his shoulder bag across and opened it up, retrieving a folder full of his completed works. Maps, notes, reports, it was all there. Avarson gratefully grasped hold of it as Levi handed it over. The folder glowed slightly as it moved into the red light, which seemingly encircled Avarson.

Avarson: And this is everything I asked for?

Levi: Every border and every owner.

Avarson's eyes widened slightly, a hint of blue briefly shining through the red atmosphere of the office. He opened the folder and pored over the sketches and copies, flicking through the notes and details that Levi had worked so hard on.

Avarson: I must say, I'm pleasantly surprised. Of course, I assumed the work would be complete, otherwise what am I paying you for, but not to such a degree of detail... The addition of Tväre's cultural history is somewhat unnecessary, I find all that far too pointless and wearisome, but the rest is more than acceptable.

Levi nodded once. He tried to remain unreactive but could feel a little bit of pride swelling up within him.

Avarson: Historical map records... land registries too. Very impressive. Were they difficult to acquire? I've found the townsfolk here can be...

Levi: Stubborn?

Avarson snorted at Levi's suggestion.

Avarson: More like tiresome.

Levi: Maybe... I've found that if you spend a little time with them, they quickly come around.

Avarson: How true that is.

Avarson suddenly glanced upwards.

Avarson You're quite close with the mother of the missing boy, aren't you? I happened to glance at her during the church service several days ago and noticed you standing nearby.

As Avarson's gaze bore into him, Levi suddenly began to feel uneasy... He weakly laughed before replying, taking care not to give too much away, thinking it best to respect Elvera's privacy.

Levi: If you're fishing for any gossip, I'm afraid you'll come up empty. I only know as much as everyone else does on that front.

Avarson hummed, showing the tiniest of smiles.

Avarson: Tragic event that, though not surprising. I did offer any services I could to help track his whereabouts, but the townsfolk decided to decline them. Maybe stubborn was the right description...

Levi allowed Avarson to finish the examination of the folder in silence. After several minutes, Avarson hummed and placed the folder onto his desk, beginning to sift through the other papers that were arranged in perfect symmetry.

Avarson: Right then... Payment.

Avarson found the slip of paper he was looking for and held it out for Levi.

Avarson: Here. Take this to the Aurora Bank when you return to Stockholm. I have plenty of assets with them so I can guarantee there won't be any issues.

Levi took the slip and quickly read it. It was very formally printed, detailing the account, the amount requested and

Avarson's signature stamp. The red glow of the office seemed to grow in strength as Levi accepted the payment.

Avarson: And I believe that's our business concluded. Unless there's anything else?

He asked the question out of politeness, but Levi could tell Avarson considered the meeting over. He shook his head.

Avarson: Good.

He quickly checked his gold pocket watch.

Avarson: The next train back leaves in an hour or so. Feel free to sit yourself in one of the carriages until then—

Levi: Thanks... But I think I'll risk the wilderness this time.

Avarson paused; he was rarely interrupted so bluntly, and for a moment Levi thought he'd upset the tense businessman. But then Avarson broke into a grin.

Avarson: Brash indeed. But I'm afraid I must insist. My workers are busy preparing the forests, so they are currently off limits to any folk, local or otherwise.

Levi didn't respond.

Avarson: You may go. And please, avoid being curious on your way out.

Locks of blonde hair fell across Avarson's sharp face as he picked up several other documents that lay upon his desk. Levi, not wanting to stay for a second longer in the suffocating office, quickly made his way out of the fiery red of the room and back into the dullness of the grey corridor, eager to return to the great outdoors, but there was something that bothered him.

Levi paused as he descended the metal steps. Something about Avarson's final words had just provoked a thought. The words had been ominous, almost threatening, and Levi couldn't figure out why. Maybe Avarson was just being protective of his work. It wasn't uncommon for businessmen to do that. In fact, it was rare to find a businessman that wasn't covering something up. Levi shook the thought from his mind, returning to the station below.

*

Skalham was waiting for him. The brute of a logger was standing by the doors of the central carriage, clearly there to ensure that the lone cartographer boarded the train. Skalham grunted as a smiling Levi passed him by.

Levi: Thanks for the gracious hospitality.

The door was shut heavily behind him, the clash of metal reverberating around the empty carriage. Levi chose a similar seat to his previous journey, ensuring that he would have a good view of the Lake and the Thorhorn mountain on his return. He just about made himself comfortable, but then something caught his eye...

Along the platform, Skalham began to shout at another employee of the factory. Drool and spittle flew from the logger's mouth as he vented inaudible abuse, signalling towards a closed door next to them. The bewildered worker kept his head low as Skalham ripped a tool from his hands and disappeared through the thick metallic door, dragging the poor worker along with him.

Levi frowned; what was that all about? First Avarson insisting that he take the train home, and now this strange interaction. No, it wasn't his business. Levi quickly tried to shut down the itch of curiosity before it grew into temptation. He knew he should just sit back and behave... but already his other thoughts were winning him over. The train wasn't leaving for a while anyway, he might as well sate his curious mind. But then again, he might risk losing his payment if he was caught...

Levi drummed his fingers against the window of the train, his mind battling with itself. And then, worryingly quickly, temptation won the day. Levi sighed and got to his feet, leaving his shoulder bag lying on the seat. He carefully reached out to open the carriage door and poked his head out slowly. Smooth and graceful, Levi skipped out from the train and quickly wandered over to the closed door. Without making a sound, he tested the door handle and checked to ensure Skalham wasn't standing right behind it. Having

111

gone too far to turn back now, Levi disappeared through the door, leaving the light of the platform behind.

He emerged into a vast, dimly lit basement, complete with metallic stairs and red, flaming gas lamps. Huge, silver pipelines hummed with energy as they journeyed from the heights of the ceiling and out through the farthest wall, separated only by colossal valves and great wheels. Looking over this vast room of machinery, Levi could almost believe he'd left the cold frost of the Northern Valleys far behind. It reminded him horribly of the great furnaces that operated across the cities of Europe, pumping out smoke and soot day after day.

Descending the stairs, Levi glanced down into the distant red glow of the room below, watching as Skalham furiously fought with one of the valves. With brutish persistence, the factory worker finally overcame the strength of the little wheel, the huge silver pipe beginning to groan and rumble as a new power surged through it. Wiping the sweat from his brow, Skalham turned back towards the other worker, his voice taut with stress and fury.

Skalham: What did I say about closing the valves!

The worker spluttered.

Worker: But Chief, the outputs are too high—

Skalham: I don't care what the outputs are! Keep those pipes open!

He began to stride away, but the worker still didn't give in.

Worker: We don't have space on the railway to keep up with the amount we're producing! I've heard the council across the lake mention the ruins. Maybe we can use that for temporary storage…?

Skalham whirled around, his face burning red.

Skalham: Stop! There!

The worker's own face paled.

Skalham: If you want to keep your job, you'll listen now without another word. The boss has it all sorted already. Those fools in the town stay out! You stay out! No one goes near those ruins. Understand!?

He leant forward, lowering his voice.

Skalham: And the pipes stay open.

The worker held his breath as Skalham glared at him one final time, before turning to climb the metal staircase. The one that led right towards Levi...

Levi dived behind a supporting concrete pillar, hiding himself from Skalham's blazing eyes as they appeared. The heavy thumps of the logger's footsteps crashed past him, rapidly fading away as they passed through the nearby door and back onto the platform. Levi's only way out was gone.

Glancing around in panic, Levi set to exploring the other routes of the metal gantry. He could hear Skalham grumbling away to himself out on the platform, there wasn't a chance he'd miss Levi sneaking back through. There must be another way out of here... Who designs a room with only one entrance!? Scampering around on the gantry, Levi's heart soared as his eyes fell upon a second metal doorway. He surged towards it, hoping and almost praying that no-one else stood behind it.

*

The platform was quiet and peaceful. You almost couldn't hear the hum of machinery here, although Skalham had been listening to it for so long now that it was normal to him. He continued the work he'd been doing before, which involved unloading tools and boxes from the train before it departed, until he glanced at the carriages... The seats were empty! That annoying, skinny man had gone! Skalham flew towards the window, pressing his face against the flecks of snow and mud splattered across the glass, his eyes settling upon an unattended shoulder bag...

Skalham flung open the carriage door and charged into the train, as if having to double check if Levi's disappearance wasn't an illusion. Somehow, his face turned an even darker shade of red as he gritted his teeth. He was going to tear the factory apart to find the arrogant upstart. He was—

Levi: Hello.

Skalham spun around to see the humble Levi stood in front of him, having just entered through the door that led to the second carriage.

Levi: I just needed to use the bathroom.

The door clicked shut as Levi closed it, walking past the speechless Skalham without a second look, and seating himself down upon his seat.

Levi: You want to join me? It's a lovely view.

Skalham blinked. He ignored the question and turned to leave the carriage, stepping down onto the dirty platform. He stood there for several seconds, whilst in the warmth of the carriage, Levi grinned.

***

The Scepticism

An aged man stood upon the ice of Lake Tväre, staring out across the harsh, arctic landscape. He shouted back towards the shoreline as another man approached, not bothering to turn and confirm who it was.

Jorunn: That you Torsten?

The famous gravelly voice replied.

Torsten: Yeah, it's me.

Torsten was wrapped in a thick coat, trying to deny the cold wind from penetrating down to his skin. He stumbled down the short, snowy hill, taking care not to slip on the frozen ground below, and approached the red markers of the Lake's secretive shoreline. Slowly he stretched out his boot and placed it upon the vast icy surface, trusting in the structural soundness of the ice to keep him safe. Jorunn stood several metres up ahead, next to another marker which had been hammered into the icy layers below, this one set with a blue patch instead of red.

Torsten: Vargard said it was urgent?

Jorunn didn't reply. Instead, he looked straight ahead, towards a great deformity in the ice. Torsten stood alongside him and joined his gaze, noticing the crater of ice and water for the first time. It was as wide and long as a full-grown man, and at least several feet deep. Tiny glaciers lay against one another within the freezing water, giving the appearance of an ice-filled bowl.

Torsten: Holy... Is that one of our fishing holes? What's happened to it?

Jorunn's deep and grim voice answered him.

Jorunn: It's as if the world's several months ahead of schedule...

Torsten knelt down and stared at the bizarre phenomenon.

Torsten: It's completely collapsed...

Jorunn: That's just the start. Over on the shoreline of my farm, the ice is thinner than a sheet of paper. As soon as I stepped onto the lake, I felt my boot go right through the surface. Completely soaked my socks!

Jorunn almost laughed in disbelief. Little whiffs of snow and ice floated in the air every time a small gust of wind travelled across the icy surface. Each one a tiny dance in the air.

Jorunn: The ice is melting. The coldest part of the year, and the ice is melting...

Torsten rose back to his full height, already trying to manage the situation.

Torsten: We're going to have to close it off. It's too great a risk...

Jorunn hummed in agreement, taking a moment to speak his thoughts aloud.

Jorunn: It's unthinkable; I only had my horses out here a week or so ago. Every damn year I use these crossings. And in all of my seasons, I've never seen anything like this...

He sighed. A breath long and deep. Before Torsten had taken on the unofficial role as leader of the Municipal Council, it had been Jorunn who had held the position. After twenty years, Jorunn had stepped down, wanting more time to spend his final years running the stables on his farm, but he had never lost the leading way he commanded his words or his people.

Jorunn: Our ancestors lived by this lake for over a thousand years... They relied on it far more than we do. They understood how it flowed, how it froze, and how it melted. And now, here I am, completely out of my depth...

He hummed quietly to himself.

Jorunn: You'd better go inform the rest of the council. Sooner word gets out, the better. I'll make sure no-one else ventures out on the ice until then.

116

Torsten nodded slowly, taking heed of the older man's wisdom.

> Torsten: What about the ice itself? Do we just sit back and let it happen?

He waited a moment for his predecessor to respond.

> Jorunn: We should act as our ancestors would have done. Patient and calm.

***

The two animated statues of Alaf and Olaf sat across from one another, staring down at a little stone table. In front of them lay an elaborate game, complete with a set of miniature figures, all carved from ice, as was to be expected. The game was known as 'Tafl', and it was like a Viking version of chess. As play continued, Alaf slowly moved her 'king' piece into a corner of the board, escaping Olaf's darker soldiers that were apparently chasing it. The game was won, and Alaf glanced up at her younger brother, a smug smile adorning her fragile face.

But Olaf's rage couldn't take it. With a great swing, and with the brilliant pettiness of a spoilt child, he swept the table with his arm, sending the tiny carved figures crashing over the floor in anger. And with that, he disappeared off into the corner to sulk, leaving Alaf to smugly enjoy her victory.

Far below the immense weight of the ice lay Sigmund, who was tucked within the confines of his sculpted bedroom, glowing blue light beaming down through the small skylight in the underground ceiling. He shivered, trying to wrap his arms around himself for warmth. His thick coat had helped him keep warm so far but at the moment, it didn't seem to be much help. Sigmund had always been taught from a very young age to never venture out into the cold and dark of the night, the stark warnings of his mother or his elders painting fears of a frostbitten death at every turn. Yet, here Sigmund was, buried deep under the mass of ice that had been his steadfast neighbour throughout his whole life... and no frostbite had set in yet. It may have been the magic of the cavern, or maybe his elders had just been massively overreacting, Sigmund did not know. All he did know, was that right now he was cold, and he was getting colder.

He pulled his forearm close to his chest. The limb was aching heavily, as if a weight had been attached and was pulling it down, straining his wrist. After a while, the feeling became too intense, and Sigmund pulled down the sleeves of his coat and his undershirt, holding his forearm into the light. Upon his skin, lay a faded blue scar. A patch of damaged skin, but damaged by what? Sigmund pulled down his sleeve and tried to curl up for warmth.

His icy guardian seemed to sense his discomfort. Fendal's concerned face appeared through the little archway that led into Sigmund's room, watching Sigmund in his discomfort. His echoing voice stirred Sigmund from his sleepless thoughts.

> Fendal: Are you cold?

Sigmund couldn't see him from where he lay, but he nodded anyway.

> Fendal: There's nothing worse than being cold and unable to sleep.

> Sigmund: Thanks... I'll keep that in mind.

Sigmund didn't hold back, his tiredness and frustration combining together to create an inevitable reaction. Fendal sat down at the end of the bed.

> Fendal: Have you tried counting goats?

> Sigmund: It didn't work.

Sigmund retorted grumpily.

> Fendal: Yeah, it doesn't work for me either. I get bored too quickly, that's my problem. Then I'm an hour closer to the morning and still no closer to the land of sleep.

Sigmund didn't react. He just continued to lay on his stone slab of a bed, which wasn't as uncomfortable as it sounded. Whatever mysterious power kept the frostbite at bay, clearly also had the ability to make a stone slab a somewhat pleasant experience.

> Fendal: You know what I do when I can't sleep?

Sigmund waited for Fendal to continue and turned to face the animated corpse when he didn't. The Ice-Man's eyebrows were raised cheekily, as if he'd had another of his weird and wonderful ideas. He got to his feet and headed for the archway out.

> Fendal: Follow me. Might as well embrace the insomnia!

Sigmund hesitantly got to his feet, pulling his coat around him snugly. He followed the icy remains on the floor that had formed around each of Fendal's footsteps, making his way into the main cavern once again. The blue aura thumped like a gentle heartbeat in the glowing roof above him as Fendal once again approached the bare cavern wall at the far end, neighbouring the revealed sculpture of the famed Ice-log. The translucent figures of Alaf and Olaf looked up as they approached, the little figures from their earlier game still strewn across the bedrock floor. Olaf gave Sigmund a polite smile, but Alaf's face immediately soured upon sight of him.

Fendal came to a stop against the bare wall. For a moment, he hesitated... his thin fingers stroking his beard of icicles. Until suddenly he reached out to grip a second stone lever, hidden alongside the one that had revealed the Ice-log earlier. The cavern rumbled and groaned, though not as loud or dangerously as the last time. Sigmund watched as a small doorway opened within the wall, revealing a beautifully carved hallway, extending for miles into the distance. On either side of the corridor were strange windows, separated by repeating sets of bedrock pillars. It almost looked like a museum. Fendal strode forward excitedly, eager to begin the next phase of his cavern tour.

> Fendal: I've been waiting to show this off for centuries...

Sigmund slowly stepped into the hallway; his eyes drawn to hundreds of different sights. The windows were actually thin sheets of perfectly transparent ice, behind each of which was a strange object or oddity, and Sigmund didn't know where to look first.

> Sigmund: What are they?

Fendal: This is my famously unfamous collection. You name it: relics, lost property, even memories! Anything that has been claimed by the lake ends up here...

Sigmund's eyes widened as he passed by the little windowed displays. Fendal happily narrated each exhibit for him, taking the noble role of curator. The first exhibit displayed a set of huge shears, complete with powerful wooden handles. The hefty tool was frozen in place, the metal of the cutters rusted and worn.

Fendal: The year is 1198. A young farmer is working on pruning the trees around Tväre, removing dead branches and allowing new ones to grow. On his return home, he slips, dropping the shears through a crack in the frozen Lake. His father gave him quite the spanking for his incompetence. The farmer was nearly twenty years old as well. It was hilarious!

Fendal began to cackle to himself as he moved on to the next exhibit, taking a moment to calm down before continuing.

Fendal: And these... These are my Frozen Assets.

Sigmund peered into the ice, seeing a collection of ancient coins stacked upon one another.

Sigmund: What are they? Coins?

Fendal: Twenty-five and a half copper pennies to be exact. Worth a lot back then, though I have no idea what their value is now.

Sigmund hummed quietly.

Sigmund: Probably not a lot.

Fendal: Once you're dead you realise how worthless these things are. They're essential, sure, but it's amazing how obsessed people get with them. Like it's a competition.

Fendal began to move on but stopped himself when Sigmund continued talking.

Sigmund: How did they end up here?

Fendal: Hm? Oh, some woman buried them on the outskirts of the town in order to keep them safe. Then the ground froze, and come springtime, she'd lost them.

Sigmund frowned.

Sigmund: Really!?

Fendal: Yep. Poor girl... She certainly paid the price for not respecting the earth...

They continued on deeper, the frozen exhibits becoming more and more bizarre.

Fendal: Aha! Now these are the best pets you could ever have.

Sigmund turned and stared into the motionless eyes of a huge, grumpy catfish whose fins and whiskers were frozen in place.

Fendal: Driven extinct only a few decades ago by overfishing in the lakes and rivers. I believe this guy is the only one left.

Sigmund: Is it alright in there?

Fendal scoffed and waved his hand.

Fendal: Ah, he'll be fine, he does this every year. Every spring he reemerges, sporting that beautiful smile of his.

The ugly catfish somehow glared at Sigmund through the ice as he gave it one final look. Beneath each window Fendal had scribbled a brief summary of the object in question, each one apparently donated out of his own generosity. As the young boy ambled on, his eyes quickly flitted from sign to sign, skim-reading their brief histories. He passed a wooden statue of a mermaid, followed by a leather strap that almost looked like an ancient, biblical slingshot and finished the section with a rusted metal firearm. Sigmund's childish eyes, however, were drawn to something else: a strange rat-like creature that seemed to be chasing an acorn.

Sigmund: What is this?

Fendal bent down to have a quick look himself, wincing slightly.

> Fendal: Ah... Better leave him be if I were you. He can get quite aggressive.

He continued on, this time turning a corner that led into a second hallway, just as long and bright as the first. Sigmund's voice echoed down the corridor, bouncing off the icy walls.

> Sigmund: How deep does this place go?

Fendal glanced back.

> Fendal: I don't know! It changes every time I visit!

His strange reply caused Sigmund to frown.

> Sigmund: But didn't you say it was your collection?

> Fendal: I did indeed. But the trick with great masses of ice is that they are always moving, always adapting, always planning... We might be hidden beneath the lake now, but we're just as vulnerable to the impacts of the surface.

Sigmund shoved his hands into his pockets as he slowly got bored with the charade. Why would Fendal be showing him all this? His thoughts were quickly distracted, however, by something else. Something dark that appeared in the depths of the distance.

> Sigmund: What's that? Down there?

Sigmund pointed towards yet another hallway, the entrance enfolded in the distant shadows. It was dimly lit and narrower than the others; the blue aura of the cavern fading into darkness as Sigmund turned towards it. He took a wary step forward... the hallway growing in power, as if feeding off his attention. Tempting him in.

Fendal looked around, seeing the young boy slowly take another step towards the uneasy corridor. In an instant, he'd returned to Sigmund's side, quicker than anyone could even blink. The white light in the frozen man's eyes flickered for a moment, as if the very sight of the dark corridor were disrupting their power.

Fendal: Easy there my lad...

He gently guided Sigmund away from the temptation of the corridor.

Fendal: Some things are best if they remain unseen... especially now.

Sigmund glanced back towards the distant shadowy entrance.

Sigmund: But then, why is it here?

Fendal didn't answer immediately. He risked a second glance towards the corridor himself, thinking on the best answer to give.

Fendal: Every scrap of light comes with its share of the dark... An evil that lies within the good. Some people can accept that, others bury it deep within their minds.

The darkness pulsed slightly as Fendal spoke, his words and attention giving it the life it so desperately craved.

Fendal: And others choose to simply ignore it and focus on the here and now.

He rose to his feet, his usual swagger and joy returning.

Fendal: Trust me. I've been doing it for centuries. Now follow me. We're close now.

As Fendal led Sigmund away from the murky edges of his museum, the mysterious, dark hallway slowly retreated and then vanished out of view, but the memory of its taunting shadows never left Sigmund's thoughts. He stumbled along behind Fendal as the white glow around him faded. He suddenly glanced around, realising that the icy exhibits of the walls were no longer present. He'd followed Fendal into yet another hallway, this one empty and bare, stretching further into the depths than any of the others. A glow of dull blue light sat in the distance, steadily growing as Fendal confidently led them both towards it. It enveloped the pair, the rays wrapping themselves around their bodies, and Sigmund suddenly found himself staring out across a cave of bedrock and ice... He was back within the cavern, only this time, he wasn't at the bottom.

Sigmund stood at the end of a small tunnel, overlooking the vastness of his most recent home. From this height, he could almost reach the frozen ceiling that topped the cavern, following each precarious crack with his eyes as it travelled across the rooftop. For a moment, Sigmund thought he could see the shadows of bootprints, appearing and disappearing way up upon the surface... Fendal, however, had to hunch himself over to avoid hitting his head for the second time. They both peered over the edge, staring down at the great sculpture of the Ice-log, its icy shards powering out in all directions. At either side, Sigmund could spot the two icy figures of Alaf and Olaf staring up at them from far below. Fendal gave them a little wave, and then turned to face Sigmund.

> Fendal: I imagine you're wondering why I'm showing you all this?

He held his hand over the edge of the overlook, and the cavern slowly began to tremble and rumble.

> Fendal: I wish it were simple, but alas no such word exists in the realms of the natural world.

Sigmund risked a glance over the tunnel's edge himself. The Ice-log was growing, expanding like a rapidly evolving tree, rising up against the walls to meet them at the top of the cavern. It was only when the icy shards brushed against the ceiling did Fendal drop his hand, the trembling and rumbling stopping with it. Sigmund stared at the frozen centre of the Ice-log, the source of all the great shards, where the blue aura of power gently hummed and thumped. But as he peered closer, the blue aura took on a new form. Miniature branches and tiny leaves came together to form a little tree sapling, its roots planted in the centre of the sculpture. Each and every twig was frozen solid, but Sigmund could still see the green pigment of each leaf through the icy shell that surrounded them.

> Fendal: This is the oldest resident of the cavern. Though exactly how old, I'm not quite sure... I have my guesses, of course, but the lake still likes to keep its secrets... Even from me.

Fendal chuckled to himself.

Fendal: What do you see?

Sigmund glanced up at Fendal, who simply nodded back, encouraging him to take a deeper look. Sigmund stared at the unmoving sapling for a moment, answering glumly.

Sigmund: It's frozen in ice...

Fendal: Good. That ticks off the obvious answer. What else?

Sigmund looked again, almost instantly groaning with annoyance. He smacked the edge of the nearest icy shard, giving in to his petulant ways.

Sigmund: Why are you asking me to do this!? What is even the point!?

The whites in Fendal's eyes glowed dangerously, forcing Sigmund to immediately back down and lower his head. When the Ice-Man finally did speak again, his voice was deeper, firmer... almost growling.

Fendal: The point... is to help you see what your fellow townsfolk cannot. You are blind Sigmund. Blind to your history, blind to your world, and blind to your consequences.

Sigmund kept his eyes low.

Fendal: Now look again... and tell me what you see.

Without another complaint, Sigmund pressed himself against the ice, staring at the frozen sapling once again. This time, he could see a hint of brown within the green of the leaves. And they bent and drooped, as if weighed down by something unseen...

Sigmund: It's wilting...

His reply was small and quiet, but Fendal swelled with pride.

Fendal: Exactly.

He stepped forward, standing alongside Sigmund and staring at the weak aura of the sapling himself.

Fendal: The miracle of nature is that it can thrive in any environment on Earth. Even in the coldest winters, when life flees from our own fires, the animals and plants somehow survive. We stand within a perfect creation, the pieces fitting together exactly as they need to. One that was designed to survive nearly anything...

Fendal's voice became somewhat forlorn. He placed a frozen hand on the sculpture, the ice reacting to the power in the faded blue of his fingertips.

Fendal: That is my purpose. To protect the sapling from the things it can't survive. The thieves, the raiders and the evil. But instead of a battle, we have poison... and it's not one we can easily cure...

Fendal's wide eyes turned to Sigmund, shining on him like spotlights.

Fendal: And that, my lad, is why the lake brought you here. As I've said before, it's never too late for change...

He turned and retreated back into the tunnel, leaving the glow of the sapling behind him. Sigmund paused for a moment, taking everything in that Fendal had said. Then he turned and yelled out.

Sigmund: Wait!

Fendal: Hmm?

Fendal stopped, glancing around.

Sigmund: Why me? I'm not like you; I haven't got any powers. I'm not special... Why does the lake want me?

The icicle beard in front of him twinkled as Fendal smiled.

Fendal: Because, like me, it believes you are capable of doing better.

Fendal disappeared into the tunnel, leaving Sigmund to sit and think at the top of the cavern. The blue aura of the sapling pulsed and throbbed as Sigmund looked at it again, staring at its motion and movement for several minutes longer. Had he stayed for another minute, as was always the case with these things, he might not have missed the small drop of brown slime that fell from the empty space above the sapling, falling and landing onto one of the frozen leaves. In that moment, the little patch of icy protection melted, and the leaf began to wither…

Far above them all, through the glistening roof of the cavern and the thick layers of ice that formed it, Chief Magnhilda and a cohort of stubborn volunteers scoured the surface of Lake Tväre, searching for any sign of Sigmund's whereabouts. Their hands lifted to cover their faces as sharp gusts of wind launched themselves at their eyes and cheeks. The hurricane-like weather was beginning to take a turn for the worse, and they all looked across at each other, all knowing that they couldn't give up the search… Once again, it was going to be another cold, dark night…

***

The blurry image of green and grey phased in and out of focus. Levi glanced down at the dials on his telescope, adjusting them slightly with a frown. A single ray of sunlight shot across his balcony, piercing through the horde of grey clouds that seemed to always dominate the arctic sky. Levi pressed himself against the eyepiece of his telescope again, this time seeing his intended image in full focus.

Across the Lake and atop the hill of the Northward Forest, lay a clearing in the trees. Within the clearing were the remains of a large stone structure, a crumbled building that lay dormant and empty. Giant grey bricks, as large as the trunks of the oldest trees, were scattered upon the ground nearby, almost completely buried in the snow. Levi wished he could see more, but that was where the detail ended. He leant back from his telescope and took a deep breath, wondering if this was worth all the effort. The so-called 'ruins' could just be as they appeared; empty and abandoned. What could be gained from that?

A brief shadow caused Levi to instantly stop in his tracks. He froze. adjusting the knobs of the telescope as something blurry and grey floated in the view. As the telescope focused, Levi stared at the haunting grey rags of a spectral figure, standing between the trees. Staring at him with an unbroken gaze…

Levi lurched back, knocking the telescope out of focus. He quickly returned the sensitive equipment to its place, realigning it with the clearing of the ruins and pressing himself against the eyepiece... But the unearthly figure was gone. He looked across the entirety of the Northward Forest hillside, from the gully in the east to the factory in the west. But there was no-one there. Not a single soul.

*

The torches along the walls were always kept alight. Almost every building in Tväre held some sort of basement beneath its wooden structures, but none were as deep or as large as the town library.

Levi ventured down into the depths of the bookshelves, his eyes scanning the narrow channels between the desks and drawers. The only sounds were the brief spits and crackles of the fiery torches, another reminder of how cold and empty this place could be without its light. But then, a rustle of claws... The scratching sound came from the shelf above Levi's head, instantly drawing his attention upwards.

Peckingham stared at him from the nearest and highest corner of the library. He seemed more curious than aggressive, not that Levi had ever known or heard of a dangerous pigeon. But still, the young cartographer remained cautious of the strange bird. He slowly and carefully held out a hand...

Levi: You going to come down this time?

The pigeon didn't shift. Instead, he disregarded Levi completely, turning his head to look another way.

The Librarian: He takes a while to get used to people.

Levi jumped, flinging himself around, the elderly figure of the Librarian materialising by his side.

Levi: Don't you ever just say 'hello'!?

The old woman chuckled.

The Librarian: I'll remember to do so next time.

128

Levi sighed as the old woman fell silent. She fitted in so naturally with the surrounding darkness, that if she ever decided to scare people for fun, she'd barely even need to put on make-up. She held out her hands, almost welcoming him.

> The Librarian: What's the purpose of this visit then? I would have thought Avarson would be busy preparing for the carnival, not demanding more work from you.

> Levi: I'm not here for Avarson.

The Librarian raised her eyebrows, the wizened wrinkles of her skin shifting with the movement.

> The Librarian: Oh? Then why are you here?

> Levi: ...Personal interest.

He reached into his shoulder bag and pulled out the battered old book that the Librarian had lent to him during their last meeting. Her face lifted at the sight of it as Levi elaborated.

> Levi: Specifically, the ruins within the Northward Forest. I had a flick through this, but the only mention involved a story and a few sketchings. Nothing definitive.

The Librarian hummed.

> The Librarian: Old books rarely are. The ruins though, that's a strange choice... Might I ask what brought on this 'personal interest'?

> Levi: I overheard a logger mention them while I was at the factory. He spoke about dealings there and mentioned the town council. I thought I might take a look... just to make sure the town weren't being taken advantage of...

He shifted his eyes as he spoke, purposefully avoiding the true reason as to his interest. The earlier sight of the spectre was most likely a hallucination. An illusion of the light caused by the glass within his telescope. Whatever the cause, it repeatedly drew Levi's mind back to the ruins. But he thought it best to avoid mentioning that to the Librarian, or to anyone for that matter. The Librarian narrowed her eyes.

The Librarian: And why would you want to help the town? You're an outsider, remember. Aside from a few weak friendships, what reason do you have to offer help?

Her question was met with a reluctant sigh as Levi replied.

Levi: A guilty conscience.

The Librarian's face softened. Her shrewd tone dropped, and she now spoke softly and quietly.

The Librarian: Sigmund's disappearance wasn't your fault.

Levi: The stares I get from the locals say otherwise.

He retorted, turning his gaze away from the Librarian's face.

The Librarian: People assign blame. It's the only way they can face the reality of things. That doesn't make what happened any less of an accident.

Levi didn't respond.

The Librarian: But if it will help ease your mind, I'll gladly offer my help. Besides, the ruins have an entire history all to themselves. Factory secrets or not, it'll be interesting to see what else you might find...

*

The tiny claws of Peckingham the pigeon tapped and clicked on the top of the bookshelves. His unblinking eyes watched over Levi and the Librarian as they toiled through various dusty drawers. It had been the Librarian's suggestion for Levi to search the ruins directly, along with stating several other judgemental comments. But to plan such a trip required a bit of research, and the Librarian was more than happy to lend him an old map or two. They just had to find them.

Levi withdrew one such sheet of paper now, dust erupting from within the drawer as it moved. He coughed and spluttered as the particles hovered around his face, prompting a quick clear of the air with his hand.

Levi: Is this the one?

He held up a faded map for the Librarian to see, the black ink of the drawing now almost grey with age.

The Librarian: That's the one.

She moved across the room to join him in his examination. The map held a wonderful, mystical style, with detailed drawings alongside perfect curving penmanship. At the base of the map was a small settlement that was labelled 'Tväre', but near the top, across the white emptiness that represented the Lake and within the depths of the Northward Forest, was a neat little tower. The Librarian spoke over it with fondness as it spread out across the desk.

The Librarian: Drawn at a time when the ruins were more than just ruins. Look at the detail on these drawings...

She brought in a candle to give them some more light, taking care not to spill a drop of wax on the map itself.

The Librarian: If I remember correctly, there was an old path that led up the hill... This line here.

She pointed towards the pencilled hill of the Northward Forest, where a small, zig-zagged line led from the Lake up towards the ruins.

The Librarian: It'll be heavily buried in snow, but better than a straight climb up the hill.

Levi followed her finger, scoffing when he saw what she was pointing at.

Levi: If that path even exists...

The Librarian: Is there a reason why it wouldn't?

Levi rolled his eyes.

Levi: Come on. You're not seriously recommending I follow a map that's hundreds of years old? Look at the drawings. It's guesswork!

The Librarian stared at him coldly.

The Librarian: The Vikings who drew this map were some of the best navigators in the world. They understood the seas and the stars better than we ever will again. To doubt the accuracy of their work, as a fellow cartographer no less, is beyond idiotic.

Her sharp tone forced Levi into a shameful silence.

The Librarian: If you want to be successful, you need to respect the ancestors of your craft.

Levi mumbled a reply.

Levi: Yes Ma'am.

The Librarian: Good. Since we've now agreed that there is a path there, the only question is how are you going to get to it? Is the train a viable option?

It was Levi's turn to point to the map.

Levi: It takes you as far as here. To the factory. But it'll be hard boarding without a ticket, and even harder to talk my way out if I get caught on the other side. They're already suspicious of me...

The Librarian pursed her lips in thought.

The Librarian: It's too far to walk around... and you'll want to avoid descending from the ruins in the darkness. Which really only leaves you one option...

Levi's eyes widened as the Librarian's finger settled on the vast blank space that represented Lake Tväre.

The Librarian: Looks like we'd better ready you for a crossing.

She chuckled and took the map away from Levi's gaze, leaving him to stand there, as still as stone. This hadn't been the way he thought things would go...

***

A small group of Tvären townsfolk sat within the slanted room of the Bergskydd Tavern, taking a moment away from the depressing, futile feeling that everyone in the town was now experiencing. The search for Sigmund was falling into a redundancy of disappointment and desperation. No-one

132

wanted to talk about it, yet it was all anyone could think about. In a bid to escape their feelings, several of the folk now gathered in Hervor's Tavern, but the gloom and loss that had settled over Tväre had beaten them there. The huge interior was practically bare. Old mugs were left on tables, the floor was dirty and wet, and Hervor looked as if her energy had completely deserted her. The only others present within the tavern were a group of Avarson's hired loggers, all of whom were draining pint after pint of mead and ale, completely untroubled by the pain of the town.

Despite the current emergency, life and business in the town still continued. People still needed to be fed and new information still needed to be discussed. Hervor had volunteered the Tavern as tonight's unofficial meeting place for the Municipal Council, hoping that the fire and cosiness would counter the cold and empty atmosphere. Joining her was Torsten and Saffi, along with Edvin, who had been invited to attend in place of Almarr, who was busy coordinating new safety measures around the Lake. All of them had a drink of sorts, mead for some, water for the rest. An extra mug lay next to Torsten's own, reserved for the apparently absent Jurgen.

> Torsten: That's the second one we've found now...

Torsten gruffly informed the rest of the council of the news surrounding the collapsing ice, having already referred to his earlier encounter at the ice-fishing hole with Jorunn. Edvin, however, immediately countered the statement.

> Edvin: Nah. Nah it's not. It's only the first—

> Saffi: It's the second one Edvin. Jorunn found one, Vargard found the other.

Saffi patiently tried to correct Edvin's assessment, but the thickset man leant back and crossed his arms.

> Edvin: Couldn't the first one also be the second one? They could just both be the same ice-fishing hole and someone's just gotten confused.

> Torsten: I know what you're trying to do Edvin. Cut it out.

Torsten nearly snapped at him, and Edvin snorted indignantly.

Edvin: I'm not trying to do anything.

Torsten: You're not going out on the lake again until further notice, you hear me!? No more fishing until we say it's safe! Council's orders.

Edvin went to argue once more, but the fire in Torsten's eyes made him back down, and he instead slumped into a sulk. He looked exactly like a spoilt child, if the child had heavy sweat patches and a dirty, messy beard. Hervor tried to calm the situation.

Hervor: It's not personal Edvin; it's for your safety. It's off limits for everyone, not just you.

Edvin: Whatever.

At that moment, Jurgen barrelled through the Tavern door, groaning loudly for everyone's entertainment as the cold outside air washed in.

Jurgen: Ugh... Sorry I'm late. My wife had a bit of a rough moment and I just stayed put a bit to help calm her down.

Saffi followed up worriedly as Jurgen placed his coat on the nearby rack.

Saffi: Is she okay!?

Jurgen: She had a run-in with one of those loggers down at the station on her way home. They said some things that I won't be repeating.

He sat himself down with an annoyed grunt. His tone seemed calm, but his blood was boiling beneath his skin, turning his face bright red.

Jurgen: It's fine. Her mother is with her now.

Torsten: How about you?

Torsten's little invitation was enough for Jurgen to open the floodgates.

Jurgen: Well, I'm infuriated! Of course I am. Not only do we have enough on our table with everything that's happened these last few days, but now we have to look out for those damn workers and what they might do to those who can't defend themselves.

Jurgen smacked his fist against the table.

Jurgen: Avarson promised us we wouldn't be bothered by his work, but so far it's been nothing but constant trouble.

With his outburst over, the little group were left in an awkward silence. Saffi gave Hervor a worried look and the tall woman silently indicated that everything was okay.

Torsten: As long as Evanna is alright?

Jurgen nodded once, his scowl unchanging.

Torsten: Then we should get onto the talking points...

Jurgen: Which have been, what so far?

Jurgen took a heavy gulp from his pre-filled mug as Hervor filled him in.

Hervor: Another one of the fishing holes collapsed on Lake Tväre. This time on the townside...

Jurgen: Another one?! But it's freezing outside!

Hervor: Exactly our thoughts. According to Jorunn, it's thawed in several places along the western shoreline. It's like summer is knocking on the door...

They fell into a short silence, pondering the perplexing mystery that was beginning to rear its head. Such occurrences of thawing and melting had been seen every year since the Vikings of Tväre had first set foot upon the ice. But usually, these occurrences were much closer to the warmth of the spring or summertime, when the thick mass was much more vulnerable to subsidence or collapse. In the depths of winter's bite, however, it was never even a consideration...

Torsten: Something's upsetting the lake...

Torsten muttered aloud. The only other sounds in the tavern were those coming from Avarson's workers, who

135

laughed and drank in the far corner. Saffi hesitantly put forward a suggestion.

> Saffi: So, what should we say? Do we ban people from making crossings until next Winter!?

> Edvin: Surely not...

He countered nervously, as if worried that Saffi's question might be the actual outcome.

> Jurgen: You're welcome to go out and risk it whenever you want.

Jurgen's retort earned him a quick smack from Saffi. They all looked towards Torsten, waiting on him for the final decision.

> Torsten: For the sake of safety, the lake has to be made off limits... To everyone.

His eyes quickly flitted towards Edvin, who looked to the floor crestfallen.

> Torsten: We'll issue the news to the town in the morning, and hope that it'll get back to some stability soon.

Everyone besides Edvin, nodded slowly in agreement. Jurgen took the chance to ask a question further.

> Jurgen: Has anyone mentioned this to the Chief?

Torsten shook his head, way ahead of Jurgen's own thoughts.

> Torsten: If you're thinking of Sigmund, it's not a possibility.

> Jurgen: Why not?

Jurgen's follow-up was instant, but Torsten was ready for it.

> Torsten: Because we searched the entire lake, twice over. No cracks or holes were reported.

> Hervor: Adding to that, the ones that we've found are all on the western side. So, unless the boy walked across the whole lake during the night...

Hervor shrugged and droned off.

Torsten: None of it makes any sense…

Torsten sighed heavily. In their moment of contemplation, a small cheer went up from the opposite side of the long room. Avarson's workers hooted, slurred and clacked their mugs together. Saffi stared at them over her shoulder.

Saffi: How can they be so cheerful at a time like this?

Jurgen: Simple. They don't care. The boy's disappearance is meaningless to them. Why be sad if it doesn't affect you?

Saffi glared at Jurgen whilst he sipped from his mug.

Jurgen: Am I wrong?

Saffi: You are beyond help…

Torsten and Hervor both smiled softly at the quarrelsome pair. The moment of humour lasted only for a second, though, before Hervor returned to the meeting.

Hervor: What of the complaints about the Carnival?

Saffi: What's this now?

Saffi quickly interjected. The question had been aimed at Torsten, who fiddled with his beard, unsure how the rest of the council would take the news he was about to break.

Torsten: We've had a couple of worried suggestions, not complaints, about whether we should proceed with the Carnival.

Saffi: Ah…

Saffi nodded understandably.

Jurgen: Including the Signing as well, I'm assuming?

Jurgen spoke up, talking about Avarson's signing of Guardianship. The additional event had been planned to coincide with this year's Carnival, designed to be the official agreement between Tväre and Avarson for protection and management of the Northern Valley lands and forests. This included the lands on the opposite side of the Lake, which lay adjacent to Avarson's dirty factory. Once the signing was complete, the railway would be opened to the townsfolk, and their economic relations with the southern cities could finally begin. Torsten knew that to cancel such an event would be one of the hardest decisions he'd ever have to make.

> Torsten: They've mentioned it yes. One or two suggested we forgo the carnival altogether and simply delay the signing out of respect... for Sigmund...

He seemed to struggle to say the final part. The missing boy had hit the hardy northern man quite close to the heart, much more than he'd expected it to.

> Hervor: Avarson's had the date set for a few months now. Even if we forgo the carnival, the self-centered git will throw a fit if we delay the signing any longer.

> Jurgen: And if we do, we'll have to keep dealing with those bastards over there...

Jurgen pointed towards the workers, who were growing louder and louder as their mugs became emptier and emptier. Their voices echoed in the Tavern as they shouted their words across the single metre distances that separated them.

> Torsten: In regard to the signing, I say we wait. Give ourselves a day to think it over. If any further 'suggestions' come to the hall, we'll speak with Avarson about a delay.

> Saffi: And the carnival?

Saffi asked with a hint of concern, aware that a consensus hadn't yet been reached.

> Jurgen: I hate to say it, but I think that fire has already died...

Hervor nodded in agreement with Jurgen.

> Hervor: It's a shame, but I think it's the right choice. The town will understand.

> Worker: Oi! Barwoman!

The booming interruption cut right across the meeting. Hervor lifted her head, seeing one of the workers waving his hefty mug in her direction.

Worker: Aren't you supposed to keep this filled up!?

His fellow loggers chuckled as Hervor muttered under her breath.

Hervor: I hate people...

She reluctantly got to her feet, returning to the neighbouring tables to refill the empty mugs that were waved in her face. The little group of townsfolk watched as she did the rounds, returning to their small conversations as they waited for Hervor to rejoin them. What none of them saw however, was the man sat by the table behind them. Hidden in the shadowy corner of the Tavern all by himself, sat a sneering, shifty little man. Avarson's loyal pet, Regan, had been subtly eavesdropping on the unofficial meeting of the Municipal Council, making what mental notes he could. As he finished his small cup of drink, he whirled his long coat around himself and quickly vacated the Tavern, ready to inform his employer of what the council now planned to do.

***

A young woman threw another log onto the fire, the strips of bark catching instantly and curling in reaction to the extreme heat. She returned to the sofa, sitting herself down carefully so as not to cause her guest any unnecessary stress. Her name was Annali, and she was Elvera's older sister. She usually lived with her husband only two streets away, but for the last two nights she'd been living here, making sure that Elvera wasn't alone in her pain.

Annali: Are you warm enough?

She asked the question gently, Elvera slowly nodding in response. She'd been silent for most of the evening, staring out into the empty space with barely any emotion. If Annali hadn't been here to light the fire or prepare some food, Elvera would likely have done neither. She just sat there, saying only a few words at a time. But Annali never got angry; for although she could imagine the pain that

139

burdened her younger sister, she had no real understanding of what it truly felt like.

Annali: I can get you another jumper or a blanket if you need it—

Elvera: I said, I'm fine.

She didn't shout, but the monotone nature of her words had the same effect.

Annali: I know you really don't want to, but you must have something to eat. It's not good to keep avoiding it... Elvera.

She tried to get her sister's attention, but Elvera didn't respond. She simply stared continuously at the fire, watching the shining embers roll and flicker over one another. Annali lost her patience with the silent treatment, despite knowing that her sister didn't mean any of it.

Annali: I'm getting you something. I don't care if you don't want it, you have to eat.

She got to her feet and wandered the short distance away to the kitchen. Sorting through the cupboards, she found herself a clean plate, but then she spotted something on the countertop. In that moment of pause, Elvera spoke quietly from the next room.

Elvera: I made Sigmund breakfast this morning...

The statement hung in the air as Annali glanced at the plate, realising there was a slice of bread and a small bit of meat. She returned to the room, looking at her sister sympathetically.

Annali: It's habit sister. Nothing to be ashamed of.

Elvera shook her head, almost telling herself off.

Elvera: I got that wrong too. One moment... One moment of distraction... and I lost him...

Annali didn't know what to say. Elvera looked over towards her.

Elvera: I can't go in his room anymore. Even though I know he isn't there I... I can't bear to see it empty.

Annali: Is there anything that needs doing in there? Bedding? Collect the washing? Anything?

Elvera shook her head.

Annali: Then you don't need to go in there today.

Annali took to clearing up the kitchen, leaving her sister in the company of the spitting and crackling fire. She cleaned and wiped the plates, using a basin of water in the kitchen that was already prepared for such chores.

Annali: There. All sorted.

Elvera: Thank you...

The whispered reply came moments later, and Annali smiled sadly, sitting herself down in one of the other chairs. She lifted a book from the table in an attempt to distract herself from her own sorrowful thoughts. After a short while, when the incinerated logs collapsed into the embers, Elvera stirred herself from the sofa.

Elvera: I'm going to bed...

Annali: Are you sure?

Elvera: Yeah... Not to sleep. I just... I just want to be alone...

Annali sighed sorrowfully and went to get up, but Elvera held out a hand.

Elvera: Alone in my room. Not anywhere else... Would it be okay if you stayed down here?

Annali: Of course I can. The whole night if you need me to.

Elvera smiled softly before heading up the stairs in a slow and painful walk. Annali stepped forward and began to poke at the fire, shifting some of the logs to free the heat that lay underneath.

There came a knock at the door. Two taps followed by silence. Annali pushed back the loose strands of hair from her face and moved to open the door, facing the shivering face of Minister Toro, wrapped up against the cold of the oncoming night.

Minister Toro: Annali. Good evening.

Annali: And to you Minister.

Minister Toro: Is she in?

He indicated to the room behind her, and Annali bit her lip.

Annali: She is. But if you're hoping to talk to her, it's probably better to wait until morning.

Minister Toro: I thought as much. I tried to talk myself out of coming, and yet I found myself at her door anyway...

Minister Toro smiled sadly.

Minister Toro: I just wanted to make sure she wasn't alone.

Annali: She won't be, Minister.

The old man nodded, his light beard creasing slightly. Even though the people of this town were not his kin, nor the people of his homeland, he thought of them like family. And they him.

Minister Toro: Thank you, Annali. Sleep well this eve...

He turned to leave, walking back into the embrace of the ice when Annali called out to him.

Annali: Minister!?

Minister Toro: Hmm?

Annali looked away for a brief moment, and then all her emotion came flooding out.

Annali: Why her?

Minister Toro blinked. He'd expected this question from many of the townsfolk, though none of them had dared yet say it. But now, in the cold of the night, it had finally emerged.

Annali: She's been through so much already. I almost feel guilty for even thinking it but... of all people for this to happen to, why would God burden her with this?

Annali's question was another in the long list that the old Minister had been struggling with. He glanced towards the icy surface of the distant Lake, trying to think how to best phrase his answer.

> Minister Toro: You know, I've grappled with that question my whole adult life. In my home country, it was not uncommon for little children to go missing. Sometimes they would appear an hour or so later, having simply been playing in the bullrushes. And other times they never came back… It is plenty enough grief to make even an old Minister question everything he believes in.

He paused in his speech. Annali's desperate expression hurt to look at.

> Minister Toro: There is little I can say that will make anything better Annali. Only God knows the true reason behind why things happen, and trusting in him to either solve them or help us through them is oh so difficult to do…

Annali's head dropped. She hadn't been expecting a quick and brief answer to one of the world's most difficult questions, but she still felt disappointed.

> Minister Toro: And no, you shouldn't feel guilty for thinking such things. It is normal, and almost expected of you.

> Annali: I don't know why, but I feel like our town is being gripped by darkness…

The old Minister smiled sadly as Annali's voice cracked.

> Minister Toro: Go back inside, child. Be in the warmth with your sister. She needs you. Even if she doesn't say it.

Annali nodded sadly.

> Annali: Goodnight Minister.

> Minister Toro: Goodnight.

He turned and walked back into the midst of the silent, slumbering town. Who knew how many were currently lying awake, thinking on the mystery of the missing child that had gripped their minds so. The clouds fell upon the peaceful town and then upon the surface of Lake Tväre, covering the shifting ice like a blanket.

* * *

Regan watched carefully as the glowing embers of the fireplace exploded and erupted, sending billowing flashes of red around the dark, dismal office. Avarson's short temper had been completely shattered by the news, and the industrialist had begun taking his volcanic anger out on the first thing he could see, which happened to be the messy pile of flaming embers that lay behind him.

Avarson wrecked the fire with raging brutality, his face red and his eyes completely black. With every kick, ash flew in a new direction, coating his expensive boots with dirty, grey blemishes. Embers scattered themselves across the floor and logs were flattened into the base of the grate below. The fireplace was completely destroyed. After several moments, Avarson began to regain control of himself, kicking a shattered log one last time before wiping his mouth and turning to face Regan, who hadn't said a word during the entire episode.

Avarson: You said there was a chance they wouldn't delay?

His breath was short and quick, like that of a wild animal.

Regan: As long as no more complaints come in, then possibly.

Avarson nodded, talking to himself as different ideas filled his mind. He rubbed his face again, the ash in the air irritating his exposed skin.

Avarson: We can make this work... Yes.

He directed his next thought towards Regan, who listened obediently.

Avarson: Find out what you can about these complaints. Names, addresses, anything. Maybe we can make it work to our favour, I don't know, but the signing must go ahead! I've already had one messenger from Stockholm telling me to get my ass into gear, I don't need any more.

Regan nodded, several ideas already forming in his mind.

Avarson: Do whatever you can, but Do Not fail me on this. You understand? Nothing else can go wrong...

Avarson was practically unhinged, almost threatening, but Regan was used to his employers being aggressive, he even enjoyed it.

Regan: You can count on me, Sir.

Avarson turned back towards the fire, not even giving Regan a second look. Without the energy of the flames, the office descended into a mess of dark shadows, the largest of these being Avarson's outline, which hunched and crawled across the bare walls. He glanced downwards, spotting the small glow of an ember on his floor that had somehow survived the output of his rage. He stepped on it heavily, instantly extinguishing the small light before it could grow into anything more...

***

The Crossing

The great expanse of the Lake seemed to stretch and grow as Levi stared over it. Like an optical illusion, the trees of the nearby Northward Forest faded further and further away, giving the impression that they were suddenly hundreds of miles in the distance. Levi gently shook his head, freeing his mind from the trickery. He knew the Lake was crossable; he'd witnessed horses and carts stand on the ice with ease. And the distance, in truth, wasn't far. With an educated guess, he imagined it would take less than an hour to reach the forest, but he didn't move yet...

Red markers lined the shore, the border hidden from sight by the snow. The icy snowflakes shined in the light of the early morning sun, glistening and twinkling. Levi only had to take one step, and then his crossing would have begun. It felt so risky, so dangerous, but he could feel the call of adventure, the temptation to step into this frozen world and walk upon the waters. The sparkling trees of the Northward Forest beckoned him from the other side, and he knew if he waited any longer, he'd risk losing the daylight upon his return.

Without another moment to waste, Levi inhaled and stepped past the red markers, his boot landing on the ice of Lake Tväre for the first time... He exhaled in relief. The ice was holding. Of course it was; it held both people and animals nearly every winter's day, but the worrying nightmare of falling through had always been in the back of his mind. Levi stepped again, grinning as the dusty snow crunched beneath his footstep. He began to stride across the ice, taking in the strange and mysterious sights that lay around him. Flaky layers of snow brushed away under his feet, revealing unlimited shades of blue. In other places, the snow had frozen to the surface in little ridges, causing Levi's ankles to wobble and bend. Icy waves and folds, formed over months of slow migration, shifted in different directions, driven by unseen undercurrents. Every now and then, the ice would creak and groan, sending a shuddering sound wave across the silent world.

Levi stopped with a jolt. Almost immediately, he was anxious and alert. A great, shattering boom echoed through the valley, a mixture of a crack and a crash. The sound eventually faded, and Levi peered ahead, now cautious of every movement he made. His gaze fell upon a huge crack that split the ice in two perfect halves, the gap descending down to unimaginable depths. He paused for a moment and allowed the Lake to settle, the warning received loud and clear. Glancing around, Levi realised how far he'd come. He was a long way from the shore, much too far for any sort of rescue, but close enough to the forest that it felt within reach. He peered down into the crack, and for a moment, he thought he saw a dim blue aura pulsing at the bottom. Just a trick of the light and ice maybe...

Levi took a deep breath. Slowly and carefully, he lifted one leg and took a giant step over the crack, avoiding it at all costs. He had no idea whether this would make a difference; for all he knew, any of his next steps could be his last... But as he tentatively continued, leaving the vast crack behind him, he felt more and more at ease. He looked up ahead, seeing the great frosted trees of the Northward Forest tower above him, and picked up his speed for the last few metres. His boots crashed upon the hard, rigid soil, and he exhaled in relief. He'd done it! The crossing was complete. Now all that remained, was the exploration of the ruins above.

*

Snow crunched and groaned beneath Levi's boots as he navigated his way through the trees. Where his steps sank in some places, they barely moved in others, the depths of the snow constantly changing. Occasionally, his steps would brush the flat grey stones that formed the ancient path that weaved through the forest. The old channel helped with the climb, but hundreds of years of neglect meant that it still wasn't easy. Tiredness was beginning to set in, and Levi's movements lacked energy, yet still he soldiered up the incline, the ruins at the top beckoning him on.

Eventually though, he had to rest. Catching his breath, Levi leant against one of the many trees that lined the path, the trunk of the great spruce strong and wide. But as he pulled his hand away, he felt something stick to his palm. He

147

looked down to see a splatter of red, smudged across his fingers like a gluey resin. Levi glanced up at the source of the mess. Across the surface of tree bark was a line of fractured red paint, a mark that could only have been put there recently...

Levi: Eugh...

Levi grimaced, trying to flick the paint from his hand. He wiped it on the bark on front of him, scraping it from his skin. But it was then that he noticed another line of red, slathered across the bark of the next great tree.

Whirling around, Levi realised that every tree in the immediate vicinity had been marked by the runes. Some were splurged with red spots, others struck by red stripes. There wasn't a single tree without a mark... Levi warily continued through the forest, wondering what the ominous signs could possibly be. It was only when he reached the heights of the snowy hill, ascending up the elevated ridge of rock at the top, did the marks finally disappear.

It was here that Levi finally came across the ancient stone ruins. The main thing he noticed was that they were actually rather insignificant. A simple set of stone steps lead to a building without a roof. Walls were cracked and broken, the hollowed-out room was stripped bare, and piles of snow filled the gaps between the stones that remained. Levi carefully climbed the steps of the crumbled entrance, peering within the centre of the remains, but an invisible sheet of black ice caught him out. He flung out a hand as he fell, catching hold of a strange stone structure for balance. He yanked his hand back, the bare stone freezing cold to the touch.

Levi took a stifled breath and pulled himself up, turning to examine the peculiar structure of stone that had prevented his fall. It consisted of a hollowed-out circle, positioned atop a stone pillar, that faced out towards the valley, where Lake Tväre lay unmoving. But it wasn't alone... Out on the edge of the stone ruins stood another pillar, with yet another hollowed-out circle at its top, this one slightly larger.

Levi peered through the circular pillar, positioning his line of sight to match the one out in the forest. He stared through the ruins like a telescope, using them together to focus on a distant target. Levi's eyes widened as he stared through the circles, the stone surrounding a part of the Lake where the ice never froze… The Everflow. Levi looked at the pillars in astonishment. They lined up with the strange phenomenon perfectly. How had they survived so long, and without so much as a crack or scar in the rock? He stared at the Everflow a little longer before turning around. There must be more secrets to explore here, and the question of why Avarson's lackey, Skalham, had been so protective of this place, still remained unanswered.

The back wall of the ruins were still intact, but even that had suffered terribly from the impact of time. The remains of a great painting had now descended into a mess of faded colours, though Levi could see the potential it once had. Thick black lines, shaded on either side, swerved and weaved around an oval-like shape that dominated the centre of the wall. Each line branched out, linking to unidentified figures. From the centre of the oval rose a ghost-like creature, splitting the earth as it shone with a powerful blue light. Levi's eyes widened as the truth of the image finally dawned on him…

It was, in fact, a giant map. The black lines were the snowy hills, the oval was the outline of the great Lake Tväre, but what Levi struggled to understand was the purpose of the strange figure rising from the ice. The drawings caught Levi's attention more than the rest of the map, painting mysteries as to what they were, and why they were there. If not for a little sideways glance towards the edge of the back wall, Levi would have stared at this map for another hour at least. But a whistle of air distracted his gaze, and he turned in surprise to see a short, stone staircase, leading down into a basement hidden beneath the surface. What was more strange, however, was that each of the steps had been gritted with salt crystals, and there were fresh footprints in the dustings of snow…

A horrid, metallic taste landed upon Levi's tongue as he descended into the underground room. He shivered; the temperature of the air dropping rapidly. But he persevered through as his eyes settled upon an unnatural sight. The entire floor was filled with wooden barrels. One after the other, stacks upon stacks. Each one sealed with a metal band and thrown on top of another, resulting in an ugly pile of abandoned material. Several of the barrels leaked with a brown sludge, dripping and pooling across the cobblestone floor… Levi rushed to cover his mouth, the stench of chemicals overcoming him instantly. He turned and retreated up the steps, desperate to return to the clean, forest air.

He sat outside the ruins, trying to cough and spit the metallic tang out of his mouth. Whatever was being stored in those ruins, it wasn't natural, and it certainly wasn't anything for the better. As Levi recovered his breath, he looked up across the great valley that held the Lake. The remote peak of the Thorhorn mountain pierced the sky, built up on all sides by powerful drifts of snow, soaring above the quaint little town of Tväre that lay in the distance below. Levi sat staring at the humble buildings, wondering if they knew of the mess that lay beneath the ruins. He rubbed his head and grimaced; the exploration having created more questions than answers.

As the sun began its short drop towards the western hills, the young explorer got to his feet and began the descent down towards the Lake, ready to make his second and final crossing of the day…

**

Levi trudged up the short hill, whimpering as each breath became shorter and shorter. The topography of Tväre changed rapidly and randomly it seemed, from the frozen grass of flat plateaus to the stone steps that countered a steep drop. Depending on your journey, the walk could either be easy, or incredibly painful, and today Levi had unfortunately chosen the latter. He'd finished his second crossing of the day, the Lake choosing to remain silent this time, thankfully for Levi. But it was the strange discovery that now weighed on his mind. The mystery of the ruins, the spectre in the painted map, and the chemical barrels that filled the underground bunker… He had to talk to someone about it, but who?

He scaled a short set of stone steps, rising to the next level of the town. Two men, each wrapped in a thick coat, leaned against one of the stone walls, conversing with one another as Levi approached. Upon recognising him, however, they became instantly silent. Their faces soured as the young cartographer passed between them, their gazes cutting right through him. Levi frowned and hunched up his shoulders, trying to ignore their horrible stares and focusing instead on his destination.

At the top of a steep set of stone steps, overlooking the entire frozen valley, lay a single, lonely house. Levi leant on his knees and tried to breathe. He'd only climbed a few of the steps, and yet here he was completely exhausted. Each one was like a full stride of his legs, and it took a lot more willpower than it should have done to keep going. Eventually, though, he reached a scratched wooden door, neatly decorated with a carved figurine of a moose. Levi held off knocking until he'd collected himself, coughing several times into his hand, before making the move towards the entrance.

It opened before his knuckles even connected, revealing the short figure of a tired young woman, who immediately scowled. Her name was Gudro, the loving yet fierce wife of Torsten. She was well respected in the community, always helping where help was needed, but the most important duty of hers was attempting to keep her short-tempered husband in check. Today, however, she was the one trying to stay calm.

Gudro: You...

Levi frowned.

Levi: Have we met already?

Gudro: No. But I've heard enough to know who you are.

She folded her arms, causing Levi to tense up in response.

Gudro: What do you want?

Levi: I'm looking for Torsten. I was told I could find him here?

Gudro's grey eyes stared back at him.

Gudro: He's down at the square. Either inside or outside the Hall of Memory. One of the two.

Levi scoffed and shook his head.

Levi: Great...

Gudro: Have you just come from there?

Levi: Yeah...

Gudro chuckled.

Gudro: It's a lot of steps. Don't slip over on your way back.

And just like that, she shut the door. Levi was left facing the barrier of scratched wood, taking several uneven breaths before turning back to the long stretch of steps that led back to the centre of the town.

*

He found Torsten outside the Hall of Memory, exactly where Gudro said he would be. The hulking man stood by the glistening wooden sculpture of the Firelog, flecks of snow having frozen to the supportive, wooden beams. Torsten moved around the great monument, picking up discarded pieces of wood and piling them within the hollow centre. He was completely alone in his task, but maybe that's how he wanted it. There wasn't another soul present. Levi approached, hesitantly clearing his throat. Torsten glanced over his shoulder in response to the sound, almost groaning when he saw who had made it. He carried on with his task, shifting lumps of wood as he grumbled a reply.

Torsten: I'm busy. And don't want to talk.

Levi: I know. But it's urgent.

Torsten: If you have a concern, raise it with someone else.

He threw another plank of wood onto the pile, causing a brief crash.

Levi: They all said the same thing. That I should talk with you.

Torsten sighed and turned around, staring at Levi with a grim expression. He didn't say another word, instead he just waved his hand reluctantly, inviting Levi to begin. Levi took a short breath.

Levi: I was exploring the forest earlier today, and I think I found something... Something that the town council might not be aware of.

Torsten frowned.

Torsten: The Northward Forest?

Levi turned, pointing across the frozen Lake towards the distant trees and blurry grey of the ruins that lay across the valley.

Levi: Yeah, the one across the valley. I crossed the lake this morning and walked up the to the ridge—

Torsten: You made a crossing!?

The brutal accusation cut across him instantly, and Levi was suddenly quite wary of the daunting man.

Levi: Is that not allowed...?

Torsten's reply came through gritted teeth.

Torsten: Crossings should only be made by Tvärens who know what they're doing... By people who live and know these lands...

Levi: But they're not forbidden?

Torsten snorted like a bull, his face turning a shade of dark red. Levi now trod very carefully, fearful of blowing Torsten's embers into a flame.

Levi: When I reached the top, where the ridge lies, I found a set of stone ruins. I'm sure you know them?

His question was answered with a hard stare.

Levi: Yeah, you do... Well, I had a look inside and there was something buried in the centre. A hundred wooden barrels, all stacked up against each other. And they all had some sort of...

Torsten suddenly rolled his eyes, the reaction cutting Levi off mid-sentence.

Torsten: Let me guess, chemical waste?

Levi paused as his statement was finished for him. Torsten shoved his bearded face down into Levi's own, his voice firm and commanding.

Torsten: We already know this, outsider. Avarson asked our permission to use the ruins, and we said yes. It's temporary storage, that's all it is. A way of holding the logging waste until it can be shipped out on the rail-train.

Levi took a short breath and mumbled a reply.

Levi: I didn't know...

Torsten: Well, why would you? It's not for you to know! Life here isn't the same, secretive mess that you have in your big cities. We talk to each other. And help each other. We *trust* each other.

Hands quickly became fists as Torsten riled himself up. Levi now felt very small in comparison to this brutal man, a feeling that only got worse as Torsten chastised him further.

Torsten: You really think a lot of yourself, don't you? You go anywhere you want, whenever you want. Ignoring the dangers that come with your ignorance until it's just too late.

Levi tried to defend himself, but Torsten wouldn't him speak another word.

Torsten: I know what this is. A desperate attempt to balance your scales. You think trying to help us in any way will make up for what you did to Sigmund!?

Levi froze.

Levi: That wasn't my fault...

Torsten: Did anyone else take him to the edge of the lake? Did anyone else distract his mother, leaving him out there *alone*?

He left the questions hanging in the air. Torsten's voice became dangerously calm once again as Levi fell silent.

Torsten: I think it'd be best for everyone if you got on the next train out. If you want to help this town, make it one outsider less.

He turned his back to Levi and bent down to retrieve another wooden panel, continuing his work as if the entire conversation hadn't even happened. Levi stood completely still, only his free locks of hair shifting in the wind. It was only after several moments that he was able to summon the willpower to turn around and drag himself away, leaving the hunching figure of Torsten to finish clearing up the wood.

***

Fendal: You know, when I first awoke down here, I thought I'd been cast into Jotunheim.

Sigmund and Fendal were laying upon two sunbeds, both obviously carved from ice, which were reclined back to receive the full beams of the blue aura that gently fell from the ceiling. Alaf and Olaf sat nearby, stationed upon weak little chairs that struggled to hold them up. From the comfort of his sunbed, Fendal clicked his fingers commandingly, summoning Olaf to his side.

Fendal: Water on the rocks again please.

Olaf paused and then nodded... He grabbed an ice-carven mug from the table beside Fendal and wandered his way back over to the makeshift bar that had risen from the ground. Olaf hesitantly began to gather up little pebbles and stones from the bedrock floor. He then deposited them in Fendal's empty mug and filled the gaps with water, returning to the wintery guardian with his proud concoction.

Fendal: Ahh... Perfect.

Olaf bowed his head.

Fendal: Would you like one Sigmund? It's Olaf's specialty.

Sigmund stared uneasily at the mess of pebbles and meltwater in Fendal's hand.

Sigmund: Um... No thanks...

Fendal: Eh. You're the one missing out.

He took a colossal gulp, swigging both water and stone. He then chewed on the rocks in his mouth, crunching them the way someone would with flecks of ice.

Fendal: But as I was saying, I didn't die in battle, clearly.

He quickly indicated towards the frostbitten frame.

Fendal: So I knew this couldn't be the great hall of Valhalla. I never knew of the Christian God during my time, so I had no idea that a different kind of heaven even existed. What else could it be? Icy tomb, tick. Frostbitten skin, tick. Oh yes, I thought, this is definitely the realm of the Ice Giants...

He paused for a moment, and then spoke again, almost to himself this time.

Fendal: Jotunheim... Coldest place in the universe.

Sigmund lifted his head, glancing across at Fendal's extraordinarily thin figure.

Sigmund: Is that where we are then? Yotun... Yooten...

Fendal: Jotunheim?

Sigmund nodded and Fendal shrugged in response.

Fendal: We might be. All myths have to come from somewhere and I wasn't the first Viking to venture down here... Who knows? We could be at the birthplace of Norse Mythology...

He swirled the remains of his drink within its mug. Tiny pebbles clinked against the icy outline as they shifted and moved.

Fendal: But one thing I know for sure lad, is that there's worse places to end up than here. Whether it be the fabled Jotunheim or not.

Sigmund glanced around, eyeing the ice-coated stalactites and stalagmites that clung to the surfaces. Fendal did have a point. Despite the quite essential drawback of not being able to leave, this vast, empty cavern had a somewhat mystical beauty.

Sigmund: Would you go back if you could? To Tväre?

Fendal blinked, the tentative question catching him off guard. Despite being such a distracted and flamboyant spirit, he often considered such notions, though never spoke about them aloud. Sigmund leaned across, eyeing Fendal from the opposing sunbed, until he eventually replied.

Fendal: Would I go back...?

Fendal clicked his tongue.

Fendal: Back to the fires and hearths that our ancestors built? To see the village traditions handed down from generation to generation? Watching the drunks desperately slip and slide their way home lest the cold remove them from life?

He sighed, his eyes shining as he turned to face Sigmund fully.

Fendal: I'd go back in a heartbeat.

Sigmund: Then why don't you?

Fendal smiled. Such questions were to be expected after all; a child's curiosity thrived on them.

Fendal: Oh, I tried. I tried many times. But I came to realise that my place was here... serving the will of the lake. My kingdom is the surface, my territory the shoreline. It is the way it is, and a Viking should accept that. Like these two numbhands...

He indicated towards Alaf and Olaf with his hand.

Fendal: They were born to become great explorers. Navigating the sea and the skies in the known world and beyond. Instead, they wrecked their ship and drowned.

Sigmund glanced over towards the brother and sister duo. Alaf rolled her eyes and snorted, Olaf glanced downwards shamefully.

Sigmund: But they're not real...

Alaf raised her eyebrows accusingly, her face becoming horribly dark. Sigmund caught himself.

Sigmund: That's not what I meant... They're not like you Fendal. How can someone like you be trapped down here!?

The frantic question echoed throughout the cavern, and Fendal gave Sigmund a long, careful look.

Fendal: What makes you think I'm trapped?

The sudden turn in his answer made Sigmund hesitate.

Sigmund: You just said you can't go back to Tväre...

Fendal: I did indeed. But you're jumping straight out of the beer barrel to the wrong conclusion. This life in Jotunheim, or wherever we are, isn't a punishment; this is my second chance! I was offered this life by the lake, and I accepted.

Sigmund shook his head.

Sigmund: I don't understand...

Fendal got to his feet, the ice of his sunbed crumbling into pieces as he left it behind.

Fendal: Come. It's time to show you why you're here.

He turned and walked away, towards his favourite cavern wall. Sigmund stood himself up as Fendal once again pulled on another of his magical, hidden levers. The result of this one was the sound of a bell dinging around the cavern. To his left, Sigmund saw a slot in the wall open up, this one leading to a small, perfectly symmetrical box, lit only by a tiny stream of light in the cave ceiling. Fendal ducked his head and entered the confining room, quickly indicating for Sigmund to follow.

Once together, and feeling somewhat claustrophobic, Fendal reached out and touched a singular point on the bedrock wall, the button giving way at the contact. The little cave rumbled and groaned as it sealed itself off from the main cavern, leaving the faces of Alaf and Olaf staring after them. And with that, Sigmund and Fendal were completely hidden from the rest of the world. As Sigmund glanced around, a small wooden sign appeared at the top of the enclosed cave, suddenly showing the number '1' in thick black Viking runes. And yet still, they didn't move, resulting in a grumbling complaint from Sigmund.

Sigmund: Are we supposed to be waiting this long?

Fendal scoffed.

Fendal: Honestly. Even when you invent teleportation, humanity will still find a way to be impatient. It's a short way up to the surface my lad. We'll be there soon.

Sigmund: The surface!?

A touch of hope filled his voice. But then, almost immediately, the cave began to rumble, and Sigmund suddenly felt himself being pushed towards the ground, as if the cave itself were rising and he himself were falling. The number on the sign began to count downwards, flicking through runes of black ink at great speed. Sigmund stared up at it, his eyes wide and wild.

Fendal glanced down, placing his hand on the young boy's shoulder. Sigmund relaxed slightly at the contact as the number on the wooden sign disappeared completely. The heavy feeling on Sigmund's body mysteriously stopped, and the enclosed cave rumbled again, this time opening to reveal the vast expanse of Lake Tväre's beautiful surface...

A frozen mass of shining ice greeted them, and Sigmund felt the arctic air on his face for the first time in days. It felt cool and crisp to his skin. Fendal felt it too, somehow using what little skin he had left. The icy guardian took a long, deep breath as he stepped out onto the surface of the Lake, his feet gliding along the surface.

Fendal: Ahh. That's the stuff. Like a deep clean for the lungs!

Sigmund slowly followed, stepping out onto the icy surface cautiously. Throughout every day of his life, he'd always been warned to be vigilant of the ice. That it could all change in the space of a second... But he hadn't paid attention to that warning before, and the enchanting world was too tempting to ignore. Glints of snow whirled and danced around him as he left the rocky cave behind, which disappeared as soon as his foot left the stone. Sigmund glanced back, seeing that the unbroken stream of the Everflow had taken its place, the water trickling and streaming over a shallow, pebbly riverbed.

Fendal: This, Sigmund, is my domain.

Fendal opened his arms, embracing the world around him. Trees covered the hillsides, hunching over with the weight of the snow. Birds and animals scurried and flitted between them, dashing from shelter to shelter. And, in the centre, the great Lake Tväre shone in the glorious moonlight.

Sigmund: Is that Tväre!?

The young boy pulled on Fendal's arm, pulling his attention towards a scattering of distant orange lights across the far side of the Lake. Like tiny flames on the hillside, the lights shifted and twinkled, sometimes disappearing, sometimes glowing brighter than the others. The peak of the Thorhorn mountain rose high above them, the ice-cap shimmering in the light of the moon.

Fendal: I do believe it is. Beautiful isn't it?

Sigmund didn't reply. He stared at the distant firelights, the orange glow calling out to him. Tväre was there! And it was within reach!

Without any hesitation, Sigmund surged forward, running through the mist and fog and across the treacherous expanse of ice, towards the town he called home.

Fendal: Sigmund...!

The outcry did nothing to stop the young boy; his destination was set, or so he thought. His ran with such energy and enthusiasm, desperate to get back home. He looked up, expecting to see the snowy buildings of his town come into focus. But when his eyes settled on the hillside, the lights of Tväre were no closer than before. The shoreline of the Lake seemed to extend itself out away from him, stretching at the same pace that he could run. Sigmund stopped and stared at the unreachable firelights, which continued to glow gently in the distance. Fendal quickly rejoined him, his footsteps almost silent as he approached.

Fendal: I'm sorry Sigmund... But maybe now you understand what I meant.

Fendal stared at the firelights himself, his tone incredibly gentle.

Fendal: It is the curse of a life below the lake. I can see the town that was my home, but never again can I return...

Sigmund grimaced, not once breaking his gaze.

Sigmund: But you said you chose this life... I didn't get a choice. I don't *want* to be here.

He closed his eyes heavily, and a wall of mist blew across the Lake, obscuring the lights of Tväre from view. Gusts of wind whistled through the valley as Fendal muttered a soft reply.

Fendal: You're right. I did get a choice. A limited choice, but a choice nonetheless. The lake saved me for a reason, or what's left of me at least. But it also saved you...

Sigmund looked up into his frostbitten face.

Sigmund: What do you mean?

Fendal: You aren't being offered a choice between death or service Sigmund. You are being offered something better... A greater responsibility... One that will take you back to the hearth of Tväre when the right time comes.

Almost in response to Fendal's words, there came a heavy groan from beneath the ice. A valiant roar of noise that boomed throughout the valley. From beneath the footprints of Sigmund's dirty boots, came the blue glow of the Ice-log sapling, shining stronger than it ever had before as the Lake's mysterious power penetrated through. A faint blue halo shone across the surface of the Lake, pulsating outward with a simple, rhythmic heartbeat.

Fendal: There's a reason why the earliest Vikings chose to settle in this inhospitable valley. A reason why the town of Tväre thrived where others starved and were abandoned...

The glowing halo hummed in accordance with Fendal's tender words.

Fendal: For centuries, people have been drawn to the lands of the lake. Even the most stubborn minds can feel the essence of its spirit. Over these same centuries, the essence became a story, and then a tale, and then a myth. But the power of the lake always remained...

The curtain of mist parted, revealing the towering Thorhorn mountain once again. The lights of Tväre returned, gleaming with renewed vigour, but Sigmund's gaze was gripped by something else... Spectral movements in the mist. The clouds seemed to flow and bend in accordance with the wind, slowly forming themselves into a variety of shapes that settled themselves upon the icy surface. The fog gathered around Sigmund and Fendal's feet, lifting them up as the ground was completely obscured.

Up upon the hillside and below the might of the Thorhorn, the mist began to condense. Colossal trees, created entirely from cloud, rose up higher than any of the green trees nearby, reaching out with extensive misty branches. Vaporous animals, from majestic birds to powerful reindeer, charged across the landscape, even passing by Sigmund and Fendal as the mist drew them further in. Fendal spoke as the passing wind blew past their faces, his words so caring and proud.

Fendal: Before the time of man, long before I ever dwelt in these valleys, was a time called the Harmony. A world that walked, ran and jumped all under its own terms.

Thick clouds rolled around Sigmund's torso. He reached out to test it with his small fingers, the vapours retracting away from his touch like a shy animal.

Fendal: Then came us...

Fendal held out his hand, drawing Sigmund's gaze towards the opposite hillside. Atop the snowy, tree-covered ridge, the mist gathered itself again. A heap of grey clouds came to rest upon the site of the ancient ruins, sealing itself between broken bricks of stone and building them back into their former glory. In just a few moments, the misty structure of the renewed ruins soared over the rest of the valley, staring down at the Lake from a terrific height. Circular stone structures rose between the trees, and a beam of pastel blue aura shot out from the Everflow, passing through the circular stone structures and hitting the ruins right in its heart.

> Fendal: We joined the world, initially for the better, working in balance with the land to benefit everyone. We took the trees we needed to live, and the food we needed to eat, but never anything more…

Misty figures appeared from the surrounding forests, coming together to chop down the colossal trees of cloud whilst leaving others to remain standing. Sigmund watched carefully as they created farms and buildings, gathering around fires for warmth and friendship. Numerous animals came and joined them, from tiny birds to formidable wolves, all enjoying the comfort together.

> Fendal: We made roads without destroying land. Farmed without causing pain. We lived in accordance with nature, helping the forests regrow when storms knocked them down.

The mist reenacted everything Fendal narrated, a show of time playing out for Sigmund's benefit. Everywhere he looked, there was something new, from cloudy characters planting saplings in the dirt, to the construction of paths and roads that laced around nests and animal dens. Then Fendal's voice dropped, becoming tight and tense. The orange firelights of Tväre fluttered for a moment and then, one by one, they went out… until the land fell into shadowy darkness.

> Fendal: But, as with all things that are good, the bad isn't far behind…

163

In the far distance, from the valleyed lands of the west, grew a cloud of horrible mist. An armada of dark Viking longships formed themselves out of the grey clouds, increasing to a colossal size as they approached. The features of these longships were horribly exaggerated, and each of them displayed horrifying banners that appeared to drip with ice and blood. Misty Viking warriors appeared on all sides of every ship, yelling a tirade of war cries that echoed throughout the frozen land. As they crashed upon the surface of the Lake, the ice thrashed and collapsed in on itself, leaving trails of destruction behind them.

Fendal continued his monologue, undeterred by the apparent onrushing threat that charged at both him and Sigmund.

Fendal: Cold-hearted people, as they are so ironically named. Set on either abusing the power of the lake for their own gain, or ridding the world of it altogether.

The evil ships tore through the realm, slicing and splitting the white clouds that formed the harmonious scenes of nature and man. On the furthest shore of Lake Tväre, behind and above all the dark figures of the Viking ships, rose the misty mirage of Avarson's ugly factory. Complete with dark and empty walls, shining silver pipes and two soaring chimneys, it speared above all else in the sky. These same chimneys churned and mulched, producing thick smoke that pumped continuously into the air. As he followed the terrible trails, Sigmund saw that it was the factory's dark smoke that was giving the ghostly apparitions their horrible power, feeding them with evil tendrils like a mother to her unborn children. A new ruler had taken control.

Fendal: Since man was put on this earth, war and battle have followed them... And when there's nothing left to fight over, man will fight out of hate for each other.

Sigmund's breathing became short as the terror of shadowy ships rose in the sky above them, misty swords and axes raised. Fendal, however, seemed to have no fear at all, instead turning his back on them to face something new.

Fendal: But as horrid and terrible evil can be, it can spawn goodness. Such is the beautiful humour of the world.

Sigmund turned to see a wonderful cloud of white mist that had been developing in the distance behind them, building itself into a powerful Viking longship of its own. One that shone with the light of the moon above.

Fendal: Folk that will give their last to defend these places and the spirits that reside in them. Folk that listen to the calls of the earth...

The longship charged forward on the air, scooping Sigmund and Fendal up on its mighty brow. Standing before them, upon the misty white of the deck, were the two icy figures of Alaf and Olaf. With their hard steel helmets and armour, they commanded the great vessel into the depths of battle. Sigmund gripped the sides of the shining boat as it speared the darkness with its great misty figurehead, which looked suspiciously like an image of Fendal. Murky shadows landed aboard the deck, appearing to jump out of the dark fog, ready to attack. Sigmund backed off as the shadows approached, but Alaf and Olaf immediately came to his rescue. The two warrior Vikings surged forward, dispatching the dark warriors with ease, the evil mist splitting and evaporating into thin air upon contact. The rest of the army began to flee as the longship tore through the rest, their losses rapidly stacking up. They retreated over the edge of the western horizon, taking the hellish view of the factory with it, but there was one shadow that remained...

A murky figure climbed aboard the great longship, having seemingly clung on the side during the rampage of the battle. Its back was hunched and there were empty holes in its head where the eyes should have been. It scurried along the vapour of the deck, unseen by any of the crew, and approached the small figure of Sigmund from behind...

Sigmund felt the hairs on his neck prickle, and slowly turned to see a nightmarish sight. The murky shadow stood directly in front of him, completely unmoving. Then suddenly, a dark hand lurched out, thrusting itself seamlessly through Sigmund's heart...

The longship came to an immediate stop, and Sigmund suddenly found himself back upon the surface of the Lake. The illustrious vessel had vanished, and the misty figures had gone, leaving just him and Fendal alone in the silence of the arctic valley. Sigmund tried to take a breath, but the shock of the murky shadow's attack had stripped the air from his throat. He jumped as something brushed by his shoulder but was immediately relieved when he saw the frostbitten skin of Fendal's hand. His voice trembled slightly as he spoke...

> Sigmund: What happened? What was that thing...?

The icy guardian looked down at him, the lights in his eyes now delicate and still.

> Fendal: That... was a product of a life of greed. The fragmented soul of a man who chose to serve himself instead of the earth.

Sigmund looked across the Lake, as if cautious that the murky creature might return at any moment. A subtle shade had now fallen across the landscape, the light of the moon now dim and cold. Avarson's factory lay dormant in the distance, and the snow of the trees lay completely still.

> Fendal: There used to be people who lived in accordance with the Lake. They devoted their lives to it. They would keep us strong and protect those who were weak... Which was most people back then.

Fendal chuckled slightly as he looked up towards the ridge that lay above the Northward Forest, the ancient ruins laying in their stony heap.

> Fendal: Few such people exist now. Those that have taken their place either deny the existence of such things or turn against them. And those that do possess any meaningful knowledge are scattered across the continents after all these centuries...

His head dropped, the runic markings of his head tattoos almost glistening as the dull moonlight crested over them. Sigmund, however, raised his head high.

> Sigmund: I can help... I can be one of those people.

That made Fendal smile.

Fendal: I knew you wouldn't let me down.

He straightened up, eyeing Sigmund carefully.

Fendal: It is a lot of work though. A great responsibility. You'll be a guide, a planner and a leader all at once. And, the worst part of all, you will have to talk to people...

Sigmund paused for a second, and then he nodded.

Sigmund: I can do it... I want to do it.

Fendal smiled again.

Fendal: Then you shall.

He patted Sigmund on the shoulder.

Fendal: I'll be in the cavern. When you're ready, come and join me.

With that, he turned away, walking slowly back towards the sparkling stream that was the Everflow. Sigmund stayed behind for a moment, taking the chance to stare at the tiny firelights of Tväre just one more time, the little flames flickering in the distance. A sharp pain shot up his forearm, and Sigmund glanced down to see that the faded blue scar on his skin had grown. It now reached from his forearm to his wrist, and stung slightly to the touch...

Sigmund held the arm to his chest, focusing instead on the lights upon the distant hillside. The clouds stopped moving and the wind ceased its breezy gusts, as Sigmund gazed longingly at his hometown...

$$**$$

Elvera stood out in the snow, her face bitter and cold. She stared out across the mist of the distant Lake, just watching as the mess of cloud and fog crawled over the icy surface. A single firelog sat beside her, coughing and spitting as it struggled against the wind of the night. Even with the protection of metal and bark, the flames were seemingly losing the battle. The sky was black and empty, and even the stars struggled to glow...

Yet Elvera continued to stand there, in the cold and the dark, looking out across the Lake.

***

The Pretense is Dropped

The wooden door of Tväre's Hall of Memory clicked and gave way. Regan glanced over his shoulder to see if anyone was watching, but no one was around on this cold, empty night. Amazing what the disappearance of a single, tiny, insignificant little boy could do. None of the locals seemed to want to venture further than their front door, which was all the better for him right now. Having never had children, nor the desire to raise any of his own, Regan couldn't understand what all the fuss was about. These things happen in life: people get sick, children go missing and sometimes you lose your job after attacking your manager.

It was a funny old story, involving a very angry Regan at the time, who had had enough of being lied to by the men who made more money than him by doing less work. One day, after a particularly difficult evening beforehand, his manager had accused him of stealing from the workplace. His response had been... less than mature, and his now ex-manager had subsequently spent the night in the nearest hospital. It had been a mix of luck and word of mouth that had landed him work as Avarson's personal assistant, if that's what you could call his position. For example, it was somewhat rare for an assistant to have to break into the hall of a humble town. But Avarson had given the order, and Regan was paid to obey.

The sneering man glided through the cold, empty rooms, looking for the one that had been used most recently. The main office of the hall, where the Municipal Council met every few days, was his primary target, and he found it without much difficulty. Near the back of the room was a table that was covered in documents, each of them desperate to be read. After a quick search, Regan landed on the treasure he'd been sent to find: the complaints made to the council surrounding the work and attitude of his employer Avarson, and the names that came with them.

Noting down each name on a spare bit of paper, Regan hid the notes back within the messy piles. Had this been a simple trespassing or intimidation job, he wouldn't have been so precise in rebuilding the scene. But this one had to

169

be done without suspicion. The people here were stubborn and somewhat aggressive at times, but they were also as sharp as tacks and would easily have guessed that someone had been where they shouldn't. But Regan had done many a job like this before, and he knew how to do it well enough to never be discovered. He grinned to himself as he snuck away from the hall, revelling under the dark coverage of night.

**

Levi jerked awake, a noise or bang from afar had awoken him, enough so that his light sleep had instantly been broken. He glanced out of the nearby window, seeing only a fragment of moonlight through the thick clouds of mist. Night was still in control. Levi tried to return to a bit of slumber, using the heat of the pillow for some comfort to no avail. He was awake now, and nothing was going to change that. It was just another annoying aspect of life that you had to deal with.

Exchanging the loving warmth of his thick blanket for the cold air of the room, Levi got to his feet, his woollen socks hanging loosely around his ankles. It was a trick that Levi had learnt from his mother many years ago, to go to bed with a pair of thick socks on during a cold winter night. It was believed that warmth in your feet led to an easy sleep, and Levi had tested this theory one night in Copenhagen, inadvertently resulting in the best night's sleep he'd ever had.

Levi stretched and yawned, taking care not to make too much noise for the other users of the town's hostel. As his eyes adjusted to the bleak darkness, he began to approach the window, interested in how the silent expanse of the Lake appeared during such a late hour... But the mist seemed to be covering most of the view. Levi yawned again and went to turn around, when suddenly he saw movement out on the icy surface...

Two figures, one tall and one small, stood alone on the great mass of ice, shrouded in the fog. They didn't move a muscle; they simply stared out into the darkness, out towards the western shore, entranced by something that Levi could not see. The cartographer broke his gaze from the mystifying sight only for a second, rushing across his bedroom to grasp his telescope. He slipped on the rug, landing hard on the wooden panels of the floor, but that wasn't enough to stop him. Levi lunged towards the window again, setting up his telescope as quickly as he could. He had to see who these misty figures were...

Levi stared out across the Lake, telescope in hand... but the misty figures had vanished.

*

The whistle of the train rang out across the valleys as Levi trudged through the centre of the freezing town. He glanced up at the Thorhorn, the peak shining in the light of the morning, desperately trying to rid his mind of the previous night's encounter. He focused on the ugly, grey clouds that hung over the snowcapped mountain, but no matter how hard he tried, the memory quickly returned. The mystery of the Lake's spectral apparitions poking fun at Levi's cynical mind. Needless to say, the sight had bothered him deeply. It had been too vivid to be a dream, Levi didn't believe that self-lie for a second, but what else could it possibly be!? He had to have been going mad... and that meant he had to keep quiet. Levi had heard of the terrible nature of lunatic asylums for the mad and insane, and he did not fancy becoming a resident of one.

The disturbing nature of last night's event had been the deciding factor in Levi's latest conundrum, which was whether to bid the town of Tväre a final goodbye. When paired with the consistently sour looks from the locals, alongside the horribly accusing and blame-ridden conversation he'd had with Torsten, he'd realised he had very little reason to stay. The only person whom he could call a friend was spending every day in unbearable pain, and there was simply nothing more he could do for her. Nothing that he could offer anyway...

The unhappy decision had led him back to the town's underground library, where he was set to return every book and map he'd ever borrowed. He plodded past the cold stone statues of Alaf and Olaf, their great battle cries more lifeless than ever before. Around him lay the abandoned setup of the town's beloved Carnival of the Fires. Half-assembled wooden stalls lay all around the town square, and the beautifully carved Firelog centerpiece was empty and hollow. The loss of Sigmund from the town's community had been such a hit to them, especially due to his significance as one of only a few. Levi found himself feeling shameful about packing his bags that morning, as if he were abandoning the town to a depressing and dismal existence. But they clearly didn't want him here, and that seemed more than fair...

Levi's footsteps echoed down the stone steps as he descended into the torchlit darkness of the subterranean library, opening the door with a great creak. Levi reached into his shoulder bag, withdrawing several of the large, folded maps that he'd borrowed during his last visit, and began to replace them in their dusty homes. That is, until something caught his eye... He glanced over his shoulder, turning to face the figure of the Librarian, who finally greeted him properly.

> The Librarian: Hello.

> Levi: Hello.

They both chortled at the exchange before the Librarian glanced towards the maps in Levi's hand.

> The Librarian: I'm assuming you've assumed your work to be complete?

Levi blinked, taking a moment to understand her phrasing.

> Levi: I'm not assuming anything. My work *is* complete.

The ancient woman narrowed her grey eyebrows.

> The Librarian: How were the ruins? Did you find anything?

Levi paused, turning back to replace the final few maps back in their drawers. The old paper crumpled and crinkled as he folded them up, eventually mumbling a short reply.

> Levi: Nothing that mattered...

> The Librarian: I don't believe that for a second. I know those ruins. They're prevailing, historic, even

paranormal. Are you seriously that narrow minded that you'll just dismiss anything you don't understand!?

The wrinkles around her face tightened as she snapped at him, but Levi was ready to bite back.

> Levi: It doesn't matter what I don't understand... or what I saw! Sigmund's still missing. And I know you said it was only an accident, but it still happened. And it happened under my watch. So forgive me for focusing on what really matters instead of things that are just sheer lunacy...

He sighed and leant against the drawers, the wood creaking under his weight. It felt good to get it all out, but the Librarian simply tutted, her tone firm and strict.

> The Librarian: I can forgive your denial... I can even forgive your rudeness, as both things can be changed. What I can't forgive is you complaining about the boy's disappearance whilst you simultaneously pack your bags.

The cartographer froze.

> The Librarian: Tell me, Levi, if it's been such a tough time for the people up on the surface, why are you abandoning them?

Levi's mouth dropped open slightly.

> Levi: Have you been watching me!?

> The Librarian: In a way...

She shot a quick glance towards Peckingham, who suddenly took an interest in cleaning his beak. Levi gave her an astonished look before putting a hand to his forehead.

> Levi: Okay. I'm not even going to ask what you mean by that. In the last few days alone, I've seen more things that have me questioning everything I've ever known. So please... and answer me clearly, just once... Why are you so interested in me?

The Librarian gave him one of her trademark grey-eyed stares.

The Librarian: Because you're more important than you think you are. Or... you will be.

Levi shook his head, scoffing in disbelief.

Levi: What's that even supposed to mean!?

Naturally, he didn't get a straight answer.

The Librarian: You seek answers for the things you cannot understand. And that is exactly the reason why your cartographic ancestors set off exploring in the first place.

She shrugged.

The Librarian: Or you can leave on the very next train if you so wish. I believe there's one to Stockholm in half an hour. But for your sake, I pray you're not on it...

Levi was stunned silent as the Librarian gave him a final word.

The Librarian: Keep an open mind Levi. Those that are closed tend to get lost...

She turned heel and left, once again leaving him alone in the dusty darkness of the library. And, once again, he was left with more questions than he'd arrived with. As he returned the last of his borrowed maps and books, he could feel Peckingham watching him carefully from the corner. He only escaped the eyes of the grey arctic pigeon when he finally exited the cold air of the building, heading back to his snug room within the town hostel.

**

Minister Toro: I know how hard it is to be here... To find the will to leave your home, or even lift yourself up from the bed, knowing the day you're going to face...

Minister Toro sat at the head of a small circle of chairs, most of which were occupied by varying members of the townsfolk, about nine or ten of them altogether. All of them were different in height or build, yet all their expressions were the same.

The support group was an idea that Minister Toro had set up several years ago. It was a short meeting varying between weekly and monthly, focusing on helping people overcome the struggles, difficulties and occasional grief that occurred throughout the year, especially in the dark of the winter months. The loss of a wise, elderly relative was the most common reason why a person might attend this group, but today they were all there to support and pray for one person: Elvera.

She sat to the left of Minister Toro, her eyes sunken and tired. She tilted her head forward and occasionally wiped her face with her hand but rarely did much more. She didn't talk, or nod in agreement, or even say 'Amen'. All she did was listen to the Minister's words of encouragement, hoping that any little feeling of relief might cleanse her of her deepest pain.

> Minister Toro: If I might echo myself from a few days ago, I said that one of the hardest trials in life is keeping your faith when going through the darkest time... When you feel ignored or forgotten... When your one prayer seems to miss the mark...

He lifted his head, addressing them all at once.

> Minister Toro: Though, I think we are all praying the same prayer today.

Everyone quickly glanced sympathetically towards Elvera, who remained dead quiet.

> Minister Toro: It is not written that being close to God means we will be free of suffering. This world is not perfect. Sometimes it's horrible. But we draw close to God when it gets so, because he wants to support us... grieve with us... even when we feel like we've fallen into darkness...

The door to the church creaked and opened as someone entered the old building. Minister Toro turned his head, looking to see the identity of the person who had interrupted their meeting, the large fur coat and blonde hair instantly recognisable. Avarson was extremely focused and walked with intense purpose, as if he knew all eyes were now on him. In his hand, he carried a small paper document, which he gripped tightly.

Avarson waited several pews back from the group. Despite supposedly being polite in the gesture, he was clearly very impatient. Subtle movements and twitches in his body indicated that he wanted someone's attention urgently. His fingers tapped the wood of the pew in front of him, drumming out an impatient tune, but Minister Toro didn't bite. Instead, he maintained his focus on those sat around him.

> Minister Toro: Let's close there for today.
> Remember, the door is always open.

He glanced around the group, locking eyes with Elvera as she lifted her head. The smallest smile of comfort appeared on her lips, but then it was gone. The group began to clear up, moving the chairs out of the room's centre.

> Minister Toro: Leave the chairs where they are. Just for now.

He smiled as the men and women began to leave, seeing them off with a smile. Elvera was the last to go...

> Minister Toro: Did you want to stay a bit longer?

Elvera paused as the Minster gently asked the question, eventually shaking her head. Minister Toro nodded understandably and slowly walked with her to the doors. But Avarson stepped in her way.

> Avarson: I'm sorry to have to do this now Elvera, but could you look at something for a moment?

Minister Toro put out his hand, astounded by Avarson's blatant confidence.

> Minister Toro: Not now Avarson.

But Avarson did not move.

> Avarson: I'm afraid it cannot wait Minister –

> Minister Toro: Surely, it can. You are very much aware of the current situation. Whatever it is you have to say, it can wait.

Avarson stood his ground against the kindly, yet firm, tone of the Minister. His voice became harder as he became increasingly frustrated by the constant interruptions.

> Avarson: This is a concern of the town council, not the church. It is extremely important that it's dealt with *today*.

> Elvera: Important to me? Or important to you?

Elvera lifted her head and spoke for the first time. There was very little energy in her voice, but her stubborn nature still fought back. Avarson blinked, slightly taken aback.

> Avarson: Important to everyone! Look, I've tried reaching you at your little house twice already so the least you can do is—

Elvera palmed him off, clearly exhausted.

> Elvera: I don't want to consider anything right now. Please… just let me go home.

She went to walk by, but Avarson put his hand on her shoulder.

> Elvera: Get Your Hand Off Me!

Elvera immediately forced his hand away. Avarson held it in the air, trying to show that he meant no harm. Minister Toro watched him closely as he now stumbled over his words; all the earlier authority in his voice now gone.

> Avarson: I just need your agreement on this… The Guardianship signing is tomorrow, and since you missed the last meeting of the Municipal council, understandably… You haven't officially agreed to the vote yet…

He slowly held out the papers towards her, along with a pencil. Elvera slowly took it from him and glanced over it, her mind barely taking in any of the words. On the final page was a set of five signatures, with a space left that should have been for Elvera's.

> Avarson: As you know, the council needs a unanimous agreement… and there's workers standing by—

Elvera hastily signed her name in the blank spot, and a small smile grew on Avarson's face. She then thrust the papers back into his waiting hands, and left the church, wiping a secretive tear from her eye.

Minister Toro turned towards Avarson, looking at him like he was something new. His old forehead somehow became more wrinkled as new thoughts about this man entered his mind. Avarson had always been obsessed with vanity, a trait evident in every aspect of his character. Minister Toro tried never to judge a person so quickly, for everyone had their own relationship and journey with life and faith, but Avarson had always been a confusing person to read... His privileged ways were often countered by his frequent attendance at the church, and he had been more than friendly when he had first arrived many months ago. In fact, he'd even given a fair portion of his profits back to the town in his earlier days, adding to the many loans he'd provided to improve the local town's way of life.

Yet now, as Minister Toro stared at Avarson, he realised that every generous statement or gift had always been made in front of the masses. Minister Toro was reminded of a saying that his own father used to live by: "those who give, so that they are seen to be giving, seek only to benefit themselves." And it was in this moment that Minister Toro realised Avarson fitted these words perfectly.

Avarson looked back at the Minster, frowning in response to his scrutinising expression.

Avarson: Something wrong Minister?

Minister Toro: There's a time and a place for such matters, Avarson. She's going through something none of us can imagine, and a man who frequents this church should know better that to demand such things from her.

Despite the harsh reprimand, Avarson simply smirked. He glanced around the empty church disinterestedly, looking all the way up to the narrow beams in the roof.

Avarson: Eh... Church isn't for men like me. I've got all I need already.

Minister Toro furrowed his brow, his tiny curls of grey hair shifting with the movement.

> Minister Toro: Enlighten me then. If church isn't for you, why did you willingly choose to regale us here week after week?

> Avarson: The same reason that you do Minister. For the people! I frequent this church because of the folk that belong to it.

The Minster's bright brown eyes widened.

> Minister Toro: You seek the favour of the people over the favour of the Lord!?

Avarson stared hard at him.

> Avarson: Favour of the people gets you things, you know that. Do you think these people would pay for your own shelter and upkeep if they didn't respect you?

Minister Toro didn't know how to respond, and subsequently fell into silence. The horrible statement was true, but certainly not in the accusing way Avarson meant it.

> Avarson: Though I wonder if even that will stop soon. Once 'missing' becomes 'presumed dead', the people of this town might realise that all you can offer them is thoughts and prayers…

The unprovoked verbal attack continued as Avarson wandered further into the church, his lurid voice echoing in the hall.

> Avarson: It's like the story you told about the shoebill and its chicks last Sunday. Do you remember? The one of the chicks panicking and fleeing the nest?

> Minister Toro: I remember.

He replied, his voice flat.

> Avarson: Well, instead of panicking, I like to think of it as growth. The loss of the shoebill shows the true darkness in life and the chicks have to realise and

become independent in order to survive. Once they do, they never need depend on the shoebill again!

The old Minister sighed.

Minister Toro: You've completely misunderstood the point of the story Avarson—

Avarson: Have I? Well then answer me this. What do we do when the shoebill doesn't come back? We wait on the Lord, and there's nothing. What do we do then...?

A sudden feeling of dread came over Minister Toro as he realised Avarson wasn't here to talk about his faith. Instead, he was here to challenge his own. He attempted a hypothesis.

Minister Toro: You don't believe prayer will do any good...

Avarson scoffed and rolled his eyes.

Avarson: Stop burying your head in the snow, Minister! It's been nearly three days now! The search will be called off soon. We're in the depths of winter, and a grown man couldn't survive a night out there, even with the fur of a wolf around him. The reality of what's happened is obvious, it's just that people can't accept it.

His words were harsh, and Minister Toro took a short breath, struggling to hold himself back from an angry retort.

Minister Toro: ...I guess that's why we have faith that the shoebill always comes back.

Avarson was ready for that.

Avarson: And when the boy is found, frozen and lifeless...

He looked the Minister right in the eye.

Avarson: What will you say about faith in a loving God then?

Minister Toro knew Avarson was trying to provoke him, but his question, however horrible, was still a valid one. He took several moments to think, silently praying that God would give him the right words to say.

> Minister Toro: I do not claim to know how the Lord works in this world. OR whether he will deliver Sigmund back to us or not…

He took a short breath, staying in control, yet answering quickly enough to stop Avarson jumping in with another accusation.

> Minister Toro: But if you base your faith purely on whether God gives you everything you pray for, be it in good will or not, then you do not understand the loving God at all.

> Avarson: Oof.

Avarson winced in mock pain.

> Avarson: Is that the same thing you're telling Elvera?

He indicated towards the church doors, through which Elvera had just departed.

> Avarson: That her faith wasn't strong enough to bring back her son!?

Minister Toro was stunned, Avarson's words cutting him like a sword.

> Minister Toro: Who are you to question the faith of someone else!? How can you even say such a thing!?

> Avarson: I'm simply a man who lives in the real world, Minister. And what I've seen, time and time again in the real world, is that the blessings in life are earned.

Minister Toro paused, trying his best to comprehend such an arrogant point of view. The door of the church creaked and opened, and Avarson turned to see his slimy assistant Regan peering in from the cold outdoors, silently asking for his master's attention. Avarson held up a finger, demanding him to wait for one more minute.

> Avarson: Forgive me, Minister but I must now take my leave. Though I hope we can continue this

invigorating conversation some other time. It's been quite fun. Good day.

He nodded politely and then turned to leave, his floating hand brushing against the polished wood of each pew as he passed them by. Minister Toro raised his voice slightly, calling out to Avarson once more.

> Minister Toro: So what happens? When the blessings eventually run out?

Avarson stopped in his tracks.

> Minister Toro: Will you just accept that? Like everyone should just accept the disappearance of a young boy? Or will it be you who buries his head in the snow?

Avarson's eye twitched slightly; no one had ever asked him such a question before. The idea of losing all that he'd worked for flustered him, and Minister Toro could see that now, clear as day.

> Avarson: Well, it's like I said... blessings in life are earned.

He held up the papers that Elvera had signed, almost as a representation.

> Avarson: Just as the curses of life are avoided. You can't have a missing child if you simply choose not to have any children.

> Minister Toro: I agree. Any child would be blessed not to have you as their parent.

Avarson tensed up as the Minister finally countered. For a moment, it appeared as if he was going to stride forward and attack the old man, who stood there without any fear. But eventually Avarson turned away, vacating the residence of the church without a glance back. Minister Toro stared after him, now wondering who that man truly was... for in that conversation, his real nature had appeared, and Minister Toro did not like it one bit.

*

182

Regan stood outside the church, smoking another of his rolled cigarettes. He enjoyed the sensation of the warm smoke swirling around his lungs, closing his eyes in relaxation as he blew the smoke back out into the air. A crunch of ice caught his attention, and he glanced over to see his employer stomping along the path towards him.

> Avarson: Ahh! For god's sake...

Avarson's boot sunk into the dirty snow and mud, breaking through the frozen layer of ice that lay above the hidden grass. He turned and glared at the ground as he lifted his perfect leather boot, kicking his foot to rid himself of the mud that had attached itself to him. Avarson seemed grumpier than usual, almost infuriated. Regan had seen him angry many times, quickly learning that despite his rather positive façade, his true temper was extremely short. The case with the fireplace being just one example of Avarson's suppressed rage. Regan was one of the few people that actually saw Avarson for what he was, a demon hidden under a beautiful guise. But that same demon was paying him, so what did he care?

> Avarson: What is so urgent that you have to interrupt me, Regan!? If you want to talk to me, you can wait at the carriage!

Regan snorted, undeterred by Avarson's reprimand. He held his cigarette between his fingers, blowing the smoke out of the corner of his mouth, and then held out a small note of paper.

> Avarson: What is this!?

He snatched the note from Regan's hand, reading the quick notes.

> Regan: Names and addresses.

Avarson's eyes narrowed as Regan gleefully continued.

> Regan: Each and every person who made a complaint against you or the day of the signing.

Avarson's eyes widened as he realised the value of the information now in his hand. Reading the paper again, he broke into a cruel smile.

Avarson: Well then... It looks like we have some more visits to make before the day is done. Get the carriage ready. I don't want to have to walk anywhere else today.

Regan: Of course, Sir.

Regan took another long inhale of his cigarette before he tossed it aside, leaving the smoldering butt to rest in the snowy ground.

***

The air itself was empty and cold, clinging to the skin of anyone who dared step outside. It wrapped around the leaves of every tree and crushed down on every little fire that had been lit in the modest little valley. A frozen river of ice meandered its way through the centre, changing course every few metres as it diverted around various boulders and trees. Little houses, complete with fishing rods and buckets, lined several areas where the river was slightly larger in width. If you hadn't explored further than the little town of Järven, then you would have no idea that this little river was just one of the several that fed the frozen depths that was Lake Tväre.

The screeching whistle of the train sounded around this neighbouring valley as it pulled into a modest little station, somewhat smaller than the one in Tväre. Out from one of the metal carriages stepped Chief Magnhilda, accompanied by her son Här. The cold hit them immediately, and they reacted by quickly wrapping their scarves tightly around their faces and pulling up their collared coats.

Här: You really think we'll have any luck here?

The young man didn't sound convinced, and his superior officer sighed, replying with a tired and strained voice.

Magnhilda: I don't know what to think. We've not found anything around Tväre, have we? Not even a hint as to where he could be... This is the next best thing we can do.

Här contested further, clearly unhappy with travelling such a distance from home.

184

Här: But Järven is miles away! He couldn't have gotten here by himself...

Magnhilda: Couldn't he?

She glanced back at the smoky beast of the train, which was still creaking and squeaking as it settled upon the cold metal tracks.

Här: If he were on the train, why would he get off here? And how would we even know if he did!?

The old police chief snapped.

Magnhilda: I don't know Här! We're here because I don't know what else to do! So please, stop asking obvious questions because I don't know the answers!

Här fell silent. Chief Magnhilda shook her head, annoyed at herself for lashing out at her son, who she knew was just verbalising his own unsure thoughts.

Magnhilda: Come on. We have to try.

They ventured up towards the local police station, which was almost identical to the one in Tväre. It was just as small, with a single cell capable of holding only one person who was more likely to be drunk than having ever committed a crime. An older policeman was the only one holding down the fort, and he was barely even awake when Magnhilda knocked on the heavy door. After a brief discussion, he agreed to assist them with their search, promising to spread the word of Sigmund's disappearance to Järven's townsfolk. Chief Magnhilda felt that this wasn't enough and, with the old policeman's permission, she and Här began to search the town for themselves.

From house to house they both went, knocking on every thick wooden door they could find. To those few that answered, they showed a faded black and white photograph of Sigmund, hastily asking if they had seen anyone that may look similar to the missing boy. Annoyed Järven folk shook their heads, closing their doors one after the other to prevent the cold outdoor air from rushing inside.

Magnhilda put her hand to her face, hopelessness hitting hard as she reached the end of another street. She'd known

185

there was almost no chance of this trip providing any sort of information, but the continued responses of "don't know" or "can't help" had started to get to her. With the sun setting over the distant hills, she began the return journey down the icy hill towards the Järven train station. She tried to suppress the tiny flicker of hope that her son, Här, may have found something, but the chances were so low, she knew it was practically impossible.

They met at the train station, and each of them shook their heads. Boarding the train in silence, they didn't speak another word to each other the entire ride home. The darkness had fully set in by the time they were back in Tväre. They returned to the comfort of the police station, feeling as if the entire day of searching had been a complete waste of time...

***

Avarson: Hello, hello?

A polite double-knock was heard at the door of the modest little shop. Freja had been busying herself with closing the store for the evening, pulling curtains, blowing out candles. She looked up towards the sound of her opening door, seeing Avarson poking in his head as the sunset gently glowed behind his perfect blond hair.

Freja: Oh! Good evening, Avarson.

Avarson: Mind if I come in?

Freja glanced around, a bit unsure. Despite the admiration she had for the handsome industrialist, it was a strange time of the day for a visit.

Freja: Uh... It is quite late... and I was just closing up.

Avarson continued as if Freja hadn't said anything, entering the shop with incredible confidence. He sifted his hand through a rail of shirts as he walked by, his voice calm and calculating.

Avarson: It won't take a minute.

Freja: No, I really need to go. I've got my father to deal with. He needs me to—

Avarson: You said only the other day that I'd be welcome anytime… Are you going back on that already?

Freja closed her mouth warily.

Freja: No… Of course not. What can I do for you?

Avarson's eyes searched around the store, glancing at the odd variety of photos that were for sale along with the many garments of clothing.

Avarson: It's about a little matter. Nothing major, just… a minor disagreement.

Freja: Oh? Who between?

Avarson: Between us. Apparently.

Freja fell silent, which was a rare thing for her to do. Avarson stopped alongside one of the baskets, picking out a nice headband, made from interweaved thread and intricately layered with wool for warmth.

Avarson: A lot of people in this town seem to be experiencing tougher times than usual. It has been a cold winter. Two blizzards already. And the case of the missing boy as well…

He sighed, almost exaggerating the motion.

Avarson: I know how hard it can be… Especially for a quaint little place such as this. So dependent on friends and neighbours.

He fiddled the headband with his fingers, testing its strength against his own.

Avarson: So I, generously, approved a small loan for you to keep afloat, well, small for me. I believed it also helped pay for the repairs to your roof?

Freja took a shallow breath and nodded, feeling the atmosphere in the shop change... Avarson smiled to himself.

Avarson: And then I learn that we have a disagreement…

Freja: There's nothing wrong with our payments Avarson. We've never missed one, nor have we ever been late.

Avarson didn't react. He simply continued playing with the headband, glancing down at it whilst Freja scrambled to provide further answers.

Freja: We agreed on a payment plan. My husband shook hands with you on it!

Avarson: This isn't about the loan, Freja. I'm simply reminding you that, as of right now, your quaint little shop is technically mine.

Freja paused nervously. Avarson continued his intimidation, very much aware of the power he held over the poor woman. But his ulterior motive for his visit was not yet clear.

Avarson: I was in the Hall of Memory yesterday. I don't know if you know, but they've offered me a nice little room to conduct my business whenever I'm in the town. I was preparing for the day of the signing, and something with your name caught my attention...

Avarson dropped the headband back into the basket, now facing her directly.

Avarson: It was a letter of complaint. Something about the cancellation of the signing? Am I correct in my assessment so far?

Freja's breathing became short and sharp, but she didn't yet break eye contact.

Freja: I was just voicing a couple of concerns. The boy is still missing, I didn't think a carnival, or a signing event was the right thing to proceed with.

She backed away ever so slightly, but she was trapped in the limited space between the shop desk and the wall.

Freja: I didn't think they'd put them on record.

Avarson: Many would say a letter with your name on it, *is* a form of record. I'm just surprised you, of all people, would do something so stupid. We are friends, are we not?

Freja subtly reached down under her desk as Avarson's tone became increasingly dangerous, trying to find anything she could use to defend herself if the need arose.

Avarson: I'll make this clear, so there's no misunderstanding.

He stepped forward, coming close enough to lower his voice. The desk still separated the both of them, but it was still too close for comfort.

Avarson: You're going to visit the council tonight and withdraw the suggestion. Say it was a nervous thought, and you've now had time to think. All clear?

Freja nodded. Avarson placed his long fingers on the desk between them, his index finger seemingly twitching.

Avarson: Because if you don't, you might find your loan repayments start getting lost...

Freja breathed a trembling reply.

Freja: The bank keeps records.

Avarson: Records can be changed. That old clerk at the bank has had troubled times of his own too. And it'd be nothing new if that old fool forgot or misread a detail or two...

Avarson's blue eyes bore into Freja's mind. The light in her store seemed to darken as Avarson shifted his position, blocking out the glow of the sun behind him. He slowly reached out his fingertips towards Freja's neck and gently brushed his finger against her skin. She instantly recoiled, and Avarson smiled as he withdrew his advantage. He began to retreat back to the shop entrance, but to Freja, it felt like an age before he finally reached the door.

Avarson: Remember... I'm welcome everywhere.

With that, he was gone. And Freja was left in silence. She didn't move for a long while...

***

189

The habitat of the cavern was a strange one to say the least. The air seemed to alternate between pockets of warmth and unbelievable cold, causing the covering of ice above to drip and trickle down the bedrock walls until they eventually froze once again. The effect was an unbroken trail of thin, bumpy ice, building layer upon layer until an entire pillar had been formed, one of many that surrounded the cavern, holding up the Lake like a crown.

Sigmund stared up at one of these shining walls of ice, running his fingers over the tiny lumps and bumps that had frozen to the side. Sometimes, the icy cold would flash through his fingers upon contact, and other times, he would feel only their texture. He frowned as one of the bumps broke away, covering his fingers in a splash of cold water.

> Fendal: We're almost ready.

Fendal called out from across the cavern, instantly drawing Sigmund's attention away from the wall and over towards the sculpture of the Ice-log. As he walked, his eyes flashed towards the side of the cavern, where Fendal's frozen museum lay hidden. A horrible dark shadow appeared to glow from behind the bedrock, somehow shining through it and making the bare rock appear like a transparent barrier. And then, in a moment, it was gone. Sigmund returned his gaze back to Fendal, who stood in front of a small desk and chair, each formed entirely out of ice, and indicated for Sigmund to sit down. A little array of sculptures lay in front of the young boy, from an icy quill and inkpot to the outline of a book, though none of them seemed to be of any practical use.

> Fendal: You should be proud of yourself Sigmund. You might just be the first Viking to bear this knowledge in centuries!

Sigmund frowned and looked up from his desk.

> Sigmund: Why so few?

Fendal shrugged.

> Fendal: Various little reasons. Lack of interest, harsh winters... war... If such things had been avoided in

the past, we probably wouldn't be in such a struggle now.

Sigmund: Then why didn't you show yourself to someone years ago? I thought you knew the future... Wouldn't it be better if—

He went to protest further but stopped when he saw Fendal's stern look of reproach.

Fendal: Word of advice, Sigmund. Don't argue when you don't know what you're talking about.

Sigmund lowered his head and fell silent.

Fendal: The future isn't set in ice. It morphs and shifts with every decision. Big changes are easier to see. But little ones are unpredictable.

He eyed Sigmund knowingly, opening out his hands.

Fendal: I cannot, for example, know for sure if someone will agree to dedicate their life to the good of the lake. And as the lake became weaker, I could only risk showing myself to the select few... Those that showed the best promise.

Sigmund: But you did to me?

Fendal's mouth curled with a small smile.

Fendal: I did indeed. Now let's get cracking!

He clapped his blue hands together and turned his back to Sigmund, striding off towards the cavern wall. Sigmund played with the icy carvings on his desk while he waited, pulling on the sculpture of the quill. The icy feather snapped in his hand, leaving only the inkpot on the desk. Sigmund looked around guiltily, quickly hiding the feather before Fendal saw what he'd done.

Over by the grey bedrock wall, Fendal pulled down one of his hidden rocky levers causing a loud click as it changed position. An icy mirage of Fendal, appearing in his more human form, came into view in front of Sigmund, like a scene from a travelling theatre group. He stood before an ancient version of Tväre's Hall of Memory, speaking loudly and aggressively to an invisible crowd.

Mirage Fendal: Hear me when I say! Canute now seems to prefer the people of the south than he does his own kin! I'm sure I speak for everyone here when I say, we don't want these Danes Anywhere Near Our Borders—

Fendal: OH, THOR'S GOATS!

Fendal rushed to pull the lever back up, cutting off the mirage and its words in an instant. He breathed out in relief, looking over at Sigmund, somewhat embarrassed.

Fendal: My deepest apologies my lad. That's very outdated and I don't stand by any of what I said back then…

Fendal turned back to the rocky wall and fumbled along for a different stone lever.

Fendal: Ah. It's this one. My mistake…

He pulled down on a second lever, and another mirage of Fendal materialised in the same place as before, only this time it was Fendal as Sigmund knew him, complete with his boney frame and frozen beard.

Mirage Fendal: The basics to being a Spirit Herald. Lesson one, understanding your spirit.

Sigmund frowned and looked over towards the real Fendal, who grinned as the mirage flickered and came into focus.

Sigmund: I don't want to be rude… But is this it?

Fendal's great eyes widened immediately.

Fendal: Of course not! I've always believed that you can't truly appreciate nature unless you experience it!

In perfect synergy, both Fendals waved their arms and Sigmund became surrounded by an icy mirage. White, transparent images appeared on all sides as his desk and chair melted away, forcing him to stand to his feet. To his left, he saw a typical Tvären winter, with snowdrifts piling high against the little houses. To his right, he saw the magic of summertime, the Lake gently pouring into the western stream as trickling water sparkled in the sunlight.

Fendal then began to instruct Sigmund in the ways of the Lake, teaching and showing him the incredible variability of the land throughout the different seasons, along with the people of Tväre that worked with the land as it changed form. Icy images swirled around figures of Fendal farming, planting trees in carefully chosen spaces and testing the Lake ice during the springtime thaw. This imagery transitioned into the building of roads and horse-drawn carriages, even showing the townsfolk trading and working with other settlements. The real Fendal narrated Sigmund through every mirage, helping him understand the wonderful balance that could be achieved if people only understood the land they lived upon, instead of abusing it. When they were finished, the images faded away... and the icy figure of Olaf stepped forward.

The cavern began to shift and change. The ice of the ceiling became brilliantly transparent, showing the sun and the moon hanging in the blue sky of the day. Without saying a single word, Olaf held his frozen hands aloft and began to shift them through the air, drawing lines in the sky that matched those of a clockface. As the sun shifted across the sky, moving slowly from east to west, a great shadow appeared above Sigmund, moving across the clockface in perfect rhythm, turning the clockface into a brilliant sundial.

As the light faded, and darkness began to take over, Olaf held up his hands again. This time, he moved each one individually, creating invisible patterns in the air. The tiny glow of a million different stars came into focus above Sigmund's head, all laying upon the purple and pink of the surrounding galaxy, known to the Vikings as Odin's Way. One of these stars began to glow with a mighty bright light, creating a halo around itself like a beacon. As Sigmund watched, enchanted by the display, the stars began to rotate in the sky, shifting around the haloed star which remained perfectly stable.

Olaf's invisible patterns began to emerge, connecting the stars together to form amazing drawings and pictures. A powerful swordsman charged across the sky, followed by another Viking riding a chariot. They surrounded the head of a wolf, which itself was balanced by a great Viking longship. Many more of these pictures surrounded the single glowing star, which led the way through the night and Sigmund realised that they were in fact a map of perfect design, allowing Olaf to navigate his way anywhere in the world.

The display came to a close, and Sigmund waited to see what was next. Alaf glowered at him from her little corner, almost making a silent statement as she refrained from moving. Fendal walked over to her, his mouth tight-lipped and his eyes furious. Sigmund watched as they argued without words, Alaf clearly pointing towards Sigmund several times during the interaction. Within his hands, Fendal created iced forms of a hammer and a saw, offering the tools out to Alaf as an invitation. But Alaf turned her face away, remaining by the Ice-log until Fendal eventually gave up.

Sigmund: Is everything alright?

Sigmund asked tentatively as the frozen man came wandering back over.

Fendal: It will be. Once she realises... They both have their strengths, and I was hoping she would be willing to share hers with you... Maybe another time.

Sigmund nodded as Fendal turned his back. Suddenly, through the wall of the cavern, Sigmund saw the circle of shadows appear once again. A flash of pain sparked up Sigmund's forearm, causing him to flinch. He quickly pulled the arm towards himself, hiding it from Fendal's piercing view as he waited for the pain to fade away. His sudden change in breathing, however, caught the attention of his icy guardian.

Fendal: Everything okay?

Sigmund kept his gaze low as Fendal peered over him.

Sigmund: Nothing, it's fine... Just felt a bit cold.

He wrapped his arms around himself as Fendal frowned slightly.

Fendal: That's worrying... Let me see what I can do—

Sigmund: It's fine.

Sigmund almost snapped, stopping Fendal in his tracks.

Sigmund: I don't need you to fix it. I'm just tired.

Fendal didn't say another word. He simply nodded once as Sigmund got to his feet and walked back towards the narrow tunnel that led to their rooms. The blue aura faded slightly as Sigmund disappeared, the shadows descending across Fendal's unmoving form...

***

Part Three

The Terrible Reality

Magnhilda: Elvera. How are you?

The tired policewoman spoke gently and carefully towards Elvera, who stood before a carved wooden desk. What constituted as Chief Magnhilda's office was simply an upstairs room with the attic above removed. This left the wooden beams of the roof exposed, giving the space an almost hollow feeling. It wasn't homely; the Chief had made sure it didn't feel that way, but it wasn't cold or bitter either. A fire had been lit and it breathed warmth and calm into the room where the two women stood. Elvera finally replied, her own voice as exhausted and stretched as Magnhilda's.

Elvera: Okay... I'm doing okay.

Magnhilda: Good. Do you need anything to drink?

Elvera shook her head.

Elvera: No, I'm okay.

Magnhilda: You sure? Don't think of it as a problem if you do—

Elvera cracked, interrupting the policewoman mid-sentence.

Elvera: You didn't call me up here for a drink Magnhilda. Just tell me what you need to tell me... Please...

Magnhilda gathered herself, becoming less of a friend and more of a police chief.

Magnhilda: Okay.

She paused, trying to read Elvera's expression. It was defensive and tight, like a set of armour. But to Magnhilda, the desperation and need for any answer at all was clear to see. She had seen a lot of faces in that police station, and had learnt to read each and every one of their expressions. She hated what she was about to say next.

Magnhilda: We're stopping the search.

Elvera froze.

Elvera: ...What...?

Magnhilda: We're stopping the search, Elvera. We can't continue; we've exhausted everything to no avail and found nothing that points to his location.

Elvera began to shake her head, her voice taut and strained.

Elvera: I don't understand... You're giving up!?

Magnhilda almost winced.

Elvera: He's still out there! You can't do this... You're abandoning him!

Her words were cruel but true, and Magnhilda had no response. She had known this was going to be hard... but not this hard.

Magnhilda: I wish I could do more...

Elvera: But you're saying you can't!?

Magnhilda tried to keep her composure as Elvera seemed to unravel in front of her, and finally gave the poor mother a firm, definitive answer.

Magnhilda: No... I can't.

Elvera suddenly seemed to understand what Magnhilda was saying... and her face fell drastically.

Magnhilda: I'm sorry...

Elvera stumbled backward. Suddenly, it seemed as if she couldn't balance herself. Magnhilda quickly realised what was about to happen and rushed past her desk to help Elvera into a chair. The young woman didn't scream, or cry. She just sat there, trying to get through the invisible pain. Magnhilda tried to comfort her as best she could but knew there would be no words that would make this better. She looked up to the ceiling, seemingly towards God, and then closed her eyes.

***

The Carnival of the Fires had arrived. Although this year it was significantly more subdued than years gone by. Normally the centremost streets of Tväre would be thriving and beating with the hearts of all the locals, and even some visitors from the nearby towns, if they were welcome of course. In a normal year, there would be colourful streamers hanging from every torch post, and candles glowing in every window that faced the central square. But this year was not a normal year...

The disappearance of Sigmund had left a permanent scar on the celebrations. The entire town had come to the collective, unmentionable conclusion that Sigmund was now permanently gone, either taken by persons unknown or perished in the cold. And now that Chief Magnhilda had officially suspended the search, even the hardiest of locals knew there was no chance of finding him. The crushing sadness in this news pressed hard on the joy and laughter that normally populated the Carnival. Enough so, that the neighbouring towns had been asked not to come at all. The town of Tväre was in mourning. One of its few, valuable children had gone...

The few streamers that had been put out hung loosely and sadly, gently buffeting in the light wind that sought its way through the valley. The candles that had been lit seemed dim and sad, and the people appeared pale and hollow to match. They glanced around at each other, not a smile upon anyone's lips, and tried to encourage one another with the words they spoke every year.

The People: Keep warm with us.

They nodded solemnly towards one another, repeating the words in accordance with tradition.

> The People: Keep warm with us.

Torsten separated himself from the crowd, his wide shoulders instantly noticeable from the rest of the people. The many hats and scarves turned towards the centre of the town square as Torsten stood in front of the majestic, yet lifeless, sculpture of the wooden Firelog. He waited until only the wind in the valley could be heard, and then began to speak.

> Torsten: Welcome, my fellow folk of Tväre, to this year's Carnival of the Fires. We have been blessed by the weather today; we couldn't have asked for anything better for the middle of winter, especially after having to dig ourselves out several days ago.

There was a small murmur of laughter. Hidden within the crowd, beneath a thick hat and a high-collared coat, stood Levi, who tried to remain out of sight from both Torsten and the townsfolk. Despite the Librarian convincing him to stay with her scolding words, the disguise still felt necessary, especially considering tonight was more about Sigmund's passing than anything else. Levi didn't want to add any more blame or pain to an already mournful evening.

Understandably, Elvera had decided to remain at home for the evening festivities. After receiving the crushing news by Chief Magnhilda, she had locked her door and hidden herself away. Levi had been told not to interrupt her time of grief but his worry for her well-being had driven him to her front door. Elvera had reluctantly answered his knock and stated that she'd rather not stain the carnival with her horrible sadness, preferring the folk to try and enjoy themselves instead of them pitying her. Levi glanced up as Torsten continued speaking, the wind cutting through several of his words.

> Torsten: I know that everyone is aware of the situation that we face this year. The tragedy that has struck our town has disturbed us all…

The folk nodded and smiled sadly at each other.

Torsten: But... It has, I think, yielded something good...

The crowd glanced up, wondering what Torsten could possibly mean with such a statement, but he was well ahead of the curve.

Torsten: Because through this darkest time, I've seen our town come together like never before in my life. Many of our older residents, and I use the term loosely...

The town chuckled again.

Torsten: I'm sure you remember harsher winters, where you spent the freezing days sharing oil and food with those who were in need. Gathering around the soup pot for any heat you could get. And though this winter may be one of the hardest we've had in recent times; it is one we will never forget...

He lifted a candle in the air for all to see. He then balanced it with a long matchstick in his other hand, which he lit with the flame of the nearest lantern.

Torsten: My wife and I know Elvera quite closely from our time together on the council. The one thing she loved more than anything else was her son. This... is for Sigmund...

Torsten lit the candle and placed it on the large table that was set up for the carnival every year. The flame fluttered in the light wind, but just about stayed alive. The folk of the town bowed their heads in unison, keeping the time of memorial in absolute silence. Candles glowed in every window, all of them respecting the memory of Sigmund's short life. After a few moments, Torsten cleared his throat, signalling the end of the silence, and the people began to chat amongst themselves.

Torsten, his duties of the evening not yet complete, now withdrew a perfectly creaseless piece of paper from within his coat. Several lines of cursive handwriting were written upon it, and underneath were the six signatures of Tväre's Municipal Council. In the top corner was a decorated stamp, displaying the sigil of the council as a representation of the official nature of the document. Torsten reached under the table and lifted a stylus and ink pot onto the table, ready for someone to add their name to the bottom.

That someone began to slowly move through the crowd, aware that their time had finally come. Avarson's blonde hair bounced with his joyful march, almost scything the people of the crowd apart with his penetrating smile as he formed a path towards the head table and the overlooking Firelog. Torsten began to speak slightly more enthusiastically, seeing that Avarson was now approaching.

> Torsten: Despite the darkness we've faced, there has also been a bright flame in our midst. One that has bathed this town in its generous glow for over a year now.

Torsten held out his gloved hand towards the crowd.

> Torsten: Avarson. Will you join me up here?

The folk began to politely and awkwardly clap as Avarson, now acting humble and graceful, walked through the remainder of the crowd. The grief of the town over Sigmund's disappearance was still very raw, more so because of the memorial moments ago... which meant that Avarson was the only one smiling.

> Avarson: Thank you everyone. Thank you.

He slowed himself down as he approached the centre of the square, putting his hand on the shoulders of the folk in thanks, and smiling at each of them in turn. He came upon Freja, who immediately lowered her head and grasped the arm of her husband protectively, who glanced down at her, confused by her actions. Avarson saw this, and smirked. Several other women did the same as he passed by, though their reason for this was known only to themselves.

Avarson began to climb above everyone as he joined Torsten on the raised ground that lay around the darkness of the Firelog. Torsten offered him the central position, and Avarson turned and began his rehearsed speech.

> Avarson: Well, I can't tell you how long I've waited for this day.

He laughed lightly as his powerful voice travelled on the air, relishing in the centre of attention.

Avarson: A big appreciation for Torsten huh?

He began to applaud, smacking his leather gloves together excessively loudly. His enthusiasm was poorly matched by the folk, who hardly applauded at all.

Avarson: It was this resilient man who first introduced me to this wonderful place, way back when I first arrived in the Northern Valleys. And in that time, I've been welcomed, greeted, and even spoken to!

He cackled horribly at his own joke. Again, he was alone in the sound. Somehow the lack of reaction from the people made the laugh even more awkward than it already was. Avarson gently pulled at his collar, withdrawing a small note of paper, from which he now read from.

Avarson: The Guardianship of the land means a great deal to me. It's an honour just to be trusted by you all. You've all enjoyed the sight and sound of my railway passing by... I know some of you have had a few concerns, but it's good to know that the majority see what I hoped you all would.

He paused. The crowd were not reacting as much as he had expected them to, and it was beginning to put him off. Avarson cleared his throat, now attempting to build off the heavy emotion the town was experiencing.

Avarson: The situation of late has of course disturbed me as much as the rest of you. I've spoken with Elvera privately, and although she isn't here tonight to say it herself, she greatly supports the work I do here, and would have done more had she not been caught up in what's happened...

Levi frowned; Avarson's words did not match Elvera's views at all.

Avarson: And I'm sure she'd want you all to forget about the loss of her son and enjoy yourselves here instead. So, lift your heads and get some smiles on your faces eh? This is a good day for us all.

He grinned and raised his hands, as if expecting thunderous applause. The crowd almost didn't know how to react. Some remained silent, some politely clapped, but most exchanged confused and awkward glances.

Avarson turned around and approached the table. He took a beautiful quill in his hand and dipped it in the pot of ink nearby. Torsten offered him the document of Guardianship and Avarson shoved Sigmund's candle out the way to give himself room to sign it.

And just like that, the land around Lake Tväre was officially under Avarson's protection. Avarson finished signing his name, smiling to himself as his moment of triumph finally arrived.

*

The document had been signed, and the very subdued festivities had been and gone. A lone fire juggler still remained, but that was as far as the entertainment went. The stalls were now empty, and the games had barely been played. The most exciting event was usually the infamous Race Down the Thorhorn, whereby participants climbed into decorated woollen sacks and sledged down a lethal icy chute, several miles in length. It began high up on the slope of the mountain, ending in the town square, and often resulted in a few broken bones, bruised bodies and the occasional crippling. But sadly, no one had felt the enthusiasm to organise it, and the carved channel of this year's race lay quiet and empty.

Avarson had disappeared as soon as the signing had been completed, leaving the town to its limited celebrations. Many of the folk had also returned to their homes, having only exchanged meagre conversation with their friends. Levi was one of the few that were left, still hiding beneath his coat and his thick hat. He didn't want to return to his hostel so early, and luckily, he found conversation in Minister Toro, who had observed the carnival from afar. He was one of the few that Levi was comfortable speaking with, for he knew he would receive no blame or anger from him.

Levi: Did you visit Elvera today?

The old minister paused before shaking his head.

Minister Toro: I felt it best to leave her to her grief...
For this evening at least.

Levi: I should have done the same...

Minister Toro glanced at him, suddenly on alert as Levi continued.

Levi: I've never seen someone look that way
before... She was so... empty.

Minister Toro sighed.

Minister Toro: I've seen the pain she is going
through many times. In my old country it wasn't
uncommon for children to either go missing or fall to
illness, though there were a lot more of them than
here. Many women in my village know of the pain
Elvera now faces... The best we can do is be there
when she needs us. And give her time and space
when she needs to be alone.

His deeply sorrowful tone only made Levi feel worse. He'd
hoped discussing Sigmund's disappearance with someone
like the Minister would help the way he felt about it, but this
wasn't helping at all.

Levi: I've only known her a few days. She offered
me shelter and food and she didn't even know me...

Levi glanced into the Minister's humble face.

Levi: She was so generous, and now she's lost
everything...

Minister Toro: It would be a fairer world if reward
and punishment were based on who gives and who
takes. It is a conundrum that all folk, whether they
be people of God or not, struggle to live with...

Levi didn't respond. Minister Toro took a deep breath and
rubbed his gloved hands together.

Minister Toro: I think I will return to my home now.

Levi nodded, feeling the chill of the cold air himself.

Minister Toro: It was good to speak to you again
Levi. Not many people here have seen much of the

world beyond these snowy hills. Not that that's a bad thing of course, but it's quite refreshing to hear a voice that came from somewhere as far away as I did... Sort of...

They both gave a weak laugh, though there was very little humour there.

Levi: Two different worlds.

Minister Toro: That they are. But the church is always open, I hope you know that. Though you may need to see if I'm free beforehand; many of the town are seeking comfort at this time and... well, I'm only one man.

Levi suddenly realised how tired the old Minister truly was. His eyes were heavy, and he seemed to be fighting to stay awake.

Levi: I understand. Thank you Minister. Sleep well.

Minister Toro: I'll try.

Minister Toro made a resigned smile before turning and walking away through the snow.

***

The screeching whistle of Tväre's new steam engine pierced through the valley. Upon hearing it, one would think that a horn or something less shrill would have been a much more obvious choice, especially considering the town's link to its Viking ancestry. This whistle was much worse though, for it was heard throughout the valley deep in the black pitch of night. The dawn had not broken, and yet the train was in full operation.

Torsten lay on his back, covered by a thick woollen blanket. He blinked as the screech of the whistle pierced through his modest bedroom. Groaning with tiredness, he pulled the blanket from his body and stepped onto the wooden floor, shivering as the cold of the floor shot through his thick socks, decorated with little knitted pom-poms, clearly the work of his loving wife. A heavy stone, wrapped in thick cloth, fell from the end of his bed, causing Torsten to curse in annoyance. His wife, Gudro, rolled herself over, having been stirred by the noise.

Gudro: Torsten? What are you doing?

Torsten: Ugh, I got woken up.

His voice was cracked and hoarse. He grumbled a bit more before lifting the heavy stone wrapped in cloth and placing it back between his blankets. The purpose of the stone was to fight the cold within the bed during the night. Heated on the fire during the evening, it was then wrapped and placed within the covers, ready to keep the feet and body warm of the person soon to be sleeping there. It was common practice in Tväre for pretty much every resident, and forgetting the duty often resulted in a poor night's sleep.

Gudro: What woke you?

Torsten: That infernal whistle from the train.

He shuffled his way over to the window, peering out into the misty valley. In the near distance, you could just about see the train station building, and the icy surface of the Lake beyond. A thin cloud of steam, caused by the late journey of the railway, billowed and dissipated in the air.

Torsten: Why does it need to run so late into the night anyway!? Surely whatever it is can wait...

Gudro muttered groggily in reply.

Gudro: Avarson said to expect a few late journeys once the signing was done. It's just for a night or two. Come back to bed.

Torsten grunted in thought and turned away from the window. Suddenly, something flashed on the other side of the valley, causing Torsten to dart back.

Torsten: The hell was that!?

Torsten stared at the distant slope again. He thought he'd seen something move in the shadows, something in the trees maybe... But it was so dark, he could barely make anything out.

Gudro: What is it now?

Torsten: ...Nothing. I must be imagining things.

Torsten climbed back under the blankets, trying to get himself warm again. Gentle snowflakes began to twinkle as they fell to the ground, with only the light of the moon and stars upon them. And along the bottom of the valley, the great train began to move...

* * *

Sigmund lay awake in the darkness. The blue aura of the cavern was almost lifeless, giving the little cave the impression of night-time. But without the sun or the moon to help guide his internal clock Sigmund had no idea what time of day it was. He rubbed his eyes, stopping suddenly as he felt another pain shoot up his arm. It was difficult to see in the limited light, but it was obvious that his abnormal scar was growing. His wrist tingled as he pulled the sleeve back down, and it was then that Sigmund saw a strange dark glow...

Shifting shadows pulsed through his bedroom entrance, instantly wiping any thought of sleep from Sigmund's mind. He got up from his bed and looked through the archway, trying to locate the source of the dark aura. It retreated as he approached, drifting back towards the tunnel that led to the main cavern.

Sigmund carefully followed, tempted in by sheer curiosity. The shadows once again withdrew towards the cavern wall, slipping behind the cliff of bedrock where Fendal's secret levers lay hidden. A gurgled snore echoed through the cavern, freezing Sigmund in his quest. He glanced over to the Ice-log where Alaf and Olaf lay against one another, the aura from the sculpture's centre as dim and lifeless as his bedroom. Another snore came from the pair of sleeping figures, but that was all.

Sigmund slowly tiptoed towards the bedrock wall, pausing before the grey set of stone. Why had the shadows led him here? He began to scan the wall for one of Fendal's secret levers, but the shadows had other plans. The wall descended without his touch, as if reacting to his very presence, the tiny rumble not enough to wake the rest of the cavern's inhabitants. A glow of blue and white washed over the boy as he stared into the familiar hallways of Fendal's memory museum. Only this time, the shadows seemed to have control. They waved and pulsed at the end of the icy hallway, drawing Sigmund further and further in… and there was no one to stop him.

*

In the depths of the cavern, settled in his personal cast of ice, Fendal's eyes flashed open, the white spotlights piercing through the darkness…

*

Sigmund journeyed through the corridor. He passed by the strange exhibits without a second glance; his interest fuelled by only one thing. Like a door labelled 'Do Not Enter', Sigmund had to know what the dark corridor down here meant. What was so dark that Fendal dared not go near it? Fendal, who had led his people into battles and helped them through the hardest winters? What could the immortal frozen corpse possibly be afraid of?

The outward facing eye of the Fendal's pet catfish followed the young boy as he moved through the corridor, watching his movements slowly and suspiciously. The light faded as Sigmund journeyed further into the depths, becoming tainted with shades of brown and grey. He glanced downwards as his boots splashed through pools of horrible brown meltwater, water that definitely hadn't been here before… It was only now that Sigmund realised the exhibits around him seemed to be melting. Icy windows had collapsed onto the bedrock floor, leaving the soaking objects lying in their empty spaces. Water dripped from every crack and crevice, even from the ceiling, landing upon Sigmund's face.

He paused. Every instinct told him to turn and run, but the shadows now surrounded him completely, cutting off any chance of retreat. In the darkness up ahead appeared a single windowpane of transparent ice. A lone exhibit that hadn't yet fallen to the meltwater. Sigmund edged towards it, fearfully curious of what was hidden behind the ice. He began to shiver, the cold in the air suddenly becoming

208

increasingly sharp, as if the cavern were warning him to stay away, and then it was gone.

Sigmund's gaze was gripped as the frozen window finally revealed its secrets. Upon an icy bed, as still as stone, lay the cold and lifeless form of a young boy. He looked to be around Sigmund's age, but who knows how long he'd been down here; he could have been alive yesterday, or a thousand years ago. The ice had preserved him perfectly, down to his tiny fingers and woollen clothes. Where time had stripped Fendal of his human appearance, it had seemingly left this boy untouched, but from the sight of the unmoving figure, Sigmund knew that there was no life left here...

Sigmund began to back away, seeing all he wanted to see. The darkness that surrounded him was suddenly very close to his skin, and claustrophobic bedrock pressed in from every angle. Sigmund's breathing became short and sharp. The cavern ceiling was lower than before, and the walls became tight and narrow. He began to run, desperately trying to free himself from the grip of the demonic cave, but he wasn't going anywhere. The hallway extended out away from him, the power of the Lake once again keeping him trapped in one position...

He glanced one more time at the window of ice. To his horror, the boy was no longer there. Instead, the window flashed, and Sigmund saw a flurry of images go past, playing like a performance at the theatre. A lone man travelled through the dense snowy forest, kicking at snowdrifts as he passed them by. He looked exactly like Fendal would have done, before his hundreds of years beneath the ice. A second, smaller kick caught the same snowdrift, and Sigmund laid eyes on a small boy, joining the Human-Fendal in the fun.

The window flashed again, and the Human-Fendal was seen running through the town of Tväre, only this time the buildings were smaller, consisting of faded straw rooftops. His eyes were wild as he yelled across the valley, but his words were silent to Sigmund's ears. He yelled twice more, turning and looking around in a frantic panic. Again, the window flashed, and Sigmund saw the Human-Fendal struggling against his Viking townsfolk. Strong men, dressed in great furs held him back to no avail. He charged out onto the icy surface of Lake Tväre, disappearing into the mist that descended from the skies. The townsfolk watched despairingly as the Everflow glowed blue through the mist, and then faded back into nothing...

The ice flashed for a final time. And, for only a second, Sigmund saw himself. This Sigmund, however, was skinny, frostbitten and covered in an awful brown sludge. It dripped from his stained dark hair onto his face, into the blue skin that surrounded his eyes. The real Sigmund fell backward as his legs crumbled. He collapsed... into Fendal's waiting arms.

The darkness withdrew instantly. The comforting blue aura returned. And Fendal's warm, frostbitten arms embraced Sigmund for as long as he needed. They held one another, supporting themselves until they had the strength to finally withdraw. Fendal looked down into Sigmund's eyes as they separated, speaking with neither worry nor anger.

Fendal: I'm sorry you had to see what you did.

Sigmund: I saw someone! I saw someone down there!

Fendal: I know. I know you did.

Fendal comforted the boy as he struggled to get out the fearful words.

Sigmund: Are you angry?

Sigmund kept his gaze low, almost in shame.

Fendal: My lad... Of course I'm not.

Sigmund: What happened to me?

He glanced back towards the corridor, which had withdrawn back into a small pocket of shadow. It no longer pulsed, nor drew Sigmund in. Fendal followed his gaze, staring deep into the darkness.

Fendal: Not everything is happy and merry in this world Sigmund. Not even down here...

Sigmund nodded, his breath still short and desperate.

Fendal: The lake is neither good nor evil. It both gives and it takes. It is a relief to those who need it but offers a cruel punishment for those who don't respect it.

Sigmund: Am I being punished?

Fendal's brilliant eyes widened.

Fendal: No, my lad! Not in any way. The lake simply showed you the truth. And sometimes that truth is harsh.

Sigmund: It's not that...

The boy shook his head and slumped, the ordeal now taking its toll. Fendal placed one of his frostbitten hands on Sigmund's shoulder, encouraging him to look back up.

Fendal: What is it then?

Sigmund looked down for a moment, and then rolled up his sleeve. His blue scar had spread across his wrist and now ventured into his palm. Fendal took a sharp intake of breath as he finally saw the hidden damage.

Fendal: How long have you had this?

Sigmund: Since the first night... It started small, and it's been growing ever since...

Fendal continued to examine it, taking great care not to cause any further pain. Sigmund continued, his voice trembling.

Sigmund: Is it too late...?

He looked up, surprised to see that Fendal was smiling.

Fendal: You know what I'm going to say, don't you?

Sigmund smiled softly as Fendal's palm began to glow with a soothing blue light.

Fendal: It's never too late.

***

Today's sunrise was darker than usual. Billowing clouds of grey and brown colours smothered any light that tried to reach the valley, leaving the land feeling hollow and cold. If

211

you stared at the vile pollution that formed the clouds, you'd notice that it had a trace. And if you followed that trace, your eyes would take you down past the ice-capped mountains and the frozen green of the fir trees until they settled on a building on the opposite shore of Lake Tväre. The factory was now in full operation.

The good folk of Tväre now gathered on the shore of their beloved Lake, looking across at the billowing smoke that now spewed from the factory's two chimneys. No one said a word, letting the shock of the immense pollution speak for them. And as more people awoke for the morning, the gathering grew into a small crowd.

Levi had awoken to the sounds of people scurrying in the snow outside his bedroom window. Everyone in this town always seemed to wake up extremely early and Levi had never understood how. He was always the more nocturnal person, preferring the late darkness of the evening over the bright light of the morning. But the way the footsteps scuffed repeatedly on the gravelly steps by his window, indicated that there was something unusual happening...

He had hurriedly dressed himself in his winter clothing before exiting the hostel. He joined several other townfolk on their march to the lakeside, glancing worriedly at the choking gas cloud that blew on the tails of the northern wind. But that was only the first of two horrors... Levi arrived at the lakeside and joined the pairs of eyes in their unbroken gaze. On the opposite shores of the Lake, where the beautiful firs of the Northward Forest had once stood, was a barren, lifeless hillside...

The land had been stripped bare of the powerful trees that once populated it, leaving only their stumps and roots remaining as any evidence they were there at all. The scale of devastation was immense; every tree on the entire hillside had been felled, their bark-covered bodies strewn across the slope like a house demolished in a hurricane. A surprise attack had come, and it had hit the sleeping army of the forest without any chance of a rescue...

The sight left the town in complete silence. As they watched, they could see the tiny figures of many unknown men crawling across the slope. Like a colony of ants, they

212

picked up each felled tree, and carried it slowly towards the factory, readying it for the next stage in the logging process. The other ants continued their dirty work, holding either side of a huge saw which they used to slice through the next great tree. And as they progressed, more and more birds began to chirp and fly away into the sky.

The whistle of the train suddenly screeched around the valley. The forewarning sound of a third oncoming horror. The tracks creaked and grinded as the train lurched its way around the eastern tip of the Lake, continuing its speed until it passed through Tväre itself, showing off its precious cargo to the onlookers. Every carriage was full of stripped, processed lumber. Hundreds of trees, torn from their home in the hill and transported away. The folk of the humble town watched without words as the train passed them by, taking their precious neighbours into the distant realms of the south... ready to be sold on for nothing more than profit...

Their whole world was being ripped away right in front of their eyes...

*

Torsten led the charge. The townsfolk hurried around the eastern edge of the Lake, following the thick laid tracks that belonged to the railway. Their faces displayed a wide range of emotions from worried anxiety to furious rage, but the focus of every one of them was on the ugly building of Avarson's brick factory. Putrid smoke billowed out from its two chimneys, darkening the sky above them as they approached the train station entrance.

As the pack of furious men and women marched forward, they began to pass more and more workers, all of them wearing the same dirty overalls and gloves, their faces grubby and curious. Many more were scurrying about on the hillside, lifting or dragging the corpses of the felled trees towards the factory, where they waited to be lifted onto the next available train. It was only now that Torsten realised why the train had been so active throughout the previous night.

Torsten: Stop...! STOP!

He charged around the factory, seeing the true scale of the deforestation up close. The last few trees were being attacked, reduced to mere stumps by workers holding huge two-sided saws. They stopped their efforts as the mass of strange locals approached, eyebrows raised more in interest than in fear. Most were chewing on a form of tobacco, either for something to do or because they were addicted to it. Despite the cold wilderness, their faces were hot and sweaty and a few displayed small cuts to their hands and foreheads.

Torsten: I SAID STOP!

Torsten threw himself towards one of the workers, pulling the huge saw away from him. A great brute of a man stepped across, his thick, black beard tight and dirty. Skalham, the chief in command, reached out his grubby hand and shoved Torsten away.

Skalham: Get the hell back Tvären!

Torsten stood his ground. He was slightly smaller than the lump of a logger, which was a rare sight since Torsten was quite the large man himself.

Torsten: You get the hell back! Look what you're doing! You're ruining our land!

Skalham: Alright! Calm down treehugger. We're just working here, alright?

The loggers began to gather around Skalham, silently electing him their spokesman as Torsten continued to protest.

Torsten: This isn't work! Look at what you're doing!

Skalham: We're getting paid. That makes it work. And it's not like we can stop. We have families back home. You thought of that!?

Torsten didn't respond and Skalham opened his question to the entire townsfolk.

Skalham: Any of you!? No, thought not. I've seen you all running around. You're like gophers. Jumping out the ground the moment someone touches a few trees!

A murmur of laughter came from his fellow loggers. Almarr, who had been standing behind Torsten, pushed his way forward with a wild exclamation.

Almarr: A FEW!? YOU'VE DESTROYED THE FOREST!

Skalham raised his eyebrows, more intrigued than threatened by this old man's outburst. Torsten grabbed the older man's shoulders, attempting to pull him back.

Torsten: Father! Stay out of this!

Almarr didn't back down.

Almarr: Don't just let them walk over you Torsten! These are our forests—

Torsten: FATHER!

Torsten held Almarr's shoulders and shook his head. Almarr paused and began to back off, until Skalham retorted with a cruel smile.

Skalham: Come on! Let the old forest ranger have his say!

The band of loggers laughed insultingly.

Almarr: You don't see it... You have no respect!

Skalham: Respect doesn't pay the debts.

Almarr could barely contain his rage.

Almarr: Get out of our land!

Skalham: Mind your manners old man. Don't make us regret anything.

Almarr: Oh I've still got some fight left in me!

Almarr's old frame charged forward, but the brutal logger stood his ground. Skalham waited until the old man was upon him, and then aggressively shoved him back, sending him sprawling on the dirty ground. Immediately the men of the town charged forward against the loggers, the two groups each forming an offensive line of battle. Almarr, meanwhile, lay a few metres away, clutching his arm and wincing in pain as two women crouched down to aid him.

Above him stood the red faces of the furious men, standing ready to defend their land.

Avarson: Whoa! Whoa, whoa...

The tender voice of Avarson finally appeared, having noticed the commotion beginning to build from the upper windows of the factory. He sauntered over towards the two groups, parting them like Moses and the Red Sea. He seemed to almost ignore the desperate expressions of the townsfolk, instead turning his back on them and choosing to address his loggers.

Avarson: Skalham. Why aren't you and your men working?

Skalham almost seemed to stutter under Avarson's piercing questions.

Skalham: Well... These lot came out from the town and—

Avarson: I know where these people are from. That's not what I asked. Why have you and your men stopped working?

Skalham: They wouldn't let us work Sir. They stood in the way of our saws...

Avarson glanced towards the townsfolk curiously, who stared back hard as if waiting in line for his attention. He spoke again, loud enough for all to hear this time.

Avarson: I see... Well, let's add a simple rule. If they get in the way again, continue as if they weren't there. Continue as if your payment depends on it.

He articulated every word, ensuring that Skalham understood the hidden meaning.

Avarson: If they get hurt, it's not on you to help them. Is that clear?

Skalham: ...Yes Sir.

Avarson: I expect this entire hillside down and stripped by evening at the latest. No more delays or you'll be working into the night to fulfil the quota.

Skalham: Yes Sir.

Skalham and his men began to step away from the townsfolk, glancing back at the group as they readied their saws and ropes to continue their devastation. Avarson finally addressed the townsfolk in his calm, condescending voice, with Torsten at the forefront, having checked on his injured father.

Avarson: You and your fellow townsfolk had better leave and leave quickly, Torsten.

Torsten's eyebrows shot up in surprise.

Torsten: What!?

Avarson continued, his voice flat and collected.

Avarson: You are trespassing. Remove yourselves now or I will have my workers do it for you.

The townsfolk stared at him, aghast by his sudden change in attitude.

Torsten: We can't trespass on our own land!

Avarson sighed and reached into his inner clothing, unfolding the document of Guardianship, which he had signed in front of the adoring townsfolk only the night before. He waved it in front of the group spitefully, rubbing it in their faces. He knew Torsten might make an attempt at stealing it back, so Avarson took care in keeping it just out of reach.

Avarson: You're right, you can't. But it's not your land anymore.

Torsten: That's only a document of Guardianship! It's about taking care of the forests!

Avarson shrugged off Torsten's desperate cries.

Avarson: Guardianship, ownership, it's all the same Torsten! We wrote the agreement together; I am not violating anything that was written. You signed the document. You gave me command over the land. It's too late!

217

Despite being the shorter of the two men, Avarson seemed to loom over Torsten, bearing down on him with wicked blue eyes.

Avarson: If you're seeing any problem here, you can only blame yourselves for causing it.

Torsten: We trusted you...

Torsten nearly spat out the words. Avarson smiled and replied, without a hint of remorse.

Avarson: I know.

And that was that. Avarson waved his hand in Torsten's face dismissively.

Avarson: Now go on. Get yourselves back to town before another one of you ends up in the dirt.

Torsten stared hard at Avarson; the fury written in plain sight across his face. Credit went to Avarson, who stood his ground all the while, and his haughty confidence eventually paid off. Torsten's face fell as he gave up the battle. He turned and began to help Almarr walk back the way they'd come, past the factory and along the risen ground of the railway line. The despairing townsfolk followed him, knowing that if Torsten couldn't do anything to defend them, then they couldn't either.

Avarson had betrayed them. Not only that, he'd taken all they held dear in this land. The train whistled and screeched as it passed the group. The wheels showered them in flecks of dirty snow as it returned to cart more of their blessed trees away in their droves. In the space of a single night and morning, the Northward Forest had been lost...

***

Sigmund fell to the ground. He clutched his arm, which felt as heavy as stone, and lay still upon the bare rock of the floor. An aching pain shot through his shoulder, and he groaned.

Fendal: Sigmund...!

Fendal rushed over to him and fell to his knees. He raised Sigmund's head for support whilst the boy clutched his shoulder and grimaced.

Sigmund: It hurts...

Fendal: I know. I know it does.

He rolled up Sigmund's sleeve, seeing the terrible growth of the blue scar, which now had conquered nearly all of his arm and hand. Fendal carefully laid a thin, frozen hand on Sigmund's shoulder, his palm glowing with the strength of his inner power. Sigmund's breath slowly returned to a calm and rhythmic beat as the healing aura was pressed against him, the blue stain withdrawing from his hand. The blue aura of the cavern dimmed all around them as the healing continued. Once the glow had gone, the young boy muttered quietly.

Sigmund: What's happening to me?

***

A harsh wind blew through the town of Tväre. Shelters and stalls from the Carnival of the Fires hung empty and abandoned. Little curtains wafted in the breeze, but there was no-one to clear them away. The town was in shock. An immense graveyard of tree stumps now replaced the beautiful greenery that had once populated the opposing hills for so many thousands of years. The natural haven exchanged for profit. Avarson's devastation extended for miles in each direction, for not a single tree had been spared on the factory-side of Lake Tväre. It was as if the hill had been completely swept away, destroyed at the order of one man.

Understandably, none of the townsfolk wanted to see such a thing, the unbearable view making them sick to their stomach. They toiled against the anger for allowing such an arrogant and evil man to get so close to them, only for him to repay them with this... And then there was the guilt for not stopping Avarson earlier. Even when they steeled themselves to stand up to the brutal loggers, they still backed away, and the heavy feeling of desperation and loss now pressed on all of them.

Avarson's great carriage rattled down the empty Tvären roads. Two horses towed the beast of a vehicle along, clacking on the stones below. It hadn't snowed for days, and the road was now becoming increasingly visible. On one of these many streets, the horses slowed to a stop, the wheels of the carriage creaking in response. Down from the driver's seat stepped Regan, who was on course to complete yet another assignment from his master. Opening the doors to the carriage, he withdrew several small nets of chopped logs, which had been stacked and packed together, heaving their weight along the ground. They weren't exactly large, probably only enough for two days fuel, but the intention behind them wasn't to provide warmth...

Regan knocked on the first door he came across, which opened to reveal a depressed looking Vargard. At the sight of Regan, Vargard's eyes narrowed, and his loyal husky dog began to growl from behind him.

Vargard: What the hell are you doing here!? You better leave quickly before I set my dog on you.

Regan glanced at the sizable form of the hound behind him, its teeth bared.

Regan: You mean that old thing?

Vargard: Have a go. We'll see which mutt comes out on top.

Regan smirked but didn't provoke Vargard any further. He lifted one of the log-nets and landed it on Vargard's doorstep.

Vargard: What is this?

Regan: Courtesy of Avarson. A gift of thanks, for your compliance.

Vargard stared at the net of logs, now realising what they were. Regan's heartless smirk returned as he bid Vargard goodbye.

Regan: Enjoy your winter.

He turned and left, leaving the speechless Vargard to watch after him as he moved onto the next house, delivering the same set of rehearsed words to another of the town's miserable locals.

Vargard glanced at the logs, then turned towards the stricken forest in the distance. It was a horribly strange feeling; logs were there to be burned after all. They had been burning them his entire life, for if they didn't, they'd no doubt freeze to death. But for some odd reason, this stack made him feel ill, almost as if Avarson were taunting them one final time...

During the course of the day, Regan went from house to house, dropping a small net of logs at every single one. He relished in the sadness and shock that crossed the faces of the locals, especially when they realised that the supposed 'gift' was nothing more than a cruel joke. Several doors were shut on him instantly, whilst many others were left as speechless as Vargard had been.

At the police station, Magnhilda barely reacted, but she did have to hold back her son, Här, especially after some cruel words from Regan, who wished them more success when the next child went missing.

At the Bergskydd Tavern, Hervor simply refused the gift, angrily throwing the logs at the carriage and shutting the door behind her. Regan left the net of logs where they were, not even bothering to reuse them for the next house.

At the church, Minister Toro didn't respond to any of Regan's subtle taunts about God or his supposed love. Instead, he simply thanked the smug little man for the logs and gently shut the door, much to Regan's annoyance.

But it was Torsten's house that Regan most looked forward to. The hot-headed, unofficial leader of the town was the wildcard in all this, and Regan was excited to see how he would react. Upon opening the door, Torsten was red eyed and tired, but like his brother before him, he fumed at the sight of Avarson's cruel servant. The rehearsed words were said, and just as Regan had hoped, Torsten's anger boiled over. He shoved Regan to the ground and charged out of the house, ready to deal some real damage. Gudro, however, lunged out an arm to hold Torsten back, knowing that any consequence of attacking Avarson's right-hand

221

man could spell even further damage to themselves and the town. Avarson's financial influence had them all in a tight grip, and if he chose to tighten that grip even further, life could very rapidly get worse...

Regan attempted to goad him further, almost wanting the attack to come. But Torsten finally listened to the pleas of his wife and stormed back into his house... leaving Regan grinning in the snow outside.

The town was at its lowest...

***

The Hope

Flaky layers of snow fell to the floor as Levi pushed them from his balcony chair. He sat himself down and stared out at what should have been the beautiful view of Lake Tväre and beyond. Instead, Levi stared out at a battlefield. A massacre of tree stumps, all of them stripped of what made them beautiful. Not a single one remained standing.

A lone bird landed on Levi's balcony, its tiny claws imprinting in the thin layer of snow that remained. Levi watched it as it jumped and searched its way around. It seemed lost, almost confused. Levi's eyes lifted towards the neighbouring balconies and window ledges, seeing more and more arctic birds land and rest on the town's nearby buildings. There were hundreds of them... all of them now suddenly without a home.

The delicate sketchings of the Tvären landscape curled slightly in Levi's hand. His delicate fingers grasped the copies of his work tightly, a month of hard effort now sitting within the fold of his palm. He always made copies, a practiced method of habit in case his work was either stolen or lost. Plus, he always liked looking back at his travels of the past, remembering the memories that came with them...

A single tear fell as Levi scrunched up his eyes, hating the devastation of the lost forest that lay before him. His sadness surprised him; Tväre was not his hometown. He owed them nothing. Once the work was completed, he could have headed back to Stockholm, and then onto Copenhagen, forcing himself to forget that this hidden gem of a valley even existed, and to be fair, he nearly had done. But Levi had grown to love the feeling of this place. The sparkle of snow, the fantastical hills and remote valleys around him. The people were stubborn and blunt, yet they were also caring and extremely loyal. The land was like something out of a child's imagination, or it had been before Avarson had abused Levi's works and ripped Earth and Sky apart for its precious resources.

The tear landed on the pencil markings of the southern shore of the Lake, smudging the hastily drawn forest. The detail wasn't exactly perfect, but Levi had clearly put a lot of effort into making the symbols of the trees as exact as possible. He never realised, however, that whilst he constructed his borders and clarified land ownerships, that he was actually marking these trees for death. And now the guilt and fury built inside, causing Levi to grip the copy of the map so tightly that it began to crease and crumple in his hand, tightening into a ball until Levi yelled out and threw it out across the street. It landed in the snow below... barely going far at all.

Levi held up the rest of his professional works. All of them were hastily drawn copies of the originals, which Avarson now owned all for himself. One after the other, Levi ripped and crumpled the maps and notes he'd drawn of the town of Tväre and the neighbouring lakes and forests. He knew the actions he was taking right now were meaningless, but it felt liberating to do so. His work felt tainted, and the idea that he played even a small part in Avarson's dreadful plans just made him angrier. The final piece to go was Avarson's payslip. Levi held it up for only a second, before ripping that up too, scattering it across the street with the rest.

His brief rebellion complete, Levi took some deep breaths to get back in control, wiping his eyes and returning to his room. As he passed through the door, his eyes drifted towards a sketching that he'd hastily made a few days earlier. A redrawing of the map within the ruins, with figures of the Northern Valleys surrounding the central image of the Everflow... Levi had yet to add the spectral figure that rose from the little stream, the idea giving him goosebumps and flashbacks to his own strange hallucinations of the previous days and nights.

But as Levi picked up the delicate drawing, a weird feeling came over him. Not a feeling of fear, or one of panic, but a feeling of elation, as if his senses were heightening themselves. There was only one other time Levi had felt such a sensation, and his mind flashed back to the night of the blizzard. Where he looked into the distance during the most terrifying storm, seeing a blue glow appear upon the Lake... The Everflow had called to him.

Levi shook his head, trying to free himself of the strange imbalance that attempted to take over him. He stumbled towards the balcony and threw the doors to the outside world back open. The cold air struck him like a train, rushing down his throat and into his lungs. After several moments, he began to feel better, and looked into the eastern distance, towards the Everflow...

A lone figure, dressed entirely in shaggy grey clothes, stood upon the ice... and Levi was immediately on alert. The figure was out of focus, the distance affecting Levi's imperfect vision. He scrambled to grab his trusty telescope, quickly leaning it against the wooden railing of the balcony and pressed himself against the eyepiece.

The spectre stared back at him, now completely in focus. Its ragged clothing gently wafted in the breeze, but the rest of it didn't move at all. It stared directly at Levi, with incredible, unblinking eyes...

Levi stared at the apparition, finally seeing it in detail after so many days. He was loathe to blink, knowing that any change in his gaze would likely mean the end of the vision, but he had to fall eventually. His instinct was true, and the spectre disappeared the moment Levi broke his stare, leaving only the trickling stream of the Everflow behind, right where Sigmund himself had seen a ghost. And right where Sigmund had disappeared...

The coincidences stacked up in Levi's mind. He didn't know what to believe anymore. He always took every story with a cynical pinch of salt, but this was no story, this was his own mind. Could he even believe himself anymore? He remained certain about one thing, and one thing only. Levi set his eyes on the Bridge over the Everflow. That very place had been searched several times already; they couldn't have missed anything. So, what could possibly be the advantage of looking again? The chances were so small, but the coincidences were too perfect.

Levi rubbed the sides of his head, fighting the indecision to act. Until then, a heavy thump from above caused him to glance up into the branches of a nearby tree, where a large white bird stared down at him... a bird with yellow eyes.

Levi took a deep breath. He didn't fully understand why, but he knew he had to visit the Everflow again.

∗∗∗

The gloomy sculpture of the Ice-log stared down at Sigmund from its great height, but it was no longer majestic and powerful. Instead, the great shards of ice had faded into a hollow shade of grey, and almost every one of them had cracks running through their centres, making it appear like broken pottery. The life and power that had so often sustained them was now completely gone from the heart of the Lake and the cavern felt so much darker because of it. The grim figures of Alaf and Olaf leant against the bedrock wall nearby, their faces low and defeated, not even sparing Sigmund a cursory glance.

Sigmund gently rubbed his shoulder, though he wasn't in much pain anymore. The power from Fendal's healing hand had reduced the blue scar to nothing more than a small mark on his forearm, but it seemed to have come at a terrible cost. Fendal stood alongside him, frozen hands hanging limp by his side, his keen eyes having lost their amazing glow. Sigmund spoke to him, without looking up.

> Sigmund: I know what you did.

His voice seemed so much louder in the silence, and Fendal peered down at him.

> Fendal: And what was that?

> Sigmund: The light of the Ice-log is gone. As are the marks on my arm... Why did you do that?

Surprisingly Fendal chuckled.

> Fendal: Your assessment is nearly correct... but still wrong.

He stepped forward, examining the Ice-log for himself as he spoke deeply, emotion flowing through his voice.

> Fendal: It is not my actions that are killing the lake, but the actions upon the surface. Of all the selfish folk I've encountered over the centuries, I have never once met a man like the one who now lives above...

226

He held aloft one of his hands and touched the base of the Ice-log delicately, sighing before he continued.

> Fendal: When it comes to greed, there is no peak of the mountain. It only rises further and further, until everything is gone. The battlefield has changed. Money and power now rule these shores. They command the people while the man strips the land and poisons the ground... killing the very power that allowed his ancestors to survive the arctic wilderness.

> Sigmund: That's not true. The people of Tväre love their land! They wouldn't ever let someone do that.

Sigmund protested defiantly, but Fendal just turned and stared at him, the white lights of his eyes briefly returning as they burned with passion and anger.

> Fendal: They are blind, Sigmund. Blind like you once were. They hide in their houses, snubbing the Earth's desperate cry for help. They are weak and corrupted, and their inactions have dire consequences.

> Sigmund: What do you mean?

Fendal closed his eyes and shook his head.

> Fendal: You see the world as my son once did. Beautiful and precious, down to the teeny-tiniest animal and plant. But that world has been lost today, and what's worse is that it's the children that have to live with them tomorrow...

Fendal turned towards Sigmund, his beard dripping with little flecks of icy crystals. They fell to the floor in droves, covering the bedrock in a layer of snow.

> Fendal: I could not save my son... But I knew that I could save you. What's more, I thought I could save your future. But alas, that longship has sailed now...

He bowed his head, but Sigmund wasn't about to let him give up yet.

> Sigmund: It's never too late.

Fendal laughed shortly as Sigmund proudly recounted his favourite saying.

Fendal: I did say that didn't I? Such are the words of a *fool*.

He accentuated the last word, the echo ringing and bounding against the dark cavern walls.

Fendal: I believed we had enough time. Enough time for you to return to the surface and change the ways of your town... but that man is so much crueller, and your town is so much weaker than I believed.

Sigmund: You're wrong.

Fendal: Hm?

He glanced up as Sigmund fought against his despairing words.

Sigmund: My people, you said they were weak... You're wrong.

Fendal immediately scoffed.

Fendal: I saw them, my lad, with my own two rotten eyes. I watched from the mist and the fog as the forest was torn down in the depths of the night. I watched as your people watched, witnessing the devastation in the light of the new day. I saw the strength of the people rise up against it like the morning sun... then immediately fall away...

He stared at Sigmund, burning as his passion and grief paired itself together.

Fendal: They looked that demon in the face, after all he's done... and they did nothing!

Fendal turned and walked away from the deathly stillness of the Ice-log, his head hanging low. Alaf and Olaf matched his feelings exactly, leaning against the dark walls without so much as a sigh. Sigmund let Fendal's dejected body pass by, until suddenly, he had a bright idea.

Sigmund: Do you have to stay? Can you not leave?

Fendal stopped and replied slowly.

Fendal: I'm afraid it doesn't work like that Sigmund. Remember, this is my home, and a Viking should never abandon his home… even if everyone else has…

Sigmund: Then show yourself to them.

Fendal paused, cocking his head at the suggestion.

Fendal: Excuse me?

Sigmund: Show yourself to the town. Show yourself to them, like you did me… They'll help you. I'm sure they will!

Fendal paused for a moment, his shiny eyebrows twinkling as he considered the idea. But then he shook his head.

Fendal: They wouldn't help me. It's like I said, they're weak—

Sigmund: They're Not Weak!

Sigmund stamped the floor in anger as the two friends faced off against one other. Sigmund's sad fury against Fendal's despair. Heavy drops of water fell from the icy ceiling as they stood in silence. And then suddenly, there came a rumble… In the heights of the rooftop above formed a giant crack in the ice, splintering across the undersurface of the Lake, but Sigmund didn't pay it any attention. He spoke with such passion that even Alaf and Olaf had leant forward to pay attention.

Sigmund: Please… I don't want to lose you. Not after everything you've shown me. You said that I was capable of better. Capable of change! You gave me a chance! Why can't you give that same chance to my town?

Sigmund droned off, the emotion getting the better of him. He didn't even want to look at Fendal, who just stood there, unresponsive. Alaf and Olaf glanced at one another, waiting to see how their master would finally reply. Fendal looked around as the rumbling slowly came to a stop, as if taking in the view of his home one last time.

Fendal: I thought I was being punished when I first woke up here. I was like you; I never cared for the town or the grumpy folk that it constantly produced. I never cared for nature or for tradition, or even the vast power of the lake... And yet now, I don't want to say goodbye...

He sighed, this time asking Sigmund a question.

Fendal: Do you really believe they'll help me?

Sigmund glanced up hopefully and nodded as Fendal asked desperately.

Fendal: ...How do you know?

Sigmund shrugged.

Sigmund: Because it's never too late to change. And if it is, then we've got nothing to lose by trying.

Fendal blinked, Sigmund's answer so simple and clear. He paused for a long while, thinking the scenario over and over in his mind, until eventually, he shrugged.

Fendal: Alright. Might as well go out with a gamble!

*

Fendal: Come on then! We haven't got much time!

Fendal grabbed Sigmund by the shoulders and moved him into the centre of the cavern. The young boy glanced upwards, seeing the tiniest ray of blue aura still present within the ice, but it was barely even a glow at this point. The cracks in the ice had spread across the roof like veins beneath the skin, splitting through the setting of blue and white. Sigmund didn't resist, but he still wanted answers.

Sigmund: Why not? I thought we had ages of time!

Fendal: Not if we're changing the plan! We did have time, but we spent most of it sharing our feelings! That's why men don't do it often; it's great but it's not very efficient! Stand here!

Sigmund obediently followed Fendal's orders.

Fendal: Remember to keep your hands and arms by your side at all times or you may lose the ability to use them.

Sigmund: Huh!?

Fendal: Okay. Are you ready!?

Sigmund shouted out, trying to slow everything down.

Sigmund: Wait! You said you were coming with me!

Fendal paused and looked at him fondly.

Fendal: They'll see me, Sigmund. I promise.

A colossal roar began to grow. From the base of the bedrock all the way to the top of the icy surface, a great earthquake was born. Faults in the ice cracked and shifted in response to the seismic vibrations, sending tiny shards of ice in every direction. The final remainder of the blue aura flickered as the trembling cut across the subterranean kingdom, but despite all of this, Fendal didn't waver in his final goodbye.

Fendal: If this doesn't work— *If* the town does nothing to help me...

He caught himself.

Fendal: I just want you to know that you were everything I needed Sigmund. As sorry as I am that you fell through the ice, I'm glad that we were able to meet. It was almost a pleasure.

Sigmund smiled through tiny tears as Fendal laughed once more.

Fendal: And one final thing you should know about me...

The Ice-Man grinned.

Fendal: I actually hate the cold.

Sigmund smiled as Fendal lit the power in his palm one final time. He reached out to touch Sigmund's chest, but then a horrible sound grabbed their attention. From above came the noise of a singular, terrifying crack, shattering along the weakest point in the icy ceiling, weaving and shifting as it continued on its terrible journey. It surrounded the centre of cavern roof, coming together to form an uneven circle. With a clap of thunder, the slab of ice broke away from the rest of the ceiling, descending towards Sigmund's body...

A sudden push sent him sprawling across the cavern floor. Sigmund glanced backward to see the icy figure of Alaf the Viking, standing where he should have been stood. Her stoic expression never changed but she eyed Sigmund powerfully as the slab of ice crashed down upon her... and she disappeared from sight.

There was no time left. Fendal rushed over towards Sigmund's lying body and raised his glowing hand above him. As the rest of the cavern came crashing down, Fendal pressed his hand against Sigmund's chest, and immediately, his world faded into darkness. The last thing he saw being Fendal's frostbitten face.

***

Edvin sat snugly upon a simple wooden chair, which was perched on the surface of the frozen Lake Tväre. He held a long fishing pole lazily in one hand, which hung above a small circle of broken ice, while the other clasped a metal flask tightly. With the fishing pole clearly getting no response, he reverted to the flask, taking a long, drawn sip. He leant back and breathed out slowly, the flavoured alcohol, for it was almost certainly alcohol, coursing through his body.

A loud crack echoed from below, jolting Edvin from his relaxation. Tiny bubbles formed and popped within the freezing waters of the fishing hole, disappearing as quickly as they formed. Cracks were an obvious warning sign for ice-hole fishermen, though they often weren't anything more than just a crack, but the displacement of air bubbles meant that the Lake was moving... and something was happening.

Another crack boomed through the ice, this time shifting Edvin with a great jolt. His metal flask fell through the air, landing directly into the icy fishing hole. It disappeared with a small splash, immediately sinking into the dark, watery depths. Edvin looked around him, bewildered. What on earth was happening!?

*

Levi stood in the centre of the Bridge over the Everflow, clutching the sketching of his map in his hands. He leant over the side of the bridge, staring down at the trickling stream of water that was the Everflow, watching as fragments of ice broke off and joined the underwater current, disappearing beneath the Lake's surface once again.

He stared at the bubbly flow of the water, wondering where even to begin with his investigation. It could just be a complete waste of time, hence why Levi had travelled down here alone. This place had been searched meticulously and Levi knew he'd be laughed out of town once he explained that he'd been called by the hallucination of a ghost. Not to mention that it had been many days since Sigmund had disappeared now. Cold and empty days. Logically, there was no hope.

Levi sighed, beginning to realise the stupidity of his little venture. He only hoped that the visions would stop... that if he left Tväre, maybe the sight of the ghost would leave him alone. He turned and began his long, arduous walk back to the town, when a huge rumble boomed through the valley. Levi lifted his head; it sounded like a clap of thunder, rolling like a wave through the ground. In the distance, a man scurried across the surface of the Lake, his little legs pumping as he ran for his life. Levi glanced back at the Everflow, this time something unusual catching his eye. The ice near the ridge's end seemed thinner now, and there was a small web of several cracks that seemed to spread out from the edges and disappear...

Jogging from the bridge, taking careful steps so as not to slip on the frozen wooden beams, Levi ran down to the Lake's snowy shoreline. He could see the Everflow in the near distance, ever present in the ice. The question was, how to get to it, and how to get to it safely. Sigmund had gone missing around here... and Levi did not want to join him. But the ghost had called to him once again, and it was against his nature not to at least explore.

He cautiously stepped out onto the ice, the grip on his boot holding firm. He stepped forward again, being very cautious of the surface below. It certainly looked thick enough, but he knew that could easily be an illusion. As he edged closer to the thin stream of water, he could see the ice had broken at the surface, almost shattering at points. Small pieces fell away and disappeared, and Levi muttered to himself.

Levi: Oh man... Why do you do these things Levi?

Levi crumpled up the map in his hand, turning it into a paper ball, which he threw towards the gaping ridge in the ice. The ball landed at the top of the Everflow's little stream, catching the gentle current. As Levi carefully watched, the ball weaved through the thin stretch of shallow water before approaching the Everflow's end. But as it neared the wall of frozen water, it dipped and sunk into a small hole, a hole that led down into the cold, dark depths. One big enough to fit a large animal, or a small child...

Levi leaned in to get a better look, his eyes widening as he saw for himself the obscured little tunnel that lay hidden beneath the ice and water of the Everflow.

*

Torsten: Vargard! Bring the torches!

Torsten stood within the trickling waters of the Everflow, shouting to the men who stood on the snowy shoreline. He balanced himself against the ice of the Lake's surface, careful not to slip down the thin ravine that now lay open in front of him. He rested upon his giant pickaxe for the moment, the metal edge coated with ice. He'd spent the last half hour carefully hammering at the ice around the hidden tunnel beneath the Everflow, opening up the depths for everyone to see.

The bridge over the Everflow had never been so busy. The wooden planks were crammed with people, desperate to observe the possible conclusion to the long mystery that had plagued this town. Many of the folk who were not directly involved in the rescue mission were either watching from the land, or above from the bridge, their eyes leaning over the wooden rail to get the best view of the icy excavation below. A few worried murmurs had been made about the strength of the bridge when holding so many people, but they'd reduced as more and more had joined, desperate to find out if the mystery of Sigmund's disappearance was to be solved.

Torsten: Vargard! Come on! What's wrong with you!?

Vargard: I don't want to fall through the ice Torsten!

The younger brother nervously stepped across the dirty surface of the Lake, the ice creaking beneath his every step.

Torsten: Hurry Up! We haven't got any time to waste!

Vargard: Give Me A Minute!

The townsfolk watched as Vargard eventually reached the Everflow, where he stepped down into the tiny stream of water. His boots landed on the rocky riverbed below as he joined Torsten, who was busy securing himself with a rope tied around his waist.

Torsten: Here, hold this...

He traded Vargard the other end of the rope for a trusty pickaxe and began to chisel the ice around the ravine. The sound of every swipe was heard by the onlookers, who craned their necks to see if Torsten was making any progress. His aim was to carve enough room so that Vargard could lower him down, though even with the extra space now created in the ice, the ravine was still horribly thin, but it was certainly deep, almost seeming to run under the entirety of Lake Tväre itself.

Torsten: Alright... Hold it hard. Both hands! I *do not* want to be climbing my way out!

Vargard sighed and adjusted his grip.

Torsten: You got it?

Vargard: I've got it Torsten!

The two brothers stared at each other for a moment. Then, without risking the structure of the surrounding ice, Torsten began to lower himself into the clutches of the earth.

Torsten: Pass me the torch.

Vargard quickly retrieved a wooden stake, which he lit with oil, and passed it down to Torsten. Very soon, his head was all the folk could see... and then he was gone.

Vargard gripped the rope with an incredibly tight strain, holding Torsten from falling into whatever depths were below him. Of the folk watching him, Minister Toro and Elvera were staring the hardest. She had been the first Levi had told, after his mad dash through the streets. Minister Toro stood alongside Elvera supportively. She held his arm tight, trying her hardest not to be disappointed when there was nothing to be found. But no matter how hard she tried; she could not quell the thought that Sigmund might at last be found. The one thought on everyone's minds though, if the young boy was indeed found down there, was whether he was alive or dead, and unfortunately, most of the folk were experienced enough in this remote wilderness to know the chances... though none dared say it out loud.

And then, from the depths, Torsten shouted up.

Torsten: It's...!

The rest of his words were indistinguishable.

Vargard: What!?

There was no response.

Vargard: Torsten! You alright down there!?

Torsten: Yes! There's Light!

Vargard: Light!?

He paused to see if Torsten would say more.

Vargard: What do you mean light!? ...Torsten!?

Torsten: Wait... Vargard! Come to the entrance!

Vargard blinked, his beard twitching nervously.

Torsten: Now, Vargard!

The commanding shout of his elder brother spurred Vargard into action. He waved at someone on the shore to come over and hold the safety rope. Hervor was the next volunteer, and once the strong woman had come over and secured herself in the Everflow, Vargard descended down into the thin ravine. There was inaudible conversation between the two brothers, which faded as Vargard yelled down into the cave.

The townsfolk waited, shivering in the cold. Many of them hadn't considered their clothing before rushing down to the bridge, and they were only now realising they should have grabbed an extra woollen layer. Then Torsten's familiar gravelly voice shouted out from the ground.

Torsten: Careful... CAREFUL!

The people stirred; something was happening, though they weren't sure what. Vargard bent down further, almost disappearing directly into the ravine.

Vargard: Hervor! You up there?!

Hervor: Yes. Yes, I'm here!

Vargard: Here! Help me up!

Hervor bent down low, keeping the rope secure, and helped Vargard back up to the surface. He immediately turned and faced the ravine, where his brother was still situated.

Vargard: Here! Torsten, let me take him!

Torsten: You got him?!

Vargard: I've got him Torsten! It's alright!

With Hervor pulling the rope from behind him, Vargard rose to his full height... and in his arms lay the perfectly still figure of a small child. The townsfolk began to chatter and talk amongst one another in shock. Sigmund had been found...

Elvera surged forward, disregarding any hazards that the icy layer posed below her feet. Minister Toro reached out after her fearfully!

Minister Toro: Elvera, wait!

But she did not. She could not... Sigmund was there right in front of her. She had to know...

She slipped on the ice and fell, rapidly getting back to her feet. No bruise or bash could prevent her from reaching her son now. Her boots slowed as she reached the Everflow. Vargard had his arms wrapped around something... Elvera looked down, and her eyes fell on Sigmund's unmoving body.

The little boy lay still. His eyes were shut, and he was incredibly pale. The skin around his cheeks, lips and fingers were a tinge of light blue, and his face, hands and clothes were splattered in strange, brown sludge, which smelt strangely of fumes. He'd looked like he'd lost a lot of weight... but then, as Elvera watched, his little chest rose and fell with short breaths.

Seeing this for herself, Elvera collapsed over her son, tears of desperate relief flooding her face. Vargard carefully handed him over as the townsfolk above muttered and gasped, shocked to their core by the miracle they were witnessing.

> Townsfolk: He's alive... It doesn't make sense...
> Unbelievable...

Sigmund was alive, and seemingly unhurt. Despite the severe cold he must have been under, his skin wasn't blistered or scarred. This was unfathomable to anyone who lived their lives in the frozen North. Anyone, adult or child, that got lost in the winter night would always experience frostbite in some form or another if not death, yet Sigmund seemed to have escaped any trace of such a thing...

Minister Toro, who had now carefully made his own way across the ice, joined Elvera as she gazed at Sigmund's sleeping face. His mouth hung open in awe at the sight of the miraculous rescue, and he smiled with huge relief. The old minister hastily removed his thick jacket and weaved it through Elvera's arms to support Sigmund's body, being careful not to rub the freezing skin for fear of causing further harm. Elvera barely moved; she held Sigmund so tenderly, as if he were a baby again. Minister Toro reached out his hand and helped guide her by the shoulder. Without taking her eyes off her son, Elvera began to walk, her steps slow and assured, spreading her and Minister Toro's weight so as not to antagonise the ice below. As they reached the shore of the Lake, the thick crowd of onlookers parted way for her. The furs and coats of the people split like the dead sea, allowing her to move slowly through the waves of shocked expressions. Every face looked happy and pleased; some were even shedding a tear in relief.

There was no cheering, but there was no need for it. The silence was glorious. Sigmund was found. And he was alive.

The parting of the people didn't stop there; every person in the crowd wanted a glimpse of the miracle. Elvera slowly walked up from the Lake shore to the bridge, and from the bridge to the road, with Minister Toro, her sister Annali and several of her friends following closely behind her. She passed Levi, who had been watching from further up the hill, and stopped. They stared into each other's eyes, no words were spoken between them, but there didn't need to be. Levi looked down at Sigmund's unconscious form, seeing the miracle for himself, and smiled.

Elvera continued up the short hill. As she reached the road that led back to Tväre, she passed by a beautifully designed horse-drawn carriage. Standing outside the wonderous carved doors and gold wheel arches, was the confused face of Avarson, his perfect clothes with their shiny metal buttons glittering in the tender rays of sunlight that fell across the valley. Regan stood over his right shoulder; his sneering expression lost for once at the sight of the miracle in Elvera's arms.

Avarson didn't say a word, merely leaning over to have a look at Sigmund's unconscious form. He almost seemed surprised that the young boy had survived the harshness of the winter for so long. Elvera paused and gave him a disgusted look, one that lasted for only a quick and brief moment. Avarson shuffled his feet nervously, and then glanced towards the face of the old Minister who followed after her. Minister Toro flashed him a smile and walked by without a single word. The large crowd soon followed in the same footsteps. each of them shooting Avarson an incredibly dark look as they passed him by. It didn't take long for him to retreat to the security of his carriage, hurrying to return to the factory.

*

With the help of his brother, Torsten pulled himself to the surface, his furs and clothes dirty from the expedition below ground. Hervor had begun cleaning and packing up their tools, discussing the impossibility of finding Sigmund in such a place and congratulating Vargard on the work they had done. Torsten didn't seem as sociable, not that he ever was normally. He stared at his boots, which were dripping with brown slime.

Hervor: Torsten, where does— Oh...

Torsten raised his eyebrows as Hervor trailed off.

Torsten: What!?

Vargard: Torsten... Your clothes...

Torsten looked down at himself as Vargard pointed at his garments, all of them splattered with a hideous brown sludge.

Hervor: Sigmund was covered in it too...

Vargard: Argh! It stinks.

Torsten lifted a sleeve to his nose and took a whiff, nearly gagging at the stench. Jorunn came walking over, his careful footsteps causing the ice below to creak.

Jorunn: Everything alright here? Don't want to stay too long on the ice at the moment. I was scared it was gonna give way when everyone started running on it.

Jorunn scrunched up his nose.

Jorunn: Ugh, Torsten you stink! What is that stuff!?

Torsten: I'm not sure... but I think I've seen it before.

Torsten glanced across the icy surface of the Lake, his gaze settling on the horrible sight of the clouded factory. A terrible thought occurred to him, and he glanced back down into the ravine.

Torsten: Wait a moment... Vargard, Hervor, secure the rope again.

Vargard: What? Why?

Torsten: Just do it!

Vargard rolled his eyes and met Jorunn's gaze, who simply shrugged. Torsten lowered himself back into the ravine.

Torsten: Pass me another firelight. I had to drop the first one.

They did so, and Torsten disappeared back into the depths. Some of the townsfolk who had remained began to turn their gaze towards the Everflow once again, intrigued by the renewed activity. Freja shouted down from the bridge.

Freja: Jorunn! What's going on!?

Jorunn: Torsten said he's found something!

The few folk who remained muttered confusedly.

Freja: Found what?!

Jorunn: How should I know!? I haven't seen it yet!

His response caused a small commotion in the crowd. Only a moment later, Torsten shouted up from below the earth.

Torsten: Vargard!?

Vargard: Yeah!?

Torsten almost seemed to hesitate.

Torsten: Get back down here!

Vargard: Why!?

Torsten: Just do it! You're going to want to see this...

Vargard glanced at his fellow townsfolk, who stared back at him with the same confusion. He sighed and held out the end of the support rope to Hervor, before lowering himself down after his older brother. After several attempts to steady himself through the narrowest of rocky gaps, Vargard managed to land upon a slanted bedrock surface, raised slightly above the rest of the cavern. He adjusted the rope around himself momentarily, before looking ahead for his brother.

Torsten stood in the darkness, illuminated only by the torchlight that he held in his hand. In the depths of the cavern, the light reflected off the ceiling of ice and rock, giving it a strange blue aura. Torsten didn't move a muscle. It was as if he were frozen in place, his gaze unrelenting from something that lived within the depths below. Vargard carefully trudged over to him, his boots getting filthy from the slime that covered the rocks beneath his feet. He joined Torsten and glanced at him momentarily, before realising what it was that distracted his brother so.

The cavern was filled with a putrid mess of brown sludge, covering so much of the bedrock floor that the ground was barely even visible anymore. Both rock and ice were covered in the sticky substance, the leaks spewing a horrendous spread of chemicals across the floor. Right above the two brothers stood the terrible source of the awful pollution. Three silver pipes, each of them as large as a man, stuck their mouths out of the rocky ground and drooled the brown slime directly into the cavern. The scars of excavation were still visible around the pipelines, and the brothers could see that each of them led directly to the east, below where Avarson's ugly factory lay...

The smell was abhorrent, and Vargard nearly threw up, falling to his knees. While his brother retched, Torsten's face remained that of a frozen scowl. He did not scream, nor cry out in anguish. The horrifying pollution that had lain hidden under his town's beloved Lake was finally found, and the reason for the Lake's strange misbehaviour now made perfect sense. But now a terrible burden lay upon Torsten's mind... How was he to tell the townsfolk above of such a horror?

What words could describe the hollow sight of humanity that lay before him?

***

An Emerging Nature

Levi and Minister Toro sat upon the small sofa in Elvera's humble living room, each of them thinking deeply about the miracle of Sigmund's rescue. They were two different people with different relationships to Elvera. One was only a few days in length, the other over a decade. Yet here they both were when she needed them. The old Minister had lit the fire and was now tending to the embers, trying to convince the flames to gain strength. Elvera had immediately taken the unconscious Sigmund upstairs, the town's best physician joining her in Sigmund's examination. They had been up there for a long while now, but Levi and Minister Toro had remained downstairs, staying there for as long as Elvera wanted them to.

The shouts of a crowd outside alerted them to something. A gathering of sorts, except this one sounded a lot more like a fiercesome mob. Levi curiously opened the window hatch and poked his head out. Several townsfolk passed him by, shouting and riling themselves up as they followed the tense figure of Torsten, who wielded his huge, powerful pickaxe. His brother, Vargard, travelled determinedly behind him, dragging what looked like a huge barrel. From it, dripped some of the horrible sludge that had stained Sigmund so...

Minister Toro: What's going on!?

Levi: I don't know... There's a lot of people and they look very angry...

Minister Toro: What could have happened now?

The old Minister asked as Levi ran over to the front door and threw it open, quickly picking Jorunn from the crowd and repeating the Minister's question.

Levi: What's going on!?

Jorunn: We've been waiting for this... We're going for him.

Jorunn kept on moving, beginning to leave Levi behind.

Levi: Going for who!?

243

Jorunn: Who do you think!?

Jorunn continued down the street with the rest of the folk as Levi glanced ahead. In the distance, he could see the great form of the factory, the torrid smoke pumping out from its two chimneys.

Levi dipped his head back into the house, seeing that Minister Toro had now joined him, overhearing what Jorunn had to say.

> Minister Toro: By God's goodness... They're actually going to do it.

Minister Toro smiled.

> Minister Toro: They're finally going to give Avarson what he deserves.

Both he and Levi paused for a moment, before glancing at the staircase where Elvera had last been seen. They both knew that someone should really stay here in case they were needed, but this was to be something neither of them wanted to miss.

> Minister Toro: You go. I'll remain here if Elvera needs anything.

> Levi: Are you sure?

Minister Toro nodded.

> Minister Toro: Trust me, this might be one of the rare times that the judgement of man is completely and utterly correct. And, if they are going to be as brutal as I fear them to be, then a man of God shouldn't really be there supporting them...

The light in the old man's eye glinted.

> Minister Toro: But... Promise me you'll rush back here and tell me what happens, won't you?

Levi grinned.

> Levi: I certainly will.

He grabbed his fur coat and ran out of the door, rushing to join the throng of angered townsfolk in their quest for some much-deserved justice. The mob-like mentality grew as the town approached the road, seeing the factory as their target in the distance. Now standing in the midst of the anger and fear, which the townsfolk seemed to feed off each other, Levi could feel desperation and hate all around him. Had he not known the lengths of Avarson's cruelty, he might have feared for his fellow man's life. But whatever cruel and unusual punishment was coming, it wouldn't be nearly enough...

*

Avarson sat at his beautifully polished desk within his fiery red office, his face buried deep in his work. He lived deep in the belly of his factory, listening to the hum of machinery from the churning equipment below. To his left stood the thug-like figure of Skalham, the logger that had earlier stood against the grieving townsfolk during the felling of their beloved forest. The other, who lazily sat in one of the more relaxing chairs in the office, was Avarson's dog on a leash, Regan. The chair was the only other in the office, and it appeared to be there purely for Regan's benefit. He sat there, uncaring, rolling one of his cigarettes with exact precision.

> Regan: Have you seen that they've managed to find that missing boy?

Skalham squinted across the office.

> Skalham: The one from the town?

Regan looked at him as if he was stupid.

> Regan: No, the missing boy from the hundreds of other towns that are up here.

Skalham closed his mouth. He was used to being hounded by Avarson, but at least he was paid for that. Regan was an outlier, a man brought in with no explanation. He had been putting Skalham down since the beginning, jumping on every mistake and response for his own amusement. Regan returned his attention to his cigarette and continued.

> Regan: They found him under the lake of all places, barely able to take a breath.

> Skalham: He was alive!?

Regan didn't look up.

Regan: I know… Mysterious, isn't it?

Avarson: Can you both be silent for just a moment!

Avarson's tone bordered on a shout. He'd been working throughout the afternoon and was getting frustrated with the white noise of Skalham and Regan's voices. Since seeing the rescue of Sigmund unfold himself only earlier that day, he'd been unusually quiet. Sigmund's miraculous rescue had been a shock to him for sure; even he knew the dangers of being lost during these cold winter nights and the boy's survival was nothing short of impossible… It didn't make sense, but it wasn't his priority right now.

Upon the polished firwood of his desk were a stack of papers, loan applications and payments from all the people in Tväre that he had taken advantage of. Loans for their businesses, public buildings and even mortgages for their own houses, the biggest given to the Municipal Council almost a full year ago. The day was coming for him to cash in on them all, and he was scribbling with excitement at the prospect of taking yet even more from the humble little town. By the end of all this, he would practically own the entire valley and beyond… And then who knew what could be next? He had already begun offering his generous loan services to the town of Järven, ensuring that he had money in the right places so that the louder personalities couldn't use it against him. Once word spread of his true nature from Tväre, he would cash in on the forests of the next valley as well.

Skalham leaned in, looking over Avarson's shoulder at his private work.

Skalham: When do you think we can begin our work on this side of the valley then?

Avarson closed his eyes and gritted his teeth, a fringe of blond hair falling across his face. He brushed it away with a flick of his hand.

Avarson: I told you this yesterday, Skalham. Earliest will be in three days if everything moves forward.

Skalham frowned.

Skalham: I don't understand...

Avarson: There's a surprise...

Regan snickered to himself at Avarson's mutter, now playing with the rolled cigarette between his fingers. Avarson continued, speaking to the heavy-handed logger as if he were a simple child.

Avarson: Do you need me to write it down for you? Or can you not read either?

Skalham bit his lip.

Skalham: I can read just fine, sir.

Avarson: Well, congratulations. You have a common skill. You're just a worker, remember Skalham. Be careful not to get too proud of yourself.

Skalham's expression became stone. If Avarson's comments hurt him, he didn't show it.

Skalham: What I meant to say, was that I don't understand the need for such a long wait until we begin our next phase. I thought you had already been given permission to use the land...

Avarson: This side of the valley was merely public land, owned by the town. The next phase is the land that belongs to each individual...

He pulled across a map, which detailed the land registry for each of the townsfolk. Beside it were comments and notes from none other than Levi, written back when he was still in Avarson's employ.

Tväre was a town that seemed to follow no particular plan when it came to its buildings. New houses were built wherever it was deemed acceptable, and the streets changed to fit around them. This had resulted in several houses extending deep into the thick forests on either side of the mountain, becoming hidden wooden cabins that looked more like they belonged in a fantasy tale. Yet, it wasn't the houses that Avarson craved, but the land that lay around them. Every plot was home to tens of thick, strong trees, all of which were worth a fortune to the right buyers in the south. Avarson outlined different points on the map with his finger.

> Avarson: You see here? From the moose ranchers to the brewers, almost all of them each own a sizable portion of forest on this side. Which, as of tomorrow, will start shifting ownership over to me.

Avarson guided Skalham's eyes over to the letters in front of him.

> Skalham: How have you managed that?

Avarson smiled cruelly, continuing with his letters.

> Avarson: Never get into debt Skalham. You, no doubt, will be taken advantage of more than these people have...

Regan spoke up from across the room.

> Regan: So be ready Master Logger. After the tantrum they threw the other day, they'll no doubt be more than just annoyed when their own back gardens are taken from them.

Skalham shifted his feet.

> Avarson: But also remember that these people are fools. They believe their trees to be special, for god's sake, rather than see them as the commodity they are. They already signed over their rights to the land many months ago, though they didn't know it. They will have no choice but to accept the way things are now.

Avarson seemed to almost relish the statement as he said it aloud. He turned in his chair back towards Skalham's side of the desk.

> Avarson: Then you and your keen workers can return to doing what they do best Skalham.

He returned to his letters, signing his name at the bottom in neat handwriting, the quill scratching against the paper.

Then, the faded sound of a crash was heard down outside the office... Avarson glanced upwards, the noise jolting him slightly as any noise in a factory would. Avarson paused and then returned to his work, dismissing the noise as a simple accident. Maybe a worker had fallen or something...

Then another crash was heard, this one much closer. Regan glanced towards the door, his usual expression now exchanged for one of confusion. Avarson put down his quill, now getting concerned. One crash was an accident, two meant there was danger. Regan slowly stood to his feet, wondering to himself what could possibly be happening.

Then came the final crash, this one the largest of the three. Avarson's set of double doors flew open, and a stream of townsfolk entered, including Jorunn, Vargard and Hervor. They all, however, were led by Torsten, who had the darkest glower on his face. In one hand, he held a huge ice-covered pickaxe. In the other was a half-empty barrel, filled with the ugly brown sludge that had settled beneath the Lake. Torsten stopped just a few metres away from Avarson and threw the barrel on the floor. It dripped and leaked over the wooden panels as it rolled its way through the office, slowing to a stop at the desk. The smell was felt immediately, and Avarson's nose wrinkled as it hit him.

The townsfolk faced off against their personal devil, neither of them saying a word. Eventually, Avarson broke the ice.

>Avarson: What is all this?

>Torsten: Oh I think you know.

Torsten's gravelly reply was instant.

>Torsten: We found it in the lake, buried under the ice and snow...

>Avarson: Oh?

Avarson continued playing innocent, but Torsten wouldn't bite.

>Torsten: And then we found more. And more...
>Enough to fill a whole damn cavern...

His voice was trembling with rage by the end of his sentence. The furious edge in Torsten's voice was unmissable. His beard was screwed up tight around his mouth, and his expression was murderous.

Torsten: First you take our forests, and now you kill our lake...

Avarson sighed and put aside the papers he was writing on, playing the whole thing off as a mere annoyance while Torsten continued.

Torsten: This town never set itself against you. None here ever endeavoured to hurt you...

Torsten shook his head in disbelief.

Torsten: What even compels you to do such things!?

Avarson shrugged.

Avarson: What do you want me to say?

Torsten blinked.

Torsten: What?

Avarson: Do you think I did this to you all intentionally? Are you that obsessed with yourselves that you think I have some sort of hidden agenda against you?

Avarson was almost laughing at the notion.

Avarson: Look at you all. This pack mentality. Coming together to blame someone else for an opportunity that you all missed, I love it.

He wiped his face and then leaned forward, collecting himself.

Avarson: No Torsten, it is not like that at all. I picked your town because it was easy. That is all. No special choice, no consideration... no predisposition against anyone.

Torsten paused in shocked silence. Avarson carried on, getting increasingly more animated, pointing at the group of townsfolk accusingly.

Avarson: You see all this; this is just you and your guilt. Guilt because someone else took advantage of something that you could not use. I came to this town and gave you everything! Each and every of one you benefitted from my work! You were barbaric

250

before I arrived! Worshipping trees and ice like cavemen!

He looked around at them all and scoffed.

> Avarson: This is how the world works my fragile friends. Instead of getting upset over some dirty ice or missing trees, you should try being grateful for the fact that I even gave you something. Because life can get much harder than it is already, I can guarantee that.

He smiled smugly, his incredible rant now complete. The townsfolk were left in silence, stunned by the true nature of this terrible man. Skalham and Regen glanced at Torsten, as if waiting to see what he would do. The town leader was silent... unresponsive almost. But if it were possible, Torsten gritted his teeth even more.

> Torsten: No.

> Avarson: Excuse me?

> Torsten: I said no. We're done with you now.

Avarson's face contorted into a horrible expression.

> Avarson: You don't have the freedom to make that choice anymore. I'm nowhere near done with you yet.

He reached across his desk and picked up the signed document of Guardianship, which Tväre's Municipal Council had consensually signed only a couple of days ago. Avarson waved it in front of Torsten for all to see.

> Avarson: You all agreed to it. The land belongs to me. I can do what I will with it. That includes the lake... and even some of *you*.

As he spoke, he eyed the women in the group. His unrepenting, accusing tone was evident, fueling the anger of the folk as he leaned back in his chair, as smug as he had ever been.

> Avarson: Do you finally see it now? This town... is *mine*.

Torsten: Tväre was never your town, nor will it ever be. You were destroying us long before we gave you any Guardianship.

Avarson's bright blue eyes twitched.

Avarson: Get out of my land Torsten.

He nodded towards Regen, whose narrow eyes seemed to widen slightly. For once, the snake-like man seemed too nervous to move. Torsten turned towards him, making a smirk of his own, deciding this was the time to raise the blunt, but still deadly, metallic edge of his huge pickaxe... Regan swallowed, eyeing the lump of metal with an anxious expression. Almost in response to their leader's action, Jorunn, Vargard and others lifted up their pickaxes and shovels behind him in a show of support and intimidation.

Regen shifted and backed away slightly, seeing for himself the furious hate in Torsten's eyes. He was far more ruthless than most other men, hence why he had been Avarson's first choice for a trusting personal assistant, but he was out of his depth here. He didn't want to risk himself against a pickaxe, especially one in the hands of an unpredictable man like Torsten... Avarson was about to learn a hard lesson: ruthless men do not know loyalty.

To Avarson's horror, Regan rapidly bailed on his post. He edged around the pack of angry townsfolk, cautious that one of them might take a swing at him. Within a second, he was gone, fleeing the factory without looking back.

Skalham was next to follow. He eyed Avarson only for a brief moment before deciding it wasn't worth it.

Avarson: No. Don't you dare... Don't You—

His voice caught in his throat as Skalham stepped away from him. The town allowed the brute of a man to pass by, his face just as hollow and nervous as Regan's had been. Once he was gone, it was only Avarson that remained. He was now alone... and at the mercy of Torsten and his trusty pickaxe.

Avarson: No... Don't overreact Torsten, there's no need for this... Please... Please...

He stuttered uncontrollably as Torsten walked slowly towards him. The blunt edge of the pickaxe slicing through the air between them.

The town descended on Avarson's struggling form, grabbing him by the shoulders and pulling him to his feet. They threw a hood over his head and covered him with the same brown poison he had polluted the Lake with, staining his clothes and nearly suffocating him in his own repulsive product. And with that, they bundled him out of his office, through the maze that was his factory and out into the wilderness...

Across the snowy plain they marched, leading Avarson's writhing form at the front. His words and screams were muffled by the soaking hood that covered his face, and as he walked, more and more townsfolk appeared, all of whom had made the long journey around the Lake to watch as their leaders finally expelled the demon that had tormented them so much. They jeered and cheered as Avarson was led down towards the vast surface of Lake Tväre.

*

The townsfolk watched without any sympathy as those at the front led Avarson's flailing form towards the dirty sheet of ice in front of him. It seemed nearly everyone in town had come to watch their common enemy finally get some justice, and they were jumping and jeering from excitement.

Upon their approach to the Lake, the townsfolk passed by the Northern Valley Railway. The great train itself lay in the factory's private station, its engine as quiet as night. The masses then passed by the great silver pipes that lay within the ground, each of them disappearing away from the red-brick beast that was the factory and vanishing into the ground below. It was only now, that the town realised the scale of Avarson's campaign to pollute the Lake, and how oblivious they had been when the man they'd once considered their generous benefactor told them that the great and gleaming pipes were purely for pumping in water.

Then the frosty edge of Lake Tväre appeared, lined with a heavy bank of snow around its shoreline. The townsfolk slowed themselves upon approach, lining up against it and forming a human line of judgement, that curved slightly as it followed the boundary of the Lake's thick ice. Everyone wanted the perfect view to what was about to happen...

Avarson was shoved to the front of the crowd, his hands and face still obscured from view. Torsten ripped off the hood, revealing the now dirty and exhausted face of Avarson. His hair was darkened by his own pollution, and he gasped and struggled for breath. He immediately began to bargain, begging for any little bit of mercy he could scrounge.

> Avarson: Please! I can give you anything! Anything you want if you let me go!

They shoved him further forward, ignoring his untrustworthy words.

> Avarson: I can make it right! I promise... I promise I can fix it! I can stop it all!

Avarson was launched onto the ice of the Lake. He fell onto his face, the harshness of the ice bruising his nose and cheeks. He scrambled to his feet and immediately began to run back towards the land, but Torsten stepped across him, brandishing his pickaxe high above his own head, forcing the dirty industrialist to stop in his tracks.

Avarson anxiously looked around for any means of escape, but there was none that existed... None except the vastness of the frozen Lake that reached out behind him. He turned to view his only route out. In front of him lay his powerful factory, still churning out dirty brown smoke from its chimneys. To his right, was the barren, stripped land of the forest, where his work had taken its toll. All around him were his infamous exploits of the beautiful valleys, and yet none of them could do anything for him now. No amount of money or success... it all meant nothing. Avarson, upon his realisation of this very fact, turned and began to plead.

> Avarson: Please... Please, don't do this...

Avarson was on his own. The entire shoreline for hundreds of metres was blocked by the townsfolk, nearly all of whom had made the journey to see him punished. Every third person carried a sledge, ice-pick or some other tool that was capable of causing real pain. Escape via the shoreline was not an option. The only other option to take was the vast Lake of ice behind him, hundreds of metres of deadly, untrustworthy ice that Avarson himself had so severely compromised. And when Avarson realised that he was going to receive no such mercy from the town, his face became a gross expression of hate.

> Avarson: You can't do this... You can't do this! I own the land! It's MINE!

There was no reaction from anyone.

> Avarson: You can't... This isn't fair!

Avarson began to breathe heavily, the realisation of his situation draining him.

> Avarson: YOU CAN'T DO THIS!

His voice tolled around the valley, but again yielded no response. The townsfolk simply stared back; every set of eyes focused on the powerless man. In the evening sun, it appeared as if their eyes shone white...

Avarson rebelliously didn't move, somehow deceiving himself into thinking that he could outlast the hardy of the north in the cold of the winter... But after several moments, he began to shiver, for his indoor clothes were not suited for the cold. Levi stood further back in the crowd. He'd watched as the game of patience had begun, and now he watched as Avarson felt the cold of Tväre's northern air penetrate through his open skin and into his bloodstream. He wrapped his arms around himself, trying his best to mitigate the bare skin from the freezing air. And yet, he still didn't move.

Torsten's patience couldn't wait. With his face stern, and his eyes shining with glee, he walked out onto the ice towards Avarson, holding the huge pickaxe out in front of him. Avarson understood the message and held up his hands.

> Avarson: Alright! Alright...

He took a nervous breath, and turned to walk away, treading on the ice carefully as it creaked and groaned under his boots. He took slow, calculated steps, taking care not to slip on the ice. He glanced backward, seeing the unmoving line of the townsfolk all staring back at him. Something small caught his eye, something below his feet... As he stared at the thick ice below, deep cracks began to open up beneath his boots. Slices in the ice that led down to the centre of the earth...

Avarson kept walking, dodging the tiny ravines that seemingly appeared under his feet with great and deep echoes. Another crack appeared just in front of him, an aura of deep blue light appearing from within. More and more cracks appeared, splitting the ice of the Lake into different shapes as they connected themselves together. Avarson began to run, his panic and fear of the ice taking over. And then, the largest of the cracks opened up in front of him, stopping him in his tracks. Avarson stared down into the dark abyss below fearfully, and as his eyes met the blue light within the depths of the Lake, the ice around him finally collapsed.

With a great scream, Avarson flailed and fell. Levi stared from within the crowd as the maelstrom of ice and water crashed and smashed around the writhing figure, as if the full anger of nature was letting loose its wrath. The frozen mass became a whirlpool, and a bright blue glow emerged from within the tiny storm. And within a single second, Avarson was gone. And with that, the Lake stopped moving. All that remained was a mess of icy shards... a scar upon the surface. The ice became still and silent once again.

The townsfolk didn't move. No-one knew how to react to what they had just witnessed. Levi stood frozen to the ground. Whatever he had just seen, it was nothing like anything he'd expected. When he'd looked out Elvera's window, seeing the folk take back their town, he knew he was watching a key moment in Tväre's unique history. But this... The punishment dealt by nature itself... It was simply unnatural... Impossible... and it would stay with him for the remainder of his life.

A brief gust wafted across the Lake, sending a tiny plume of snow over the newly formed lakescar. It was almost as if the Lake was sighing in relief...

***

The old Minister gently dabbed Sigmund's forehead with a cloth of warm water, that had been heated in a kettle over the fire. It had been a day and two nights since his rescue, but he hadn't yet awoken from his ordeal. The only doctor in the town had insisted that he was healthy, a miracle in itself considering where he'd been. He was now clean of the awful pollution that had coated his skin, and his various cuts and scrapes had also been treated. And throughout all of this, Elvera had barely left his side, vacating his room only to relieve herself. Late into the night, both her and Minister Toro stayed with him, hoping and praying.

Then, in the darkest point of the night, when the mist covered the mountains and rested on the surface of the Lake... Sigmund awoke.

***

Levi: How did you know!?

The young cartographer charged into the underground library, demanding an answer to the question that been haunting him for the last few hours. The aged Librarian, however, stood her ground.

The Librarian: Excuse me!?

Levi came to a stop within the dark recesses of the library. He'd come late in the day, somehow knowing that time would not be an issue for the mysterious Librarian or her ever faithful pigeon companion. If she wanted to speak to him, she would be there. If not, she would be long gone. Levi didn't understand it, but now he didn't know what to understand. His mind was a mess, a swirling tornado of logical thought and reason mixed with the revelation of the Everflow, the secretive Librarian and Avarson's supernatural demise... He'd heard strange stories from faraway lands: from haunting hounds terrorising the British countryside to the ghostly samurai of the Japanese islands. Even his current home of Copenhagen had legends of mermaids coming ashore to steal away the souls of lonely men, but he'd always thought of them as just that... Legends. Now he was part of such a story, and he wanted answers.

Levi: The ghost. The ruins... All of it!

The Librarian: Ah! You've finally connected the dots.

Levi didn't have the patience for this.

Levi: You knew about the Everflow. You knew what it was and what lay hidden within its waters... Which means you knew about Sigmund...

The Librarian sighed and returned to organising the shelves, which had been her previous activity before Levi had charged into her domain.

Levi: I've seen some unexplainable things. Things that don't make any logical sense. But the one I really don't understand is why you've done nothing throughout all of this...

The Librarian closed her eyes briefly, as if this had all been expected.

Levi: If you knew where he was, why didn't you say anything!? You could have helped him!

The Librarian: The boy is healthy, is he not? Maybe a little in shock from his ordeal but I've heard he's now getting on quite well. Better than before even.

Levi took a short breath.

Levi: That's not the point. All the sadness could have been avoided. All the sorrow.

The Librarian: And the town may never have freed itself from the evil that lay within it. We cannot say what the alternatives would be... We must simply accept that there must be a reason to life's occurrences. A plan behind the madness...

From above came the cheerful applause of the townsfolk, having now begun their celebrations in the town square. Levi glanced upwards, wondering how those people could continue with happiness and joy after the impossible sights they had seen. The Librarian, however, kept her grey eyes firmly on him, almost reading his thoughts.

The Librarian: You see? They celebrate the life that was saved, not that it was saved today or yesterday... That is what matters.

Levi lowered his gaze, readying himself for the question he was most afraid of asking.

Levi: Then, answer me this... Was it your doing?

The Librarian stared hard at him, replying curtly and definitively.

The Librarian: No... Though I do understand your suspicion, I can assure you I was not involved.

Levi shook his head.

Levi: Then... Who are you?

The old woman almost smiled, her thin grey hairs falling around her eyes as she turned to face him fully.

The Librarian: Most people lead simple lives. But there are some that learn to see more than others. Those who see the world in its amazing colour, instead of simply in black and white.

Levi almost shook his head again. The Librarian noticed and softened her voice.

The Librarian: And now, after seeing the unexplainable, your mind is hopefully more open. Which means you're almost ready.

Another cheer came from above, this one louder and full of laughter.

The Librarian: Go. Enjoy yourself while you can. These occasions are rare. Don't lament over the knowledge you don't yet have. It will all become clear... You'll just have to patient.

She stepped back, intending on leaving the bewildered Levi to his thoughts.

The Librarian: Farewell... Mapmaker.

And with that, she disappeared up the stairs. Peckingham flicked out his wings, readying himself for flight, and took off after her. Levi was left alone in the darkness, his mind even more in a mess than when he'd first arrived. He hated not knowing...

*

Firelogs glowed in every corner of the town square! The fiery wicks of joyous candles were lit in every window, and the flaming stakes of the local fire jugglers rose high into the pitch-black sky.

It had been two weeks since Sigmund's miraculous return, and the town had changed significantly. The boy had awoken after only a day, much to the relief of Elvera, along with the entire town. His scars of frostbite had quickly been treated, and he'd wolfed down any food provided to him, but it was his change in mindset that was most unique.

Sigmund had told the town of a great power within the Lake. A power that had taught him to respect the ways of the land and work with it in perfect balance. He'd proceeded to demonstrate this by revealing knowledge of the land, sun and the stars, knowledge that no adult could claim to have taught him. It had been Sigmund who had led the removal of the horrid pollution from the Lake's underground cavern, and Sigmund who had suggested that the town begin growing little saplings, in preparation for their replanting of the Northward Forest. His change in attitude had stunned no-one more than Elvera, who couldn't help but tear up every time she looked at her child.

In celebration of all that had happened, Tväre's council had unanimously decided to hastily rearrange the Carnival of the Fires and return the beloved festival to its former glory. Despite being a town of extremely stubborn tradition, enough so that it was almost renowned for it, no single person had any opposition to a second Carnival in just as many weeks. The celebration had been sorely missed this year and the townsfolk needed no excuse to reignite the occasion... though their reason was definitely cause enough.

Trumpets and horns playing a rapid tune of notes filled the air as Levi wandered through the town square, surrounded on all sides by stalls, works of art and makeshift games. To his left stood Freja, who was offering her scarves and hats at discount prices. To his right stood Almarr, who was proudly showcasing his incredible paintings of the mountains around Tväre and beyond. Stalls selling every imaginable recipe of warmed Glögg stuffed the gaps between, and there, at the edge of the town centre, stood the nervous entries into this year's Race Down the Thorhorn mountain, each of them lining up, ready to begin their climb.

Hervor's brewery stall was situated nearby and, as custom would dictate, every contestant was forced to down a pint of her strongest bitter before heading up the mountain. The goal here was to numb the body as much as possible, in case a more terrible crash resulted in severe injury. It was that or face the pain without it, and Hervor was more than happy to provide for this year's insane entrants, pouring pint after pint for those both participating and observing.

Levi watched as Jorunn approached, marching over towards him.

> Jorunn: Care to place a bet yourself, traveller!?

> Levi: What's this?

Jorunn more than happily began to enlighten him.

> Jorunn: It's our wagers! Who will be the first down the mountain! Surely you have gambling where you've come from?

> Levi: Yeah of course... just not on people throwing themselves down a mountain.

Minister Toro joined their conversation from within the shadows.

> Minister Toro: Ten on Hervor please.

> Jorunn: As always. Here you go.

Jorunn handed Minister Toro a small stub of paper. The old Minister then turned to Levi, a twinkle in his eye.

> Minister Toro: I don't promote gambling of any sort, but if you were to happen to pick someone, pick Hervor.

Levi raised his eyebrows.

> Minister Toro: Last two years have been hers by a mile.

> Levi: Alright. Ten on Hervor for me as well.

Jorunn smiled as Levi handed over a small sum of money, trading it for a similar paper stub. His business here done, Jorunn now moved on to his next willing customers. Levi held up his new betting slip for the Minster to see.

Levi: Guaranteed win then?

Minister Toro: Oh, don't ever make that mistake; nothing is guaranteed, especially not in this sport. I've lived here over twenty years, and never have I seen such a chaotic, unpredictable mess.

Levi laughed.

Minister Toro: You're betting on two things really. Alongside winning, you're just hoping that your contender even makes it down the course.

Levi: Has anyone ever died?

Minister Toro: Not recently no... Is three years ago recent?

Levi raised his eyebrows, struggling to tell if Minister Toro was being serious. The crowd in the town square began to grow as the main event neared. The firelights that followed the carved halfpipe course zig-zagged down the lower half of the mountain, allowing the folk to watch the participants as they flew themselves down. The ending of the course came right through the square and was complete with a blue ribbon set across the finish line.

Minister Toro: When is it you'll be leaving us then?

Levi glanced at him.

Levi: Who said I'm leaving?

Minister Toro: I just presumed, with your work now complete, you'd be considering the next step on your travels. Forgive me if I'm wrong, but I can't see a lad like yourself trading adventure for settlement just yet...

Levi: Didn't you do such a thing?

Minister Toro smiled, realising he'd been caught in his own words.

Levi: I think I'll stay awhile longer. There is much here that I've yet to see. And much more that I need to try and understand.

The Minister chuckled, his laugh smooth and warm.

Minister Toro: I think even a lifetime here wouldn't be enough for that. The lake alone is a place that has always been shrouded in mystery. Who knows, there might even be an element of truth in Sigmund's words...

Levi nodded slowly. The Lake's mysterious nature, tied with Sigmund's own tale of his impossible adventures underneath the ice, were almost frightening to him. What if the young boy's testimony were true?

Levi: Then I'm a lot further from home than I realised...

Minister Toro patted Levi on the shoulder.

Minister Toro: Elvera will be pleased to hear you're staying though.

He turned and faced towards the Lake. In the near distance, Elvera and Sigmund stood together, staring out across the town's lower rooftops and the valley beyond them.

Minister Toro: She's spoken of you frequently since Sigmund was returned to us... If you haven't already guessed from the obvious way she looks at you.

Levi glanced over towards Elvera himself.

Levi: No... No I hadn't.

Minister Toro frowned slightly.

Minister Toro: Maybe I've said too much then...

He made to leave but stopped at the last second.

Minister Toro: Just ensure you get back in time for the race. It'd be a shame if someone took your winnings on your behalf.

He winked and went to join the rest of the crowd. Levi stood for a moment, staring at the near-distant figures of Elvera and Sigmund. Elvera heard the approaching footsteps in the snow and turned to see Levi joining them. Her face lifted upon seeing him.

Elvera: Levi!

Levi waved gently.

Levi: It's good to see you.

Elvera: We're happy to see you.

She wrapped her arm around her son, and Sigmund smiled along with his mother.

Levi: No separating you two now.

Elvera: Oh, he's not leaving my sight again.

They all grinned. Levi turned his attention to Sigmund, who held a small pot. Inside was a bit of soil, surrounding the tiny buds of a little sapling.

Levi: What's this?

Sigmund: It's a sapling. For the new Northward Forest.

Elvera jumped in.

Elvera: We're growing them now so that they're ready to plant during the springtime thaw.

Levi: You're regrowing the forest...

He glanced across the valley, staring towards the devastation where the lost forest lay.

Sigmund: We're helping the valley recover. As best as we can.

Elvera: We can only pray that it's not too late to fix it.

Sigmund gripped his mother's arm supportively as a set of heavy footsteps approached and the three of them turned to see Torsten approaching.

Torsten: Hello Elvera... Levi...

He nodded politely towards Levi, who replied in kind. If there was any bad blood between them, it had been long forgiven.

Torsten: I was wondering if I might borrow Sigmund for a moment. We're almost ready.

Elvera hesitated for just a moment, but Sigmund laid a hand on her own.

Sigmund: I'll be fine. I need to do this.

She nodded, smiling softly.

Elvera: Okay.

Sigmund walked away, following Torsten towards the centre of the town square where the great wooden construction of the Firelog stood tall. Levi turned back to face Elvera, the two of them now alone.

Levi: It's amazing how much he's changed.

Elvera nodded, her brown hair bouncing around her shoulders.

Elvera: It's amazing how much everything's changed. Even the factory.

She glanced out across the Lake, Levi matching her gaze. The shining factory stood on the distant shoreline, each of the chimneys now clean and free of smoke. If Levi focused his eyes, he could almost make out the scar in the ice where Avarson had fallen. It was incredible how quickly the Lake had covered up the impossible incident so rapidly.

Elvera: Torsten said he's negotiating for it to be repurposed. Use it to help serve the town instead of ruin it.

Levi: That's what it should be for.

Levi nodded agreeably as Elvera continued.

Elvera: But Sigmund... he's a miracle. The way he talks to people now. He speaks of things he shouldn't yet know... And when he recounts what happened to him...

She shuddered.

Elvera: It's not something I'll ever understand.

Elvera caught herself and shook her head.

Elvera: I'm sorry. I can't imagine you're all too interested in make-believe things like this.

Levi frowned and looked away.

Levi: Well, maybe such things shouldn't be so quickly overlooked.

He reached into his shoulder bag and withdrew a new drawing, showing it to Elvera. She stared over the newly revealed map, amazed at the cartoonish design Levi had given to his sketch. The accuracy had dropped dramatically, but the map wasn't intended to be factual. Mountains adorned with trees covered the background, the Northern Valley Railway wrapped itself around the icy Lake, and little handwritten labels hung above each curiosity of Tväre that Levi had found, including a quaint little drawing of the Everflow.

Levi: A map made for those who may never make the journey for themselves. The mysteries of Tväre... What do you think?

Elvera stared at the map and then smiled at him.

Elvera: I think it's amazing.

She reached out and grasped Levi's hand gently.

Elvera: Thank you for finding him.

They stared into each other's eyes for what could have been hours. It was only until Elvera broke away, did Levi realise the trance he'd been in.

Elvera: Oh! That reminds me, I got you this.

She reached into her coat pocket and pulled out a long, woollen scarf. It was formed of a soft black material, decorated in a variety of stitched patterns around the hems. Levi took it gratefully.

Elvera: I thought it might help the next time you're caught out in a blizzard.

Levi: You mean, I shouldn't be expecting a rescue next time?

Elvera rolled her eyes.

Elvera: The scarf is so that I don't have to rescue you. But if you were to crash against my door again, you'd always be welcome inside.

They smiled at each other, but Elvera's happiness quickly disappeared.

Elvera: You can wear it to remember us after you've gone... The soil will begin thawing soon. I guess you'll be heading home before then...

Levi glanced at her as she lowered her gaze. The Minister's earlier words ran through his mind.

Levi: Maybe... I haven't planned anything yet. Although, I think it'd be a shame if I left without planting my own sapling first...

Elvera lifted her eyes excitedly.

Levi: And the railway that brought me here is out of commission for a while. Something about the owner going missing?

Elvera smirked, playing along with Levi's shrewd game.

Elvera: Yeah, I heard the man who used to own it had a tragic accident out on the lake...

Levi: Oh, there was nothing tragic about it.

They laughed together, smiling.

Levi: How long is it until the soil thaws?

Elvera: Probably two months...

Levi nodded to himself, contemplating the suggestion. Elvera quickly added to it.

Elvera: It has been a cold winter though... It might take longer...

Levi: How long do you think?

Elvera: Three months... Maybe four?

Levi grinned. And Elvera grinned back, staring deep into Levi's icy blue eyes.

A tiny sparkle drifted between them, floating gracefully on the air. A singular snowflake, falling gently to earth. Elvera and Levi looked around, eyes widening as more and more appeared out of the dark. They turned and stared out towards the Lake, where the snow began to fall in droves, twinkling in the moonlight as the devastation of the lost forest slowly disappeared. Buried under a blanket of pure white.

Elvera held out her hand, letting the snowflakes fall onto her palm. Levi joined her, reaching out into the air with his own hand. They stood there together, their lips almost touching...

*

The cheering townsfolk gathered around the giant wooden Firelog, applauding and laughing as Sigmund and Torsten walked along the cobblestone path. They passed under the two statues of Alaf and Olaf, Sigmund pausing to stare at them both from below. Despite roaring their cries of battle, their eyes seemed to be full of life and cheer. Sigmund resumed his walk and approached the wooden Firelog happily and proudly. Torsten handed him a great torch, which he lit with a candle. The flame burned ferociously in Sigmund's hand, flicking embers in all directions as the boy gently touched it against Tväre's great Firelog. The sculpture ignited, and the arctic townsfolk cheered.

*

Sigmund awoke late into the night. There was no noise. No unusual activity or fault that had caused him to awaken... so what had? He lay in the warmth of his blankets for some time but could not get back to sleep. Something had caused him to stir... but what? He got himself up and went over to the window, which overlooked the eastern edge of Lake Tväre. The icy mist hung low over the frozen surface but the sky above it was beautifully clear. The only light came from the glittering moon above, watching over the sleeping town.

As Sigmund stared out across the freezing expanse, his keen eyes caught hold of something. In the distance, skulking across the Lake, was the shadowy figure of an ice-bitten man. His eyes were shining white, and his speckled beard twinkled in the moonlight. He was like a ghost, seemingly floating across the Lake... Then he stopped.

And from the distance, the Ice-Man met Sigmund's gaze, raised a frostbitten hand... and waved.

***

"When the last tree is cut down, the last fish eaten and the last stream poisoned, you will realise that you cannot eat money." Indigenous American Prophecy attributed to Chief Seattle (c. 1786-1866)

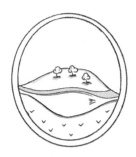

Pronunciation

The Names/

Aigetoro: Eye-Ee-Geh-Toh-Ro

Alaf: Al-Aff

Almarr: Al-Mar

Annali: Ah-Nah-Lee

Avarson: Ah-Var-Son

Benjamin: Ben-Jah-Min

Edvin: Ed-Vin

Elvera: El-Vair-Rer

Fendal: Fen-Dall

Freja: Frey-Ya

Gudro: Good-Ro

Här: Har

Hervor: Her-Vor

Jorunn: Yor-Run

Jurgen: Yer-Gen

Levi: Lee-Vy

Magnhilda: Mah-Hill-Der

Olaf: Oh-Laff

Regan: Ree-Gun

Saffi: Sah-Fee

Sigmund: Sig-Mund

Skalham: Sk-Al-Ham

Torsten: Tor-Sten

Vargard: Var-Gard

The Places (Though there aren't many)/

Järven: Yar-Ven

Tväre: Tuh-Var

And finally/

Glögg: Gl-Urg - A drink of warmed wine, often served with sliced almonds, raisins and orange. Recipe subject to experimentation.

AFTERWORD

How about... Illusion? That's a good word.

But seriously, I'd like to thank you for reading what is my debut novel. You reached the end of the story, and hopefully, you even enjoyed it.

It's been a great pleasure designing this remote arctic town. There are so many elements that go into its creation, from the intricacies in its history, the geography of the buildings and the land, and of course, the stubborn locals that give it such a remote, hardy nature.

Is Tväre a real place? Well... yes and no. Naturally, there is a town in the heart of Sweden that matches it better than the rest, and the wonder and mystery of its ways were there long before I first visited. The frozen lake and Everflow are very much real, with a little magic of course. Sadly, there is no Carnival of the Fires, although some people celebrate a similar event called the Winter Solstice or something. And, as far as I'm aware, there is no frozen Viking that lies under its lake... though I don't dare assume such a thing. As Levi has now realised, seeing isn't always believing.

I could not have even attempted this project without the support of my family. But another portion has to be owed to my own favourite authors, despite obviously not knowing it. Paolini's Inheritance cycle (my favourite series) inspired me to write the element of fantasy, whilst Cline's 'Ready Player One' (my favourite novel) inspired me to attempt clever and interwoven storytelling.

What I must say is how much the natural world means to me and to my stories. The genre of Adventure or Nature-fiction is quite unknown at this time. If you hadn't already guessed, the aim of this book is to highlight this love of nature and the forest. I believe this book's message still rings true in our time despite coming from the 1890s. Greed and profit still seek to rid us of our amazing landscapes, and we risk losing them forever unless something changes... Hopefully we won't have to throw anyone into an icy lake to do that... yet.

In the meantime, I will be moving on to my next project, which will take us much further south to another part of the world. But if it's snow and ice that you love, then don't fret; the town of Tväre is explored further in the free short story: The Fall of Fendal, which can be accessed by signing up to the newsletter on my website. If you're after even more, then just sit tight, more will come.

Rest assured, the maps and stories won't be stopping here... The next ones are already being drawn up...

Oh, and just so I don't get in trouble for encouraging this...

Please take extreme care when walking upon frozen ice.

Did you enjoy the book?

How about leaving a review?

Self-published writers thrive off reviews. Literally. Our future careers depend on them. I'd appreciate it massively if you left one on Amazon or another book site.

It really would mean a lot.

Interested in more?

I have a Website and an Email Newsletter! I'd love to have you on board, so you can keep up to date with exclusive content!

Including... the Free short story: The Fall of Fendal. And, the first hint of my treasure trail. Explore it all for yourself!

Visit addowntonwriter.co.uk for more.

ACKNOWLEDGEMENTS

Firstly, to my family. I know it sounds cliché, but they really have been my best supporters. Ironically for an author, there are no words that are enough to describe what their support has meant, but I'll give it a go. My mother, Sam, who has been my work-buddy and best advisor. My father, Martin, who provided the time and stress relief as we supported Southampton's promotion victory in 2024. And finally, to my sister, Pippa, for being herself.

Thanks extend to Jonathan, who provided my first edit. To my first proofreader and author friend Sue; her support since we met has been unmatched. My friends Lizzy and Amy who helped in proofing and publishing advice respectively.

To my illustrator and cousin Emilie for producing supportive artworks. To Stuart Cohen who permitted me to use his artwork in the promotion of my author brand. My cover designer Kelley, (Sleepy Fox Studios) who was available right when I needed her and provided such a great cover. Keep an eye out for the next one.

Not to mention all the facebook groups out there. The advice I've received from countless other authors and writers has led up to this moment. It is thanks to them that my first, of hopefully many books, is in your hands/tablet/or other reading device.

Finally to my friendship group. You may bully me for my rank, but I couldn't have done this without you guys.

A.D. Downton

A self-qualified explorer, A.D. Downton writes Adventure and Christian Fiction. Traveller of unique landscapes and frequent volunteer at Animal Sanctuaries. Once chased after the great Martin Freeman in St James's Palace. Reckless black-run skier, hockey fan and supporter of Southampton FC. His main goal? To redefine Adventure.

"To truly explore, you must first discover…"